Canaan Tomorrow

Canaan Tomorrow

by

Florence Beans

1995

Cover: Original watercolor by Rhoda Knisely

Copyright © 1995 by Florence Beans

Unless otherwise noted, all Scripture quotations are from the King James Version of the Bible.

Library of Congress Catalog Card Number: 95-92671
ISBN: 0-9648833-0-9

Printed by: Ray Printing Company, Inc., Jackson, Michigan

Canaan Tomorrow

ACKNOWLEDGMENTS

To all who have helped fulfill a dream:

My father William Amstutz and cousins, Ruth Grunder and Ed Amstutz, have passed along many of the incidents that occurred in the early days of the Mennonite community in southern Iowa which have since found their way into this novel.

I am deeply indebted to my immediate family, Don and Dianne Beans, Bob and Margaret Burritt and the grandchildren for their patience, support and encouragement during this writing experience; especially to Don and Dianne. Without their endless hours of counseling, typing and revising, this book would never have reached the publishing stage. Many thanks to Margaret for her many hours of work on the book's cover design. Thanks also to Rhoda Knisely for her original water color painting that was done expressly for the book cover.

Special thanks are due Garry Holton for his many helpful suggestions during the writing process, for insisting I keep the written lines grammatically correct and for editing the completed manuscript. My appreciation, also, to Beth Maybee for graciously taking over the critiqueing in Garry's absence.

There have been countless other friends along the way who, with kind words or a smile, have encouraged us to "keep on keeping on" when writing became tedious and dull. Above all, I am indebted to our all-knowing, caring Lord, who through the years, has led (and often carried us) through the changing seasons of life to our own Land of Canaan. If the retelling of the journey is an encouragement to the reader, it is

Because of Him,
Florence Beans

CONTENTS

1. The Meeting House 9
2. The Reaper 15
3. The Tornado 21
4. School Days 31
5. The Night Riders 37
6. The Friday Night Forum 43
7. A Touch of Silver 51
8. Wedding Bells 57
9. Westward Ho! 65
10. Return of the Traveler 71
11. New Beginnings 77
12. Apple Butter Time 83
13. Arrival of a Princess 93
14. Friend in Need 99
15. The Blizzard 103
16. Christmas at Bromes Dell 111
17. The Box Social 115
18. Telephone Poles 123
19. Treachery on the Creek Bottom 131
20. Out of the Pit 139
21. To Find a Nest 145
22. I Do – I Do 151
23. Their First Year 159
24. A Son is Born 165
25. Greener Pastures 173
26. Goodbye Iowa 179
27. Michigan 183
28. A Home in the Wilderness 189
29. A Stump in the Garden 197
30. Dawning 205
31. Building 211
32. Enough and To Spare 215
33. Revival 223
34. Huckleberrying 229
35. As Sparks Fly Upward 233

36. Grim Harvest 237
37. Christmas Interlude 243
38. Mending Fences 249
39. The Valley 255
40. Lonesome Road 259
41. Homeward Bound 263
42. Journey's End 269

CHAPTER ONE

The Meeting House

The wagon wheels creaked rhythmically as the Eschman rig moved slowly beneath the blazing July sun. The pungent sweetness of ripening berries and buckbrush hung heavy on the still air and the occasional cry of a mourning dove broke through the shimmering heat waves in mournful cadence. The summer of 1887 would become long remembered for its extreme weather through the Midwest, and this Sunday was, perhaps, the hottest day of the season.

The occupants of the rig sat languidly, making no attempt at conversation, as the horses' hoofs raised small eruptions of dust with each step.

Suddenly, a wail of protest rose from the back seat.

"Mamma, make Willard stop nudging us!"

Anna turned her head slowly, for the high stayed collar of her white waist clung tightly to her moist throat.

"Willard, du bist still back there!"

"How can I sit still with Mary and Annalie squeezing so tight to me? They're trying to smother me."

There was a swish of stiffly starched dresses, as the two sisters flounced themselves to the outer edges of the wagon seat.

Anna turned still farther around to examine the rest of her brood. They had slumped, listlessly, from the seat to the floor of the wagon.

"Ach, Sammy—John! Get up off your knees! You'll have your Sunday pants dirty before we even reach church."

The boys pulled themselves up reluctantly, in response to

9

their mother's command.

Turning forward again, Anna drew the yellow lap-robe over Baby Minnie's face to protect her from the sun.

Willard continued muttering in the back seat, "Believe me, when I grow up, I'm going where there's plenty of elbow room and no women folks to bother me."

Jacob chuckled as he sat holding the reins loosely in one hand. With a sigh of vexation, Anna turned to her husband, "How can you sit there and laugh when they talk so spiteful?"

Jacob shrugged his stocky shoulders, "Now Mamma, don't fret yourself about them. This heat's enough to make anyone snappish."

"But it's not just the heat with Willard," persisted Anna. "It's a habit, lately."

"Yes, I know," agreed Jacob. "His chief trouble is being thirteen. But don't worry!" A twinkle flickered in his pale blue eyes. "Give him a couple years, and he'll move heaven and earth to find a girl to torment him."

"Oh, you!" chided Anna with a short laugh.

Jacob drew a heavy silver watch from the pocket of his worn, black trousers and regarded it for a moment. Then he slapped the reins lightly, and the horses quickened their pace. A turn in the road revealed, beyond the cornfields, the Mennonite meeting house, set gleaming and white against a background of huge elms. The meeting house was the hub of a thriving Swiss farming community.

Jacob stopped long enough at the church entrance for his family to dismount, then drove to the nearby horse shed. He reflected, as he tied the team in the cool shade of the shed, "Ja, Dan thought of everything, even to the comfort of the horses, when he insisted on building these horse sheds along with the new meeting house."

Jacob's friend, Dan Meister, was endowed with the happy faculty of seeing the promise in a situation and persuading others to follow his dream. Fifteen years earlier Meister had left his Swiss homeland to visit a cousin, Emil Zimmerli, in the American Midwest. While there, he was captivated by the fertile Iowa acres bordering the Missouri line. After making a substantial down payment on all available land around Bloomfield, the county seat, he sent back a glowing report to his friends and family in Switzerland.

A few months later, Meister met eight weary immigrating Swiss families at Fort Madison, where they had ferried across the Mississippi River, and he led them along the Missouri line to their waiting acres in Davis County, Iowa. Jacob Eschman was forever grateful to this friend, Meister, for taking the initiative. After the tax-ridden, rock-bound fields of Switzerland, his parcel of prairie acres seemed like a slice of the Promised Land. He marveled at how swiftly those fifteen years of settling, building and raising a family had flown by. But enough of reminiscing — his family would be waiting impatiently for him in the church.

The service had begun, and the congregation was singing a German hymn as he entered the building. Strong voices blended in long sustained notes, without accompaniment. The songleader, Rudolph Sprenger, waved his tuning fork gently in time with the singers. His gold-rimmed spectacles tilted slightly on the bridge of his nose, and a smile of kindliness lit his thin features. On his right sat the women with black kerchiefs on their heads. Across the aisle were the men, browned by days beneath a parching sun, heavy-shouldered from wrestling with plows.

During the lull after the hymn, the Eschman family made its way into the service. Anna, with the girls and Sammy, found a vacant place near the back of the women's section while the two older boys followed their father down the aisle on the men's side.

There was a slight stir in the congregation following the singing. Then Uriah Tschantz stood up, and with work roughened hands, opened the massive brass-bound Bible before him on the pulpit.

After scanning the page silently for a moment, Uriah glanced at the congregation from beneath dark, beetling eyebrows and announced, in a deep, gutteral voice:

"I shall now read from the thirteenth chapter of Numbers. And the Lord spoke unto Moses saying, 'Send thou men that they may search the land of Canaan which I am giving to the children of Israel.'"

Willard, seated by his father, remembered a woodcut print in their German Bible at home. There, twelve Israelite spies stood ready for the journey with their tunics girded up for walking, turbans on their heads, sandals on their feet and long staffs to help them on their way.

As the preacher continued reading through the long list of twelve tribes and their representatives, only two names were familiar to Willard – Caleb and Joshua.

"And Moses sent them to spy out the land of Canaan, and the people therein. And they came to the brook of Eschol and cut down from there a branch with one cluster of grapes, and bore it between them on a staff."

"Wow!" with wide eyes, Willard recalled another woodprint in the Bible at home. "Just imagine! One bunch of grapes so big, it took two men to carry it!"

As Uriah paused to turn a page, the congregation stirred restlessly. The stiffly starched blouses of the women clung to the back of the varnished seats. Willard glanced through the open window at the blue, shimmering sky outside. Then wondering where his friend, Joseph Meister, might be sitting, he began to turn around. He was stopped by a nudge and forceful whisper from his father.

"Willard, sit still!"

Willard straightened himself in the seat and with a scowl of concentration, fastened his eyes on the preacher. Words faded to a murmur, and the bearded face of Uriah Tschantz became blurred as images in the creek when he tossed a pebble into the water. His mind drifted into the mists of oblivion.

He was roused suddenly from his dozing, as Uriah, in a thunderous voice, hurled the Almighty's curse upon the faithless Israelites:

"Tomorrow, turn you, and get you into the wilderness!"

So near – and yet, so far! Betrayed by their own doubts, grumbling, and rebellious spirit, the hapless Israelites had failed to reach their goal, the Land of Canaan.

But at thirteen, Willard's concern for the Israelites was soon forgotten. He turned in his seat during the last hymn and finally located his friend, Joseph Meister, beside his father in the back row.

"How come you were so late this morning?" Willard asked after the boys met outside.

Joseph answered with a grimace, "Jim Snellinger came to buy a horse just as we were leaving. Pop didn't like it much, but he did talk a few minutes. Told him to come back on a week day and he'd talk business."

The two boys wandered to the outer fringe of the group of men gathered by the horse shed. The men had paused a moment in their discussion and were studying a cloud formation in the northwest.

"I believe you're safe from rain for another day yet, Meister," observed Jacob Eschman. "Those clouds have been gathering like that for several days now, but so far, they have always gone around."

"Well, one day is all we need," assured Meister. "If that reaper does all they claim for it, we should have the wheat cut and shocked by tomorrow night."

A speculative murmur ran through the group. "Why, such a field would take a crew of men at least two days to cut with cradles or scythes, besides tying the grain into bundles and shocking it."

All eyes were upon Dan Meister whose rolling prairie acres flourished as the bay trees, whose sleek mares and spirited colts were the envy of every young fellow for miles around. He was the guiding light of the Mennonite community and the shining example that Righteousness brings reward.

Looking up at him, Willard thought, "Some day, I, too, will drive sleek horses and own a fine farm. People will ask me important questions – just like Dan Meister."

CHAPTER TWO

The Reaper

The next day arrived bright in spite of Sunday's threatening skies. Though the Eschmans arrived at the Meister farm by 7:30 that morning, they found a sizeable group of rigs already assembled in the barnyard. Anna and the girls dismounted at the yard gate and walked up the flower-bordered path to the kitchen. Meister's wife, Rose, was busily flouring chicken to fry in the large iron pan on the range. "Come right in!" she called cheerfully. Eleven-year-old Miriam was placing silverware beside the plates on the long, extended table.

Anna paused by Meister's sister, Martha, sitting at the kitchen table with a dishpan full of potatoes in her lap. "Here, let me finish peeling those for you. By the size of that crowd out there, it looks like you'll need enough mashed potatoes to feed all the men in the county."

Rose wiped her hands on the apron over her blue gingham dress and glanced outside. "Yes, this is a big day for Dan. He has been planning this demonstration of his reaper for a long time."

Meanwhile outside, Jacob Eschman, having tied his horses with the other teams along the fence, walked over to the wheat field where a crowd had gathered around the brightly painted reaper. The new machine stood gleaming red against a background of blue sky and golden wheat. Meister's voice rose above the undertone of the admiring group about him.

"For many months now, both Hussy and McCormick have been advertising in the farm magazines, each claiming the greatest improvements in their reaping machines. Personally, I don't think they differ too much. When this year's wheat crop looked so promising, I decided it would be a good time to contact one of the reaper companies.

"I finally decided on McCormick's Harvesting Machine, it being located in Chicago, which is nearby. Not only did they deliver the reaper but also sent along an agent to explain it's working. Well, here he is — meet Mr. Samuel Hite!"

Sam Hite stepped forward. He was a stocky, middle-aged man with a dark mustache and the stub of a cigar in his mouth. His Panama hat, fine checked vest over white shirt and tie, along with business trousers, set him in a class apart from the assembled farmers in their faded denim overalls and coarse blue shirts.

Without further ado, Hite walked over to the reaper and began pointing out its dominant features, the cigar bobbing in one corner of his mouth as he spoke. With a look of concern, Meister stepped close to the agent and asked in a low voice, "Sir, are you sure there's no live ash in your cigar? This wheat field is tinder dry!"

With a deprecating wave of his hand, Hite held the cigar out between two fingers. "As you can see, there's nary a spark! It hasn't been lit since before breakfast this morning." He put the cigar back, where it remained, punctuating one corner of his mouth as he continued talking.

"As I was about to say — this cutting bar is made up of a series of vibrating blades fastened together. The reel is capable of being raised or lowered according to the height of the grain. It's used to bend over the stalks for cutting and layering. The divider is for separating the standing and the cut grain stalks; the platform here, receives the cut grain and delivers it neatly on the stubble beside the reaper."

Meister's aging neighbor, Ben Traschel, rubbed his stubby chin and concluded, "Well, it might be all right, but I reckon if the Almighty had intended for us to use such a contraption, He would have described it in the Bible like He did the Ark."

Meanwhile, Willard had been searching for his friend, Joseph. "He's probably around the barn," Joseph's mother had directed Willard, earlier. A mother hen was scratching in the dry bedding of the horse stall and clucking loudly to her baby chicks. A gray cat mewed as she brushed against Willard's ankles. But there was no sign of Joseph. Willard wandered over to the group of men by the reaper. He was going to inquire about Joseph when he looked up and saw him sitting astride one of the horses hitched to the reaper.

"What in the world are you doing up there?" Willard demanded of his friend.

Joseph grinned from ear to ear. "Well, Mr. Hite told Pop that it worked best if someone rode one of the horses instead of trying to drive them from the reaper. That would leave the men free to tend the machine, and I was the one chosen to ride."

A twinge of envy swept over Willard. Not that he begrudged his friend a ride on the horse, but he had counted on spending the day with him. In Willard's mind, Joseph might as well be in the next county, as sitting astride a horse.

At the starting signal, the horses pulled the reaper to the edge of the field of ripened grain. With a clatter of shuttling machinery, the huge reel revolved like a four armed giant. The wheat fell in tiers onto the platform, and at given intervals it was deposited in neat piles on the fresh-cut stubble of the field. Sam Hite, sitting on an improvised "beam-seat", handled the controls, while Meister, rake in hand, walked beside the machine should extra assistance be needed.

The other men stood gazing for several moments in wordless amazement as the vibrating machine moved away from them, leaving in its wake a neat row of wheat bundles. Then they fell to work gathering the sheaves, tying them and setting them up in shocks.

Jacob Eschman noticed the dejected look on Willard's face and laid a hand on his son's shoulder. "Would you like to try a man's job today? Here's how it's done!" So saying, Jacob scooped up a bundle of wheat and pulled out a few wheat stalks. These he twisted into a fiber rope which he used to tie the bundle securely.

Willard took to the work enthusiastically setting the sheaves upright. Then, together, father and son topped or "capped" the shock with a final bundle, bent in the middle to shed rain like a thatched roof.

Young Louie Sprenger joined the Eschmans' shocking. Jacob straightened from his work for a moment and rubbed a head of golden wheat briskly between his hands. He blew lightly over his open palm, scattering the light chaff and leaving a group of plump, uniform kernels nestled there.

"H-m-m-m, look at that, will you Louie. Did you ever see plumper, cleaner wheat? It ought to make at least forty bushel to the acre!"

"Ja, Meister sure knows how to grow wheat. But your fields look every bit as good to me," declared Louie.

"Donke Shane!" grinned Jacob at the compliment.

By now the reaper had rounded the field and the din of shuttling machinery drowned out their voices momentarily.

"Look at that reaper go!" exclaimed Willard. He waved as the machine clattered by, but he was too late to catch the eye of Joseph who was riding and guiding the horse next to the standing grain.

"That's what I aim to have when I start farming on my own!" beamed Louie.

Jacob regarded the young man quizzically. "Meister told me that machine set him back over three hundred dollars. That's a lot of money unless you're pretty well fixed."

The suntanned features of young Sprenger took on a still deeper hue. "Ja, I guess you're right. That is a lot of money."

Louie Sprenger had earned the reputation of turning the straightest furrow of any young fellow in the county and was a "credit" to the Rudolph Sprengers who had raised him after his parents had died. Everyone in the community also knew that Louie regarded Jacob Eschman's daughter as his girl, and one day he hoped to marry her.

At noon Willard and Joseph ate together with the working men at the first table. Uriah Tschantz's usually long prayer was shortened on this occasion. There was a lull in the conversation as the men began eating. Platters of fried chicken, biscuits and mashed potatoes were passed and refilled. Coleslaw, pickles and tomatoes also made the rounds of the table. When the women could urge no more of the "plain food" upon the men, they brought in cakes along with apple and cherry pies.

Finally with groans of satisfaction, the men pushed their chairs back and filed out to resume their work, leaving the dinner table to the women and children.

As the afternoon wore on, the square of standing grain diminished in size. The reaper clattered on persistently, and the men, with tireless rhythm and skill, set the sheaves into an expanding colony of shocks.

When the final stalks of wheat had been dispatched, the men wiped the perspiration from their faces, looked up and grinned with a sense of comradeship and a job well done. Meister voiced his gratitude and promised the use of his reaper when it was their turn to harvest.

With slightly subdued banter the weary farmers hitched their teams and assembled their families to go home to their waiting chores. The setting sun shed its long rays over the departing rigs and bathed, in a golden glow, the neat rows of wheat shocks on the well ordered farm of Dan Meister.

CHAPTER THREE

The Tornado

Anna fanned herself with her apron as she gazed anxiously out through the open kitchen door. Ordinarily, the trees which shaded the sloping expanse of lawn would be teeming with the sounds of warbling wrens, squirrels swishing through the pines and the shrill cries of blue jays. All these were now hushed. The rustling of the cottonwoods had ceased, and over the place hung a silence as if life itself had been suspended.

Anna sighed deeply as she studied the motionless trees and wondered why she should feel so depressed — she was usually too occupied with gardening, washing, ironing, and cooking for her family to be unduly concerned with changing weather or passing moods. She realized she was still exhausted from helping Rose Meister with the harvester dinner the previous day, but work had never depressed her before.

She turned and glanced hastily at the clock.

"Ach, what foolishness to borrow trouble when I should be starting dinner this minute!"

"Annalie! Mary!" she called to the girls who were sewing on quilt blocks under the pine tree. "See that the lettuce is fixed for dinner. Set the table and bring the butter from the cellar. The men will be in from the field any moment now."

Very shortly thereafter, Jacob and the boys dragged themselves in from the cornfield where they had been pulling weeds and sank wearily into the chairs around the table. Their shirts were soaked with perspiration. The usual chatter at the

21

dinner table was missing. Only the sounds of silverware scraping dishes were heard as the fried potatoes, lettuce and hard-boiled eggs were passed.

"It's almost too hot to eat," answered Jacob as Anna urged more food on them. Sammy spoke up suddenly, "It's getting awfully dark in here, Mamma! Why don't you light the lamp?"

Jacob rose from the table and looked out the back door. A strong wind from the west was lashing the cottonwoods into a fluttering mass of silver against the indigo sky.

"Boys!" he called. "That storm is blowing up mighty fast! She'll be here in a few minutes. Run and shut all the barn and shed doors."

Anna, roused to action, called the girls to help her gather the baby chickens and turkeys into their safe coops. The dinner was left on the table, uneaten, as the family hurried to secure their possessions against the oncoming storm.

Willard and John raced up the hill to the barn with the wind pushing them from behind. Jagged streaks of lightening slashed the darkening sky. Tugging frantically, the boys finally succeeded in closing the huge barn doors.

Familiar objects merged into a strange, unreal scene as they made their way downhill against the wind. The homestead, below, lay dim in the wild semi-darkness with the cottonwood trees lashing like black and silver whips. The white apron of their mother billowed like the sail of a ship as she and the girls shooed the last of the young turkeys into the coop. And beyond, the dark figure of Jacob herded the young calves up from the creek bottom onto higher ground.

Gasping for breath, the boys reached the kitchen door at the same time as Anna and the girls. Rushing inside, Anna snatched up the wailing baby and Sammy. They all waited for Jacob, now crossing the yard.

The black shroud from the west was much closer now, revolving, billowing and accompanied by constant blinding flashes of lightning and reverberating thunder.

Jacob, nearing the house, shouted something about a "twister" and pointed to the storm cave. Anna clutched Baby Minnie in one arm and clung to Jacob who carried Sammy.

"Hold on to each other!" he shouted to the rest of the family.

By now, the rain was slashing down in fury, drenching the Eschman group as they formed a human chain, pushing their way to the cave. Will and Annalie brought up the rear. Annalie kept tripping over her long, wet skirt that clung to her legs, and Will would pull her back on to her feet. The cave door presented a final problem in frustration; the wind pressure was too great for one man to lift it. Willard and John crept over by their father while the rest of the family waited in a soggy huddle. Slipping their fingers under the door, Jacob and the boys forced it up.

Then cautiously, the group made its way into the dark depths below. Jacob, after watching each of his family make it safely to the refuge beneath, glanced skyward and saw the writhing mass of clouds concentrate into a funnel of destruction and tilt earthward.

With Will and John's help, he once again pulled the door to an upright position, then let the soggy wooden panel ease down over his head as he slid down the cellar steps.

In their haste to leave the house, they had made no provision for a light in the cave. With the cave door shut, the interior was pitch-black without a glimmer of light. They listened to each other's voices and using their sense of touch, they slid across the clay floor until they collided with each other and found the warmth of companionship.

"Mommy, M-o-m-m-y," wailed Sammy pathetically.

"Yes, Sammy! I'm right here!" Anna reached over in the darkness and placed her hand on him.

"Mommy, I've got to go potty!"

"It's all right, Sammy, just go."

"But where, Mommy?" the plaintive voice persisted.

"Go right where you are — in your pants."

A short incredulous silence was followed by Sammy's comment, "Oh, all right, Mommy."

After an interval that seemed timeless, the outside roaring finally ceased. Jacob pushed up the door of the storm cave a few inches and looked out. The clouds were somewhat lighter but it was still raining hard. With a mighty boost, he pushed the wooden door all the way back, letting in a heavy spray of rain and a waft of beautifully clean, fresh air. Leaning far out of the cave, with the rain streaming down his face, Jacob looked toward the house.

"Praise the Lord!" he shouted. "It's still there! Our house is still standing!"

The good news, the sudden light, and the burst of rain and fresh air roused the family to a state of exuberance. The boys sprang up and down, shouting; then turning around, they helped Anna and the girls off the floor of the cave and escorted them up the cave steps.

Once outside the cave, the children danced jubilantly in the rain, letting the streams of water wash their bodies clean of the pit's clay and the fear of destruction.

Back in the house, they shed their soggy clothes on the kitchen floor and streaked through the house to find dry clothes in their own rooms. Glancing through the east window, Jacob could make out the dim outline of the barn on the hill. "Thank the Lord again!" The tornado had cut a narrow swath between the house and barn and mercifully spared both buildings.

So great was the relief of the family in their deliverance that the rest of the world was forgotten, until they were reminded by the sound of a galloping horse's hoofs on the road outside. The rider jumped from his steaming horse and in excited tones told of the storm's destruction. "Some folks on the other road mighty badly hit. The Meisters, for instance — both house and barn gone! And Mrs. Meister — "

"Ach mein Gott!" exclaimed Eschman. "Bring them here, of course. Wait, I'll go back with you!"

In a few minutes Jacob had hitched the team to the spring wagon and was driving off at a gallop through flying mud. Meanwhile, Anna and the girls cleaned the mud-tracked kitchen and put fresh linens on the beds.

The chores were finished and the hanging lamp over the dining room table had been lit before there was any sign of Jacob's return. Finally, the bobbing light of a lantern appeared as the wagon made its way slowly up the road.

The door opened and a strangely quiet procession entered the house. Jacob and several neighbors bore a sheet-covered body which they carried immediately to the back bedroom. Behind them, Dan Meister supported his daughter Miriam, bandaged and whimpering softly. Joseph followed his father, and last came Aunt Martha, tall and angularly built, with one arm in a sling.

After the injured child had been made comfortable, the group gathered around the dining room table where Anna had prepared coffee and sandwiches. The Eschman children, awed and silent, sat in the background, listening as long as they could hold their eyes open. Now and then, Willard glanced uncomfortably across the room at his friend, Joseph, who sat numb with grief beside his Aunt Martha.

But Willard's eyes were chiefly upon the face of Dan Meister, now deeply lined by the weight of misfortune.

Far into the night, the grown-ups reconstructed the events of that disastrous afternoon.

"I remember," recalled Meister, "watching the barn go, and thinking if we had to lose a building, it was better for it to be the barn than the house. We were caught completely off-guard when the 'twister' veered in its course and returned. The house just seemed to explode. I believe it was a flying beam that struck Rose in the head. She fell on Martha and Miriam, who were already part way down the cellar steps. Joseph and I didn't have time to reach the steps. We just flattened ourselves by the stone fireplace which, somehow, remained standing."

Meister's voice broke in a short sob. Then he resumed, "It's mighty good, having neighbors like you to come through at a time like this."

Jacob responded huskily, "I began to wonder if we were going to get through for awhile. With the creek bottom flooded, the water was up to the horses' bellies when we reached the bridge. Thank God the bridge remained intact so we could cross over."

Next morning, an extra board was added to the Eschman table to make room for the Meisters. When the breakfast of oatmeal, toast and eggs was finished, Jacob took down the worn family Bible and turned to Psalm 90:

> *"Lord, Thou hast been our dwelling place in all generations. Before the mountains, earth and world were formed; from everlasting to everlasting, Thou art God."*

Even as Jacob read the words in his guttural tones, there was a bonding of wounded spirits about the table and a rekindled hope that the ravages of time, tornados and death could not dim. Soon the sounds of sawing and hammering rose from the summer kitchen at the rear of the Eschman's house as neighbors joined Jacob and Dan Meister in nailing the six-foot pine boards into a final resting place for Rose Meister.

Meanwhile, Anna and Aunt Martha tenderly washed Rose's body and clothed it with some of Anna's garments, using a white blouse with lace trimming and stand-up collar for the top. (The Meister's clothing along with all their other possessions had been scattered by the fury of the storm.)

The coffin, when finished, was placed on two saw horses in the living room and Rose's body was gently placed in the quilt-lined box.

On the following day, Uriah finished his address to family and friends crowded into the white Mennonite church. "Our dear departed sister is now in the presence of her loving Savior, but woe to those who perish outside the fold! There awaits for them only eternal judgement."

Once the church service was over, Rose's plain pine coffin was placed in a horse-drawn black hearse, and the preacher climbed into the front seat beside the driver. The funeral vehicle, with a long queue of somber buggies in its wake, moved solemnly over the muddy roads to the cemetery where Rose was laid to rest.

In the days that followed, neighbors stopping by the Eschman house added freakish details to the saga of the storm. Sprenger's cultivator had been picked up and deposited on a tool-shed roof, rods of fencing had been torn loose and rolled up on the Traschel place, and Meyer's chickens were as bare as if they had been plucked for market.

As nature, in a miraculous way, covers her scars with a new growth of moss, leaves and vines, so did the people, following Rose Meister's funeral, set about the complete restoration of their community. The debris was cleared away, and from morning to night was heard the incessant pounding of hammers as new buildings rose out of the ruins.

At the insistence of Jacob and Anna, the Meisters stayed with the Eschmans until their own machine shed could be reconstructed into living quarters. Each day at the Eschman house brought a new stir of activity as Martha and Miriam Meister helped Anna and her girls with the work. Vast quantities of produce were canned, dried, pickled and preserved, all later to be divided between the two families.

Through the long August afternoons, the women-folk sat in the cool summer kitchen and peeled apples by the bushel. As their fingers flew, the heaviness of spirits gradually lifted, and even laughter occasionally rang out as neighborhood tales were recounted.

Thus as days passed, each accessible roof became a huge drying rack for apples and corn, all covered with yards of cheese cloth for protection against flies. The shelves in the basement were crowded with bright colored jars of fruit and rubescent jelly.

There were golden days when Joseph was excused from working with his father and allowed to join Willard and John in exploring the creek bottom, fields and orchard. But in his time alone, Willard's thought always turned to the father, Dan Meister, rather than Joseph.

He recalled the dark words of Uriah Tschantz, uttered from the pulpit, that misfortune and punishment followed the sin and wickedness of men. "But why Mr. Meister?" he kept asking himself. He remembered Meister's brave, tired smile, the sympathetic word to his children and the patient days of rebuilding. "Surely those were not the traits of an evil man!"

Finding his mother alone one morning as she bent over the tub washing the family clothes, he challenged her belligerently, "What did Mr. Meister ever do that was so wicked?"

Anna glanced up from her washboard, shocked. A cluster of shimmering soapsuds slid down her arm into the frothy water of the tub.

"What sort of talk is that? Of course, he didn't do anything wicked!"

"Then why did God punish him so hard?"

Anna sucked in her breath quickly, as if her own inner doubts had been suddenly revealed. She gazed thoughtfully a moment before answering.

"The Bible says, 'Those whom the Lord loves, He chasteneth'."

"But why would the Lord want to treat Mr. Meister like that if He loved him?" pursued Willard.

Anna threw up her hands in dismay. "What a child for questions! Who are we to question the Lord's judgments? Here, run, get me another pail of water for my rinsing – and be quick about it!" she added with unusual sharpness.

Willard picked up the pail and started off on the run, then turned to ask, " – But why – ?" Anna was bent over the washboard, scrubbing vigorously on a shirt cuff. With a shrug, Willard trotted down the path to the well.

Though his mother had not actually answered his questions about the Lord and Mr. Meister, Willard sensed that she, too, shared his concern and affection for the man. With all the fervor of a young hero-worshipper, Willard sought ways of showing his love for Mr. Meister. He filled the manger of Meister's horses with hay and dumped an extra measure of oats into their feed boxes. By that time Meister had entered the barn. His shoulders seemed to sag, and he moved more slowly than on other evenings.

"Oh, hello there, Willard!" He forced a smile.

"It's good to have you home, Mr. Meister. Where's Joseph?"

"He stopped off at Sprengers down the road. But he should be here by supper time."

Willard removed the bridle from one of Meister's horses and proceeded to put on its halter. He bent down to unbuckle the cinch strap beneath the horse. Looking up into Meister's face, he confided, candidly, "You know, Sir, when I grow up, I want to be a man just like you!"

Meister, deeply touched by the frankness and admiration of the boy, laid a hand on Willard's shoulder and replied, "Thank you, Willard." Then repeated again, softly, "Thank you!"

"Can you tell me, Sir, how to begin?"

"Well, I would say for a start to keep on being the obedient, helpful young man that you are now. Don't be afraid to dream big! Then follow your dream, whatever the cost! One thing more, Willard; we have a great God who controls the universe! Be sure you leave the reins of your life in His hands!" Meister turned his face away as he finished speaking, his eyes brimming with tears.

"Thank you, Sir!" Willard leaned his head against the horse's shoulder and dug his bare toes into the dry straw of the horse's stall.

He felt he was standing on holy ground.

CHAPTER FOUR

School Days

*W*ith the coming of September, the Meisters moved into their new living quarters. White clapboard siding helped transform the machine shed into a house and added insulation against the chill of coming winter. Two oversized windows, flanked on either side with imitation shutters, let in light. A flagstone threshold beneath and a small portico above the centrally located door added to the cottage appearance. Martha and Miriam placed the final cozy touch by "dressing" the windows with freshly washed curtains and putting red geraniums in bright containers on the window sills.

To be truthful, fall also brought a sense of relief to the Eschman household. There were fewer people coming and going, fewer dishes to wash and fewer beds to make. But there was also a feeling of loneliness for the gentle folks who had for awhile become a real part of their family. Anna found herself recalling recipes to pass on to Martha. John secretly missed the shy smile of Miriam as she bantered back and forth with his brothers and sisters. Willard missed Joseph, for the Meisters lived in the adjoining school district. But even more, Willard missed the father, Dan Meister, who had become his model of the ideal man.

The days were now cooler and the nights frosty. The Eschman children put on their store-bought shoes and with swinging dinner pails, walked across the creek bridge to Bromes Dell School.

At the corner they were met by those coming up from the "Missouri Line". The Burrows twins, Carl and Kate. The three

31

Devers, Agnes, Hank and "Towhead" Jimmy. And there was Oscar Snellinger.

Oscar would fall in step with Willard. Together they made an odd pair. Willard, long and rangy with patched overalls and denim chore cap, would stride ahead with a determined gait. Oscar, short and pudgy in checked store pants and coat, hustled with quick steps to keep up.

Each morning Oscar would dig down into the pockets of his store-bought suit and bring forth some trinket or piece of candy for Willard's approval. "Paw brought this from Memphis for me last night. Want a piece?"

The peppermints, gumdrops and licorice sticks were usually consumed with relish — by Willard. (After satisfying eight hearty appetites, the Eschman budget did not provide for store candy.) The store-bought whistle from Oscar's pocket met with disdain. "Huh! I can make a better sounding whistle than that by myself when the willow is slick in the spring."

The group of children on the road quickened their pace as shouts and laughter greeted them from the schoolyard.

Bromes Dell School, with its accompanying woodshed and outhouses, was nestled in a cleared nook at the foot of a hill owned by Julius Brome. It was a pleasant spot shaded by overhanging elms. Young birch and buckeye trees skirted the edge of the schoolyard, and from there, the land fell away into lowland, rank with willow and marsh grass.

The game of Prisoner's Goal was in progress on the playground. The center group, those already "caught", waited expectantly for Meriel Browning to take off. Meriel, her slight figure clad in gingham, stood a moment laughing and panting for breath before darting across the yard with the grace and speed of a white-tailed deer.

The game ended abruptly as the group from the road entered the schoolyard and the ringing of the school bell summoned them all in from the bright September sunshine.

The interior of Bromes Dell resembled that of countless other one room schools throughout the land. There were rows of stationary desks profusely carved with initials, and at the front of the room, a long recitation bench built of hand-hewn planks. A huge pot-bellied stove dominated the central foreground. In winter, when the back of the room was frigid, a group of shivering children usually surrounded it, turning around slowly as one side became "broiled". Permeating the building were mingled scents of chalk dust, dampened slates and musty copy books. Here the homespun philosophy of McGuffy and the acquirement of the "three R's" were firmly interwoven into the warp and weft of the rising generations.

Friday afternoons were given over to "ciphering matches" after the regular classes had been finished. At 2:30 the contestants lined up at the blackboard. The teacher, Sam Zurich, called out the numbers with deliberate clearness and finality. Then, after a pause, he gave the command, "Add!"

There was a staccato of chalk clicking against slate as the arms of the five contestants moved across the blackboard in unison: the leather-patched sleeve of Hiram Heath, the long, rangy arm of Willard, the thin gingham clad arm of Meriel Browning, the short pudgy arm of Oscar Snellinger, and the plump arm of Kate Burrow. Five hands began to work their way down the final column of numbers — when it happened.

A clattering sound interrupted the thoughts of the contestants. A couple of hands paused at the board, then resumed their way down the column. Another object hit the floor, and then an avalanche of sounds followed like corn popping. Snickers were heard in the room, and all eyes turned toward Meriel as she stood surrounded by an array of buckeyes on the floor.

"Well, just what's going on?" demanded the teacher.

"I — I didn't mean to," Meriel broke out in distress. "My pockets sprung a leak."

Mr. Zurich suppressed a smile with difficulty. "Go sit down, Meriel, so we can finish our ciphering. You can pick them up after school."

Later, a curious group gathered around Meriel as she picked the troublesome nuts off the floor.

"Say, what were you doing with all those buckeyes in your pockets?" questioned Willard.

Meriel's lips quivered as she tried to speak lightly. "I just picked them up at noon to make a p-portiere."

"A portta — what?" asked Willard, puzzled.

Kate Burrows joined in. "You know, a portiere! You string together wallpaper beads and corn and buckeyes — and anything else bright and shiny that you find. They look real pretty hanging in a doorway."

"You should see the one my Maw is making," put in Oscar. "Paw got a lot of real beads at Memphis. They sure sparkle in the lamplight."

"I know where there are bushels of buckeyes," stated Willard. "I can get lots more for that porti — whatever you call it."

The next Monday morning Willard marched to school ahead of the others. He never slowed down as Oscar called for him to wait. A well-filled flour sack bobbed up and down on his shoulder as he walked.

Meriel's eyes sparkled as Will opened the sack and lifted a handful of the brown satiny buckeyes for her inspection. "Thank you, Willard! That should be enough for a whole portiere!"

Meanwhile, Oscar Snellinger had pushed his way between them and opening a pouch from his pocket, held out a handful of glittering beads before her eyes.

"M-m-m-m," appraised Meriel. "Where did you get all of those?"

"Oh, from my Maw's collection. She has so many, she'll never miss them."

"They're pretty," agreed Meriel, "but I couldn't take them." Her eyes returned to Willard and his sack of buckeyes.

Oscar, filled with fury, turned on Meriel. "Yah! Yah! It's always Willard! You're sweet on Willard and he's stuck on you!"

Without warning, Willard's fist smashed into the center of Oscar's round face, knocking him off his feet. Oscar howled as he stood up with one hand over his bleeding nose.

Sam Zurich, called to the scene by the commotion, collared the boys and led them into the school. "All right, you two!" The schoolmaster's face was flushed as he forcibly sat the contenders down in their seats. "Stay there 'til you can act like responsible human beings."

As the day drew to a close, Meriel turned around shyly in her seat. "Gee, Willard, I'm sorry!" she whispered, her cheeks crimson from embarrassment.

"Aw, that's all right!" he answered with a shrug.

With school over Willard faced a greater problem of keeping the news of the fight from his parents. Due to his many stormy encounters with Oscar, his father had made the rule: Any more trouble or fighting at school meant punishment at home.

John and Mary were both sworn to secrecy on the way home. However, at chore time John decided that such confidence deserved some reward. A little extra leisure was the most alluring prize he could think of. As their father was not near, John called out to Willard, "How about milking 'Old Jerse' for me? My hands are getting most awfully tired."

"Sure," agreed Willard.

At calf feeding time, John again broached Willard. "Would you just as soon feed my calf with yours?"

"Aw, I guess so," answered Willard indulgently.

The silence of the barn was broken by an occasional rustle of hay and the cows chewing their cuds. Looking out through the opened barn door, John could see the house lights glimmering through the deepening dusk. Another idea entered his mind. If he could just unload the pig feeding on Willard, he would have a few extra minutes to play on the swing under the elm tree before dark.

Since 'Old Jerse' was newly fresh, her milk was used only to feed the calves. The remainder of the milk was dumped into the swill barrel and mixed with ground feed for the pigs. With a pail of swill in his hand, John sidled up to Willard and asked, "How about slopping my pigs for me?"

"Slop your own pigs!" snorted Willard disgustedly with a shove that sent John and the swill sprawling on the barn floor.

At that moment Jacob entered the barn and saw John wallowing in the slippery gutter. "What in thunderation is going on here?" he demanded.

"Willard pushed me!" John wailed to his father as he picked himself up, soaked with swill and cow manure from the barn floor. "And that's not all, either — " John's voice rose in accusation. "He had another fight with Oscar Snellinger at school today!"

Jacob stiffened. "So-o-o, fighting again, eh! And what about, this time?"

To admit fighting over a girl was unthinkable. Willard thrust his hands deep into his pocket and mumbled, "Aw, nothing — "

"So-o-o, now you fight for nothing! I'm sorry, but I promised to use this, next time you fought at school." So saying, Jacob reached for a leather strap hanging on the barn wall.

John slipped quickly and silently out of the stable door. The barn was now deserted save for the two, father and son, their faces indistinct in the semi-darkness.

With deliberate effort, Jacob's arm swung in an arc and the leather strap snapped across his son's buttocks with a sharp whack.

Willard's hands remained in his pockets. Hardly a quiver moved his body from the blow.

Jacob's arm fell limply to his side in futility. There had to be a better way to teach responsibility. With stooped shoulders he turned to leave the stable.

Willard watched his father's defeated figure, and within himself there rose a feeling of pity, not for himself but for his father. Standing motionless, head down, he called, "Papa!"

Jacob stopped and turned slowly around.

"Papa, I'm sorry!" Willard continued.

Jacob stepped quickly to his son's side and, without a word, embraced him. Then the two returned to the house together.

CHAPTER FIVE

The Night Riders

The Eschman family was growing up. Minnie, no longer a little tot now, proudly carried her books and dinner pail to Bromes Dell School along with Sammy. Annalie kept steady company with young Louie Sprenger. The Eschman house received an extra polishing each midweek in preparation for Louie's Wednesday night call. The library table was rubbed to a gloss, and in its center was placed a lamp after it had been filled with oil and its chimney cleaned with damp newspaper. Sugar-stiffened doilies were arranged beneath knickknacks in the corner cupboard. Then the heavy double doors were closed, barring children from the "inner sanctum".

Annalie and her mother hurried through the daily housework so they might have extra hours for quilting and hemming sheets for the home of the future Mrs. Sprenger. Mary, as she helped with the quilting, would try in a teasing manner to extract from Annalie bits of what Louie had said the night before in the dimly lit parlor.

It was the older boys whose responsibility weighed heavily upon Jacob and Anna. Willard, now eighteen, restless and craving adventure, spent many nights riding horseback with other young fellows of the neighborhood. At first, Jacob had tried to discourage this nightly practice. Then he finally gave up the effort. After all, Willard did a man's work at home. He earned a man's wage helping the neighbors and so was allowed to choose his recreation. John now clamored to join the band of night riders, but there Jacob put his foot down firmly. "Nein! It is time you should roam

37

the countryside when you can do a man's day of work as Willard does."

Weight was added to the parents' anxiety at the Sunday services. With the passing of years, Uriah Tschantz had become more vindictive in his sermons. Under his touch the massive brass bound Bible on the pulpit invariably opened to passages of judgment, and with bristling beard and burning eyes, Uriah would thunder, "He also shall drink of the wine of the wrath of God which is prepared unmixed in the cup of His anger; and he shall be tormented with fire and brimstone."

Particularly did Uriah the preacher lash out at the rising generation and predict for them dire consequences as in Elisha's time when insolent children were devoured by a she-bear.

The preacher's views were heartily shared by sterner members of the congregation. Chief among these was Josef Schillig. Ramrod straight, with imperative eyes, Schillig let it be known that as head of the family, he would tolerate no frivolity on the part of his offspring.

"You'll never see my children running around like the other wild ones at church," he announced smugly.

To the casual observer, the Schillig young folks were, indeed, models of decorum, quiet and reserved with impeccable manners. Only those who knew them best realized that beneath their calm exteriors seethed emotions of frustration and resentment.

Easy-going Sammy Eschman was attracted to the withdrawn Emil Schillig and determined to become friends. Seeing him standing dejectedly by the hitching post one Sunday after church, Sammy walked over to him quickly with a friendly, "Hi Yah!"

"Hi," ten year old Emil responded, barely moving his lips.

"How are you?" asked Sammy, edging up closer.

"All right," shrugged Emil with his head still down.

Bound to start a conversation, Sammy persisted. "What made you late for church this morning?"

"Becky's petticoat." Emil barely raised his sullen eyes.

Sammy now pursued the conversation with the eagerness of a puppy digging for a bone. "How could Becky's petticoat make you late for church?"

"Well, as she was climbing into the rig, Paw noticed she had fancy lace on her petticoat, so he made her go back in the house and change it. He said no daughter of his would desecrate the Lord's house with that kind of trumpery! So we sat and waited until she came out with a plain petticoat under her dress." Emil spat the final words out in disgust.

"Oh-h-h-h," Sammy's voice sank guiltily as he felt he had stripped his friend bare of his self esteem and betrayed him. "I'm sorry!" Sammy faltered. Then finding no more words to say, he reached into his pocket and pulled out a hand-carved whistle. "It's for you!" he said as he handed it to Emil.

"Thank you!" exclaimed Emil with a flicker of a smile. He stroked the whistle lightly, then, slipped it into his pocket.

Despite Uriah's preaching, Willard continued to ride nights with his neighbor, Carl Burrows, and Jimmy Dever, who lived near the Missouri line. Seventeen year old Jimmy, sometimes called 'Towhead' because of his pale, sunburnt hair, looked up to Carl and Willard as big brothers.

Jimmy's father, when not in the town bar, lounged in the kitchen in a half-sodden stupor. Jimmy's mother had learned years before that life went smoother when she did not rouse her husband. And so Jimmy, since childhood, had done all the field work with his thin shoulders wrestling a plow almost as tall as he was.

Will and Carl felt a protective air toward their young friend who had grown up without ever being a boy.

One evening Carl rode over to Willard's with a newcomer, Fritz Zimmerli. "I hope you two hit it off," Carl commented. "Fritz is my cousin from Kansas. He plans to stay with us."

Willard found himself closely drawn to the sandy-haired newcomer from Kansas. Fritz, friendly and witty with a store of travel tales, made an interesting companion. Jimmy Dever dropped out of the group soon after Fritz' arrival. Willard did not give it much thought. His full attention was focused on Fritz, the newcomer. As he rode with Fritz and Carl, their horses' hoofs beat a tattoo on the hard clay roads, while the three fellows sang out lustily:

"Oh carry me to the lone prairie
Where the coyotes howl and the wind
blows free;
And when I die you can bury me
Beneath the stars on the lone prairie."

When Jimmy rejoined the group a short time later, there was a new rider with him. Will groaned inwardly as they approached close enough for the newcomer to be recognized. The stocky Oscar Snellinger had not changed much from Bromes Dell school days. Somewhat heavier, he walked with the same swagger and his chin thrust forward. Will spotted the new belt with a shiny buckle Oscar had used to buy Jimmy's friendship.

The clear, frosty night in mid-November was ideal for riding. A full moon rose behind the black silhouettes of leafless trees and shed a silver sheen upon the ragged corn shocks in the fields below. Rabbits scampered from the bright ribbon of roadway into the sheltering shadow of nearby bushes. From the distant cluster of farm buildings came the barking of a dog.

Carl, Fritz, and Willard were joined at the crossroads by Jimmy Dever and his gang. Oscar and his two cronies from Missouri had been drinking. Their speech was loud and blotched with profanity. After riding a short distance, the group drew up their horses into a huddle. One of Oscar's friends passed his flask. It was flatly refused by Carl's group. Without warning Oscar let out a yell and swatted Carl's horse on the rump. The startled beast gave a lunge that sent Carl sprawling into the roadside bushes. Oscar's group galloped off, roaring with laughter. Jimmy Dever glanced uncertainly between the two groups. He reined in his horse and lingered a moment beside Fritz and Will as if expecting an invitation to join them.

"Hey Dever! Ain't cha coming?" Oscar's hoarse voice bellowed from the road ahead.

Jimmy finally turned his horse about and trotted off to follow Oscar. Carl, furious, picked himself up and remounted his horse.

"Idiots!" muttered Fritz to Willard. "Maybe, if we hang back, they'll go on without us."

The thickening voice of Snellinger bawled out in the distance,

"Here comth a rig down the ro-oad. Watch me givth 'em a surprishth!" As they approached the buggy, Oscar let out an Indian war whoop that sent the horse shying into the ditch. He then galloped on.

When the weathered rig of the Traschels pitched into the ditch, one of the rear wheels fell off, leaving the shrieking Mrs. Traschel tilted in midair. Mr. Traschel had sprung from the buggy and was chattering with rage and excitement. His high-pitched voice pierced the night air. "Whoa, Daisy, whoa! By the great Jehoshaphat! If I ever lay hands on those heathens, I'll break every bone in their bodies!"

Willard drew up rein by the stranded couple. "I'm sorry, sir, about your accident. I'll help you get that wheel back on."

At the sight of Willard, Traschel broke forth again, "What! Willard Eschman! You're riding with those lowdown hoodlums? I'm surprised to think that a son of Jacob would — "

Willard broke in impatiently, "I said I would help you fix your wheel. Let's get at it!" Fritz and Carl joined Willard in the repairs. With scarcely restrained laughter, Fritz put his shoulder to the back of the buggy while Willard slipped the wheel back on and secured it.

"There, Brother Traschel. Your rig is as good as new," Fritz spoke in a placating tone.

Whatever Traschel's response might have been, it was interrupted by a splintering crash in the distance.

"That must be at Meyer's bridge!" the three fellows exclaimed in unison. Jumping on their horses, they galloped to the ancient plank bridge spanning Meyer's Creek.

The old weathered rail of the bridge was shattered where Dever's horse had struck it. On the dry creek bed below, the horse, bleeding badly from a chest wound, whinnied and floundered about. It tried to stand on its broken leg, then fell back, helplessly. At one side lay Jimmy Dever, crumpled and motionless. He had hit his head on a rock in the fall.

The group stood about, shaken and incoherent. Snellinger's swagger was now gone. "It can't be! God no. Say it ain't so! We were just racing. Jimmy and Tom were ahead, neck and neck on the bridge. I was going to pass between them when Jimmy's horse struck the bridge. They just build bridges too narrow these days!"

Meyers, hearing the confusion, left his house and came running down to the bridge. He bent over Jimmy for a moment, feeling for his pulse and listening to his chest. Then he shook his head. "I'm afraid he's done for! Let's get him to my house. Then someone go for his folks and Dr. Shelton."

At the house Meyers picked up his gun, and going back to the scene of the accident, put Dever's horse out of its misery.

The accident was narrated and repeated many times throughout the Mennonite community. Each time in the retelling, the details were exaggerated or new bits added to suit the narrator's fancy.

Uriah Tschantz preached a scathing sermon in which he denounced the young galloping hoodlums that made the roads unsafe for decent folks to travel at night.

Fritz, Willard and Carl rode no more at night. Oscar Snellinger, realizing how unpopular he had become in the community, sought companionship south of the Missouri line. And thus the clatter of horses' hoofs died out on the night air.

CHAPTER SIX

The Friday Night Forum

Then was Uriah Tschantz gathered unto his fathers. The funeral was austere with neither music nor flowers to soften its bleakness. The pine board coffin dominated the front of the church. Starkly etched on one side of the room were rows of men in black suits. Across from them sat the women shrouded in black veils. Josef Schillig spoke on the brevity of life and the certainty of eternal punishment in the Hereafter for the unsaved. Thus was Uriah Tschantz, in death as in life, a pillar of warning to the unbelievers.

The congregation was desirous of an "outside man" being brought in to fill Uriah's place. Through the snows and rigors of winter, the church members gathered faithfully without a shepherd for the flock. Rudolph Sprenger continued to lead the singing, and Dan Meister was chosen for the Sunday service Bible reading until a new pastor could be provided for them. The frost-bound landscape gradually thawed into slush and mud, and finally spring arrived.

The budded tree boughs were bursting forth in bloom when the Mennonite board sent the long-promised minister, Brother Mueller from Indiana, to the "Germany" Meeting House.

Though preaching with firm conviction, Brother Mueller was gentle in manner, and new life began pulsing through the congregation. Along with the plaintive German hymns were mingled occasional English ones. Childish voices rose in joyful songs during the Sunday School sessions. Garments of brighter hue began to brighten the hitherto expected somber attire in the Meeting House, and hats began to replace the black veils of the women.

The sick and needy found Brother Mueller an ever-present and understanding friend. The congregation welcomed him into their hearts. That is, with the exception of a few, Schillig among them. They contended with alarm that such mildness encouraged young folks to question church authority. Why, this new preacher was inviting young people down the primrose path to destruction. The church continued to grow despite Schillig's muttering.

The farming community surrounding the church was also blessed that summer with favorable weather and abundant crops. The farmers, in an expansive mood, were buying more equipment for bigger and better yields in the coming year. Chief among them was Charles Bauman with a black Angus ranch east of Pulaski. The cluster of red cattle barns and the spacious white house with its wide veranda supported by large columns attested to his affluence.

Bauman, as a young man, had met his wife, Alice, while in Chicago on cattle business. Her father, Max Haywood, a well-to-do meat packer, had taken a special interest in the young cattleman from the Midwest, noting he had integrity and the driving power to succeed.

When some of Max's associates had expressed concern over a rich city girl making out as a farmer's wife, Haywood answered genially, "I've never seen a Haywood yet that didn't land on both feet when tossed into a new situation. And as for Alice, don't worry! She has enough of her mother's good taste and business sense that no place is going to look 'run down' very long after she arrives."

True to her father's prediction, Alice proved to be not only a good farm wife for Charles Bauman but also a gracious hostess and social leader in the community. With Charles' expertise at cattle raising and his father-in-law's interest and financial support, when needed, the Bauman Stock Farm flourished. And those stepping through the polished oak doorway of the Bauman house were greeted by an even greater surprise as the deep piled rugs, the period furniture and brocaded draperies transported them into the domain of a fashionable city dweller.

Alice usually accompanied her husband on the train trips to Chicago. She sometimes took the two children, Steve and Ruth, much to the delight of the Haywood grandparents. At other times the children were left at the Meisters.

On these occasions Alice was free to shop in downtown Chicago with her mother or take in entertainment such as the theater, musical productions or lyceum lectures with family members or friends.

"You know," Alice confided to her husband on one of the return trips from Chicago, "there's just one city thing I miss here at home. That is any form of social life outside of going to church. Don't get me wrong, church is fine – but – " (she traced her finger around the lapel of Charles's coat) "it just seems there should be somewhere else to go in between. All we do is go to church!"

Charles shrugged his shoulders, "Well, you know the old saying, 'If you can't bring the mountain to Mohammed, take Mohammed to the mountain.' Your pa says, 'Whatever you set your mind to, you can do!'"

"Bring an opera, musical, play or Lyceum lecture to 'Germany'!"

Alice shook her head at the incongruity of the idea.

"Well, maybe if we got the neighborhood folks together once," Charles reasoned, "we could find something they were interested in doing. How about inviting them to a picnic at our place? I have a hunch they might go along with your ideas. Just so they don't think you are cramming high society down their throats!"

The picnic was planned for fall, shortly after the beginning of school. It included all families from the two adjoining school districts of Big Fox and Bromes Dell.

On that Saturday afternoon a good-sized crowd gathered to eat at the long tables beneath the maples on Bauman's broad lawn. The autumn sun filtered down warmly through the red and gold leaves. With eating over and the remaining food packed back in baskets, the folks gathered in a semicircle, sitting either on benches or on the ground. Ideas were exchanged as to what might be of general interest to the group.

"What would you call such a meeting?" demanded Cyrus

Heath, hunching his massive shoulders forward that he might hear better.

"Well, I went to such a meeting once," volunteered Amy Traschel. "They called it 'The Literary Society'."

Heath's beard jutted forth as he snorted, "No self-respecting he-man could be dragged to a 'Ladeez Literary Societee'!"

Meister came to the rescue. "How about 'Forum'? Does that sound he-mannish enough?"

A murmur of assent rippled through the group. It was agreed to have the meeting once a month during the school year, on the second Friday, and it would be called 'The Friday Night Forum'.

The programs were made up of school talent, debates and outside speakers. Its popularity grew until it encompassed all families and ages throughout the countryside. On 'Forum' nights, the chores were hurried through and suppers hastily eaten. Then the families, bundled into straw-littered bob sleighs, drove off in the deepening winter dusk for Bromes's Dell.

At the school house they were greeted with the glow of many oil lamps fastened along the walls of the schoolroom. The polished reflectors behind them gleamed like shining armor. The newcomers made their way past the friendly warmth of the huge iron stove to the rows of desks. Women with many ruffled petticoats and full woolen skirts squeezed with difficulty into the narrow confines of the stationary seats.

Mothers held their babies in their arms and small children sat perched upon desktops. Men and boys stood in the outer aisles along the wall after the supply of extra chairs had run out.

As the evening wore on, children nodded, fell asleep and were laid across the desks. The black iron stove continued to radiate heat and the atmosphere of the closely packed room became stale and humid with the perspiration of heavily clad feet and bodies.

Programs were as varied as the individuals making up the district. Debates waxed long with homespun oratory. The weightier portions of the evenings were interspersed with "readings" and songs by the school children. On occasions Cyrus Heath, the blacksmith, brought along his violin and in the intervals "fiddled" out "The Arkansas Traveler" and "Red Wing", his gray beard swaying to the rhythm and his foot tapping out the beat.

On the night Tom Burrows was chairman, the program pitched into the ridiculous. He rose and solemnly announced the topic: "Resolved: That the hen who lays the egg is the mother of the chicken."

Barnyard anecdotes were reeled off with hilarious laughter. Among them was the sad plight of Meyer's hen who reared a setting of baby ducklings only to drown herself trying to coax them out of the pond.

To Willard, the highlight of the Friday Night Forum was the debate between Fritz Zimmerli and Dan Meister. The school house was packed with folks drawn by the prospects of a match between Zimmerli, favorite of the young folks, and Meister, outstanding citizen.

Willard, glancing about the crowded room before the debate, singled out Joseph Meister with his girl friend, Ruth Bauman, dark-haired, attractive and vivacious. Her lips parted in a flashing smile whenever she glanced upward at Joseph. A faint flicker of envy crept over Willard as he noted that his friend, Joseph, always seemed to arrive first with the finest. Then as promptly, Willard squelched the idea.

The debaters stepped onto the raised dais at the front of the room: three neighborhood gentlemen and a petite young lady with auburn hair swept neatly upon her head. A murmur ran through the crowd, "Who is she?"

Zimmerli tapped with the gavel, cleared his throat and began, "Resolved: That more can be learned by travel and observation than by reading and meditation. Emil Meyers and I will take the affirmative. The speakers for the negative will be Dan Meister and his colleague, Miss Caroline Steiner from Big Fox Creek school district."

Following Emil's opening, Fritz continued by describing colorful scenes from his travels through the states: the eruptions of Old Faithful, the awesome majesty of the Grand Canyon and the grottoes of Mammoth Cave. That night the horizons of Bromes Dell were pushed beyond the cornfields to the alluring terrains of mountain, desert and canyon. Willard, along with other young farmers present, was fired with enthusiasm for travel and adventure.

Meister's approach to the subject was practical. "Travel is expensive! That counts most of us out, right there. There is a wealth of information to be found at home in the realm of nature. And then there are books. I leave that resource to my colleague, Miss Caroline."

The room was hushed as Caroline Steiner rose to her feet. Her slight body was attired in a beige cashmere dress with leg-of-mutton sleeves and high stayed collar. She began by quoting Emily Dickinson, "'There is no frigate like a book to take us lands away!' No home is so humble that it does not contain three building blocks of wisdom: the Bible, the almanac, and McGuffy's Reader. Emerson has said, 'Raphael paints wisdom, Handel sings it, Paidias carves it, Shakespeare writes it, Wren builds it, Columbus sails it, Luther preaches it, Washington arms it, and Watts mechanizes it.' With biographies and writings of many masters at our fingertips, we can learn more of the world's history, literature and religion by reading a few minutes each day by our own fireside than by traveling to the far corners of the earth."

Willard Eschman sat captivated by the manner and words of the winsome speaker before him. He had grown up with an assortment of sisters. There was Annalie who could be cajoled into pressing his trousers or shining his shoes. Mary, tender hearted and sensitive, was the target for much of his teasing, and irrepressible Minnie, the tomboy, rode horseback like an Indian and romped with her brothers.

Outside the family, his relationship with girls had been casual. There had been Meriel Browning, shy and retiring, who sat in front of him in the Bromes's Dell School; Rebecca Schillig from the Meeting House, crisp and sedate; and Carl Burrow's sister, Kate, plump and jolly with an ever ready line of amusing chatter.

Oh yes, when occasion demanded, he appeared with a girl, but he preferred the company of a gang of fellows. With them he could be at ease, do and say what he pleased.

That was before he had seen Caroline Steiner and thrilled to her warm voice and calm poise. Here was a woman who appealed not only to the sight but was a challenge to the intellect as well.

She was the kind of woman for whom he had been waiting. How could he reach her?

He was talking to Joseph and Ruth Bauman when Meister approached with Caroline at his side. The coveted introduction was forthcoming.

"Miss Steiner, may I present Mr. Eschman?"

"How do you do?" the cool, soft voice responded.

Willard, looking steadfastly at her, was aware of the green glints playing in her eyes.

"You did very well tonight," he complimented her.

"Thank you, Mr. Eschman. It's been a pleasure being here!"

The crowd was dispersing and Willard seized the opportunity to extend his acquaintance.

"You came with the Meisters?"

"Yes, I did."

"My cutter is waiting outside. May I have the pleasure of taking you home?"

Caroline glanced questioningly at Mr. Meister.

Dan Meister chuckled softly, "I release you from all further responsibility tonight, Caroline, and turn you over to Will and his cutter."

Out under the stars, away from the crowd, a sudden shyness swept over Willard. He was keenly aware of the trim, petite figure beside him with a dark fur cap over her hair and a fur muff enclosing her hands. His mind worked feverishly to find the right words to begin a conversation. He leaned over and carefully tucked the heavy lap robe about their feet.

"Why have I never seen you before?"

"It's probably because my home is up near the Wapello county line. I came to Big Fox Creek district just last fall to teach. Dan Meister is my uncle. Of course, you live near Bromes Dell, Mr. Eschman?"

"My first name is Willard. Better yet, just call me Will! I feel you're talking to someone else when you say Mr. Eschman."

"Will — That's a good solid name. I like it! At home I was never called anything but 'Carrie'. Now with everyone saying 'Miss Steiner', I, too, feel as if they are speaking to a stranger."

"May I call you Carrie?"

"Please do, Will!" she smiled.

The small teacher at his side snuggled down in the seat. Her hands reached deeper into the muff to keep warm. For a while they rode in silence over the silver bosom of the snow. Only the soft thud of the horse's hoofs indented their thoughts.

At the door of her rooming place, Will received permission to call upon Carrie the following Sunday night. There were many succeeding nights that Will also called. They went together to church, to the Forum, the homes of friends or just riding in search of new scenery.

By the following spring, folks linked their names when speaking of them — Will and Carrie. They belonged together!

CHAPTER SEVEN

A Touch of Silver

The farmers of the community were passing through troubled times. The lean years of the early "nineties" had descended upon them, not with panic and a sudden crash of fortunes as in the large cities, but rather with the slow ebb of currency and lower farm prices that left their debts looming above them and the icy clutch of fear in their hearts.

Wherever men gathered in the neighborhood, the defects of the gold standard and the greediness of the capitalistic interests were discussed. Speculation ran high as to how much lower the price of corn and hogs could fall. Fritz Zimmerli quoted a letter from his folks in Kansas that said, due to the severe cold weather and the low price of grain, they had burned their corn to keep themselves warm.

President Cleveland was denounced as a mere servant of Wall Street, and a young, gifted lawyer from the neighboring state of Nebraska was hailed as a champion of the laboring man and farmer. Already the speeches of William Jennings Bryan, the Boy Orator of the Platte, were sweeping the country like wildfire.

Nor was Jacob Eschman untouched by the hard times. He turned restlessly in his bed at night, seeking a solution to his financial problems. The previous spring he had bought a family carriage and some new machinery, giving in return a note which he felt was amply covered by his litters of growing pigs. However, by the following fall the price of hogs had fallen to 2½ cents per pound, leaving Jacob with barely enough to pay the interest on the

51

note.

"Ach! Mamma," he confided in anxiety to his wife. "If only I had not bought that new plow and cultivator. How I can ever pay for them I do not see. There is just no money to be had."

Then from the comforting warmth of his wife beside him in the darkness came the reassuring murmur, "Do not fret yourself, Jacob! Try to go to sleep. We have come through hard times before. The Lord always provides a way!" Her hand patted his weary shoulder beneath the covers.

But alone with her thoughts Anna, too, would sigh as her weathered hands smoothed the faded work clothes she had patched and repatched. Though chambray and percale had dropped to a new low of ten cents per yard, it was still nigh impossible to replace the family clothes with no cash on hand.

Only the youth remained undaunted. The weeks flew by with Will and Carrie joining the other young couples at neighborhood gatherings: box socials at Bromes's Dell, taffy pulls at the gracious home of the Meisters and warm Sunday afternoons under the pines of the broad lawn of the Eschmans.

However, when the group was invited to the Charles Bauman home, Carrie found some reason not to go. Will was puzzled by the repeated excuses considering that Carrie and Ruth Bauman were close friends. He mentioned the fact to his friend, Joseph Meister.

"Oh, didn't you know?" Joseph replied. "Carrie and Ruth's brother, Steve, used to go together. He cared a lot for her, too! But Carrie just wasn't interested in him, nor in anyone else apparently, until you came along. Lucky fellow you are! Or do you realize it?"

The thought was at first incredible and then flattering to Will that of all the fellows in the area, he should be the first to interest Carrie. "By the way, what does Steve do now?" asked Will. He recalled seeing him in the neighborhood only a few times.

"He hasn't been home much lately. Most of the time he is on the road buying and selling for his father's stock farm. They say he is a real keen judge of animals. Spends much of his time in Chicago and Omaha."

Though most of Joseph's words were lost on Will, his mind

did register the words: "He cared a lot for her!" Will was just as well pleased that Steve's work kept him away from home. The thought of taking Steve on as a competitor for Carrie did not appeal to him.

Will, helping other farmers in the community, was striving to save enough from his weekly wages to buy one of Dan Meister's horses and put aside a nest egg for the future.

The small teacher from Big Fox Creek was ever in his mind. Her voice whispered to him in the rustle of corn leaves as he cultivated the long rows, and her face was before him in his sleep. His evenings away from her were spent poring over books she had loaned him.

In the young teacher, Will had met a challenge and an enigma. He reveled in the scope of her conversation, her ready smile and the green glints in her eyes as her spirits rose. He was baffled as she deftly turned aside his more intimate remarks and advances, as elusive as quick-silver — gentle to the touch, only to slip through the fingers.

May had tripped through the depression-worn community that year with her winsomest smile. Each lane and side road was transformed into a blossoming bower. The spring air effervesced with the song and twitter of birds as Will took Carrie home to her boarding place. The horse, drawing the family buggy, walked ever more slowly until it finally stopped beside a clump of wild cherry trees in full bloom. Without warning, Will gathered Carrie into his arms.

"I love you, Carrie!"

He was aware of her closeness for a moment, then her hands pushing them apart. Startled, he asked, "But you do care for me?"

"Yes — " the words came slowly. "Yes I do."

"Enough to marry me some day?"

"Will, I'm not ready to marry anyone, yet. Until then, can't we go on just being friends?"

Will's eyes lit up, "Will you seal that with a kiss?"

She raised her lips to his and his arms enfolded her. "My Darling!" he breathed as their lips met. He felt her body relaxing in his arms, her heart beating against his. Then her body grew tense and she drew away.

With a sigh he picked up the fallen reins and spoke to the standing horse.

Excitement ran high in the community when it was learned that William Jennings Bryan would be speaking at the Bloomfield Fairgrounds. The committee spared no effort in preparation for the event. First, the grounds were rid of litter, then the tall grass was mowed and raked. By the appointed day, a platform with a thatched top had been erected before the grandstand bleachers. Red, white, and blue bunting was draped across the speaker's platform and the lower tier of seats.

Rigs from all parts of the county lined the perimeter of the fairgrounds. Will and Carrie sat about a third of the way up the well-filled bleachers, a spot within good viewing and listening range of the speaker's stand. From their vantage point, they searched for familiar faces in the mass of men in light shirts and women in bright-colored dresses.

Expectant glances watched the road for the arrival of the speaker. At last the polished surrey of the Meisters appeared, drawn by a span of blacks. At a given signal the strains of "Yankee Doodle" burst forth from the trio before the platform: Hiram Heath with the flute, Carl Burrows with the fife, and Harold Browning on the drum.

A hush fell over the crowd as Dan Meister and a stocky built man made their way to the speaker's stand. Then wild cheering broke forth as the guest was introduced. William Jennings Bryan began to speak in a simple, direct manner. The neighbors nodded to each other. Here was a public man who was not going to talk down to them; he spoke their language.

The speaker gained momentum as he progressed into his subject with a voice as silver as the crusade he championed. The abuses of the common people distressed him. He suffered with them under the heavy yoke of high freight rates and low prices for farm produce. He promised them relief if he were elected president. The assembled farmers wildly applauded his suggestions for bettering the economy.

"That man is what this country needs for President!"

exclaimed Will, as he and Caroline made their way to the Steiner home. "What he could do for the common man!"

Carrie nodded with reservation. "An eloquent speaker, yes — but not necessarily good presidential timber."

Will rose to Bryan's defense. "His plan would be bound to work. Coin more silver; the farmer would have more money to buy equipment. He could produce more and the public would have money to buy his products."

"The theory sounds good, but it wouldn't work," replied Carrie.

"You mean you wouldn't give the working man a chance?"

Carrie's eyes flashed. "After all, my folks are farmers, too. But you can't better a situation by tossing out free silver!"

Will's jaw set. It was Carrie who made the conciliatory move. "Let's not quarrel over politics. You stay Democrat, Populist, or whatever! I guess I'll always be Republican."

Will relented, "You know," he said, "you're much sweeter as a lady than a politician!"

Carrie chuckled dryly.

"It's a wonder you didn't call me a Suffragette!"

"Never a Suffragette!" bantered Will. "I have too much respect for your taste in clothes to feature you wearing those atrocious ankle-length bloomers!"

"Will! Now is that nice?"

"Probably not, but nevertheless true!"

They were approaching the neat white house of the Steiner's. Carrie realized that not once had Will made any overture of affection on their drive home. She felt a bit of resentment that Bryan's speech should eclipse all of Will's softer emotions.

"When will we be meeting again?" asked Carrie disliking herself for even asking.

"Probably a couple weeks — " Then he added with a wicked twinkle in his eye, "We laboring men don't have much leisure time on our hands, you know."

CHAPTER EIGHT

Wedding Bells

Louie Sprenger and Annalie Eschman were married the last of May with their love and the intrepidity of youth to bridge them over the uncertain times.

The heavy oak doors to the parlor had been thrown open for the ceremony. Brother Mueller joined the two in matrimony before a bower of white dogwood entwined with ivy. Annalie was radiant in a simple white dress, her cheeks rosy with the glow of happiness. Louie stood beside her, tall in his new dark suit and grave with the importance of the day.

Mary Eschman, demure in a matching pink dress, attended her sister as maid-of-honor. To Will, who served as Louie's best man, the ring ceremony provided a foretaste of the nuptial bliss he had envisioned for Carrie and himself.

Later, the newly wedded couple sat at the head of the long wedding table with its snowy linens. On either side of the festive board were gathered the friends and relatives. Among the guests, Carrie, lovely in a pale blue linen dress, sat next to Will. Only Aunt Celinda cast a dubious glance upon the newly wed couple, "My, how foolish young folks are these days to set up housekeeping in such troublesome times. Even the older and more experienced ones can scarcely keep their heads above water. I was telling Emil the other day he should be thankful he didn't have a house full of children to feed. It keeps him hustling to support the two of us--and me a good manager and 'housely gefrau' at that!"

Emil Meyers glanced uneasily at his wife and at those about

them. Her complaints were drowned out by the booming voice of Uncle Fred calling up the table to the bride and groom, "How are you fixed for housekeeping?"

"Well," replied the groom shyly, "we have a range, a table, four chairs and a bed."

Annalie patted her husband's shoulder. Then reaching up, she placed a firm kiss on his cheek. "Come this winter when the snow flies," she quipped, "we'll have our love to keep us warm."

There was a burst of laughter about the table. Carrie glanced up questioningly into Will's face, rolling her eyes. Then she looked down at her plate.

The men's conversation turned to the familiar topic of farming. When Louie mentioned that he could use a hired man to help repair buildings and fences on the run-down farm they were renting near the home place, Will readily agreed to help.

Will began working with Louie the following week, attacking the most urgent needs first; the holes in the barnyard fence and the missing hinges and latches on the barn doors.

As he shared meals with Louie and Annalie in their small farmhouse with crisp white curtains and meager furnishings, he was intrigued with the couple's zestful approach to married life. At lunch time a kettle of soup with a soup ladle and a loaf of bread centered the small kitchen table. A bowl and spoon marked each place.

Following Louie's brief blessing, Annalie spoke up, "Just help yourself to what's on the table. We have apple cobbler for dessert." When the ladle had scraped the bottom of the kettle and the apple cobbler was gone, the trio pushed back their chairs from the table and with parting jokes went back to work.

Each week saw improvements on the Sprenger place as a new barn roof replaced the missing shingles and a new porch and steps graced the front entrance of the house.

One Monday in early fall, the kitchen table was covered with a pink and white lunchcloth. Annalie, in a dainty white apron over her house dress, ladled the contents of the kettle into the waiting bowls for the two men. "Today, we're celebrating with chicken and dumplings! Louie and I found out this past weekend that we're to become proud parents!"

"And when is this momentous event to take place?" Will glanced over his sister's trim form as he finished chewing a mouthful of chicken.

"Probably the end of February. You're one of the lucky ones to know first."

An intense desire filled Will for a wife, a home and a family of his own. On his next date with Carrie, he related the happiness of Louie and Annalie in their new wedded life and the prospects of their first child.

Carrie sat silently, twisting her handkerchief in her lap. She finally answered with eyes downcast and a tinge of reproach in her voice. "Will, you couldn't live like that, could you, in a bare house – with your wife expecting a baby?"

Will answered defensively. "I don't know but what I could. They love each other, and they're happy!"

A tear trickled down Carrie's cheek as she looked into Will's face. "Well, I couldn't!"

He slipped his arm around her, "Darling, I'm not asking you to live that way. It's just that Louie and Annalie have something that I wish we had!"

"Please be patient in your planning – you won't be sorry," pleaded Carrie.

Will wiped her eyes with her handkerchief and kissed her. "That's all right, honey. We'll work things out."

As Will stepped out of Carrie's home and closed the door, a cold chill swept over him. He shook his head, puzzled. Was it the premonition of a long cold winter – or the dashing of another dream?

To the prairie farmers, the coming winter meant a respite from field work: a time to mend harnesses, a time to inspect machinery and to plan for spring planting. To Louie and Annalie, January meant the approaching birth of their first child. Annalie looked up into Dr. Shelton's face as he finished his routine pre-natal examination. "I'm so enormous! Does that mean it's time now, instead of February, for this young one to be born?"

The doctor leaned over his patient once more and listened

with his stethoscope. "What it means," he announced with a slight grin, "is that you'd better be prepared for twins. There are definitely two sets of heartbeats!"

"Oh my!" exclaimed Annalie in shocked surprise. "That means we'll need twice as many baby clothes. And Louie!" she added with an imperative tone for the first time in their married life. "You'll have to get busy on that second cradle, right away!"

Louie mopped his forehead. "Here I thought I could begin to relax after finishing the first one."

Dr. Shelton laughed heartily. "Unexpected babies aren't that perishable! I've even known parents who used dresser drawers to bed down their offspring in an emergency. Knowing you two – you'll make out just fine. Good luck with your twins!"

True to the doctor's prediction, the twins arrived on schedule the last of February. They were named Thomas and Timothy. Because of Louie and Annalie's doting families, there was an abundance of baby clothing and a lot to spare, and the proud father had two shiny cradles in which to place his newborn sons.

Following his stay with Louie and Annalie, Will spent every day that he was not needed at home in working for other farmers. Through the winter months he assisted at butchering or buzzing and chopping wood. As the early spring sun and rains released winter's frozen grip on the soil, Will followed the team and plow in preparation for the new year's planting.

By the last of April, the rush of spring planting was over. Will counted his earnings of the past year and found he had saved over two hundred dollars – more than enough for the long desired horse. He smoothed the bills fondly as he returned them to his wallet. Then mounting one of his father's horses, he rode over to the Meister farm. He found Dan Meister in the tool shed working on his farm machinery. Will came directly to the purpose of his visit; he wished to buy a horse.

Meister laid down his wrench and wiped his hands on a piece of old toweling that lay nearby. "Let's go out to the horse corral and talk it over."

Perched on the corral fence, the two men watched the horses

for a few moments in silence — an assortment of blacks, grays, chestnuts, bays and roans. Some were grazing quietly; others were galloping about with arched necks and flowing tails.

"Now, just what did you have in mind?"

"Something in a road horse." Willard, who for years had envisioned his dream horse trotting smartly down the road, now found it difficult to single out one from the group of sleek horses before him.

"Which would be your choice, Mr. Meister?"

Meister seemed pleased at the deference to his judgment. "Tell you what I'll do! I'll pick out two or three of my favorites, but the final choice must be yours."

He led out a chestnut-colored horse, a spirited black filly, and a deep bay with a white bell-shaped spot on her forehead. Will noted the rich golden tints of the chestnut and the graceful flow of its mane and tail. The spirit and fire of the black reminded him of a picture of "Pharaoh's Horses" he had seen somewhere. However, his attention was fixed on the bay, her deep, confident eyes and the calm grace of her movements. She whinnied softly and arched her neck as he approached.

"I'll take the bay. What do you call her?"

"I leave that to the buyer."

"Then her name is 'Belle'."

Meister led the bay out of the corral.

"You made a good choice, Will. You'll find she's tractable, nimble on the road, and has stamina not possessed by the highly spirited — such as the black, for instance — and that counts on a long drive. By the way, such qualities count well in a woman, too!"

"Do you know where I can get a buggy to go with her?"

"Cyrus Heath, the blacksmith, had a good-looking one there the other day. You'll probably want to get the horse shod there for road driving, anyway."

"By the way, where is Joseph today?"

"He's over at Bauman's helping put up the second hay crop."

"Oh, I see! Jacob serving for his Rachel!"

Dan Meister laughed heartily. "That's about right, Will. Only it's a good thing there is no Leah in the picture! I doubt whether Joe's ambition would hold out seven more years . . . Say, it's noon! There's Martha calling for dinner. You're not leaving before we eat."

So Will stayed for dinner at the Meisters.

Miriam hustled about, helping her Aunt Martha put food on the table. Her dark curls clung to her forehead, damp from working in the warm kitchen. With blushing cheeks, she enquired about each member of the Eschman family — especially John.

It was mid-afternoon when Will reached the long, low building that housed Cyrus Heath's blacksmith shop. Will made his way up the road winding past apple trees laden with delicate white blossoms.

Two red oxen browsed, knee-deep in meadow grass beneath the trees. Their dark eyes gazed patiently from white faces. A decade earlier they had drawn the heavy wagon loaded with Heath possessions from Indiana to these rolling acres. Their Herculean task of breaking the virgin prairie sod was over. The hickory yoke now hung upon the low wall of the blacksmith shop as they grazed contentedly nearby.

At the entrance to the shop, Will dismounted from his father's horse and led the young bay mare to the door. From the interior of the shop, dimly lit by the dull glowing forge, came the mingled scents of old leather, smoldering coals and scorched horse hoofs. Wagon axles and half-bowed ash rims lined the walls, and high on a peg hung a two-handled draw-knife used for dressing handles.

Cyrus Heath laid down the plow share he was working on and stepped out from behind the anvil. "Aiming to have your horse shod, eh?" he repeated. "Yep, reckon we can take care of you right away — oh Hiram!" he called to his son who was whittling out wagon pins at the rear of the building. "Just lend me a hand at the forge, will ya?"

A young man with dark mustache and snapping black eyes walked to the forge and began working the bellows. The dull red coals quickened into life and gleamed brighter until they became incandescent. The iron horseshoes placed upon the glowing mound, chameleon-like, took on the glowing colors of the coals beneath.

Then Cyrus, squatting on a low stool by the bay mare, carefully pared away the outer portion of her hoof as he held it firmly on his leather apron, his beard swaying gently with his movements.

Conversation drifted to the recent political rally at Bloomfield Fairgrounds and Bryan's speech. "Yep, I reckon that man would do our country good," stated Heath. "I aim to vote for him myself. What we need is more silver in our pockets. And if Bryan will scatter it, my brother, Caleb, will dig it for him. Caleb is working in the Summit Valley, Montana silver field now, you know."

Heath still had the buggy Meister had mentioned. It was in good condition, the paint job on it black and shiny, with a fine red pencil-line trim on the body and wheel spokes. The thills, axles, and single-tree showed no trace of wear. Will left the blacksmith shop with the young mare, Belle, hitched to the buggy and the family horse tied behind.

The following Sunday afternoon found Will calling at the Steiner home. Carrie, wearing a pale green dress of frosty dotted Swiss, joined Will as he was tying Belle to the hitching post.

Her eyes sparkled as she surveyed the new outfit. "Oh, Will!" she beamed. "What a beautiful horse and buggy! And, how well matched they are!"

"Glad you like it," answered Will casually. "You may have to ride in it for a long time. Shall we try it out now?"

For several miles Will put Belle through her paces for Carrie's benefit. Gradually the horse's gait slackened. They were now on a seldom-traveled road. They reached the top of a hill as the sun was sinking behind distant woods.

Will drew the horse to a stop by a row of honey locust trees. The spot had once been the site of a home, marked now only by crumbling foundation stones. Sweetbrier clambered over the ledges as if to soften the ruins with its fragile pink petals. A clump of lilac bushes and a couple gnarled apple trees were the only evidence that human hands had once cared for those deserted acres.

"What a beautiful sunset!" murmured Caroline, as the last arch of the sun dipped behind the woods in a flaming glow of crimson and gold.

Will regarded her longingly: the burnished gold of her hair, the soft light in her eyes, the smile upon her lips. "You are lovely tonight!"

Suddenly he swept her into his arms. "Carrie, I've got to know! You do love me, don't you?"

Her eyes were dewy, her voice caressing, "Yes, Will, I do!"

"Enough to marry me?"

Her voice was very faint, "Enough to marry you, Will."

"Darling . . . " He held her close. His head swam with the sense of her nearness, the exquisite perfume of her person. "You'll never know how long I've been waiting and praying to hear you say that!" He buried his face in her hair and kissed her warm pulsating throat.

"How soon can we be married?"

She drew back a bit in his arms. "Don't you think we should wait until next spring?"

"Another year?" Disappointment welled up in Will's voice.

"Let's not rush into it! I have my school contract for another year at Big Fox. If we both worked in the meantime, we could buy the things that make for gracious living — I mean like furniture, rugs, silver, china and linens. Then we could be proud of our home."

The idea was a far cry from the simple economics of his family where furniture was chosen for its durability and bought only to meet the needs of an expanding family. He recalled Annalie's wedding and the joking reference to the necessary bed and range for housekeeping.

"If you would rather, we'll wait, Carrie." He kissed her again. "After all, we'll have the rest of our lives together!"

Will's heart was singing that night on the way home. The horse traveled surefootedly along the dim margin of the road, past barnyards redolent with the warm, milky scent of cows, past fields of fragrant new-mown hay.

But Will's mind was not on the roadside nor even the newly acquired horse and buggy. His thoughts were racing days, months, years ahead. Carrie was his! Only a few more days until he would hold her in his arms again, to hear her repeat his name tenderly. In a few months she would be his wife! Only a few years and they would have built a home with the fine things Carrie desired and deserved. Yes, and a family of their own in their tomorrows.

The stars were very near that night!

CHAPTER NINE

Westward Ho!

The voice of Fritz Zimmerli rose high in its enthusiasm. "I tell you, Will, there's nothing like it! You look down into those canyons a thousand feet below, then turn and look up a sheer wall hundreds of feet high. It's magnificent! Reaching out before you is the desert, blooming like a flowered carpet −. Man, it does something to you!"

"I'll go with you!" exclaimed Will. "When do we leave?"

"Oh, in a few weeks now."

Fritz wondered vaguely how Caroline would take to the idea of Will taking an extended trip at that time, but he was too judicious to raise the question.

A few days later, Will, in high spirits, drove over the Big Fox Creek School to pick up Caroline. The early March winds had dried the heavy clay roads to a crumbly consistency. The air was penetrating, and he turned up his coat collar against it. Yet the sun was shining and there was a general hint of spring in the air. The grass on the southern hillslope was already green. The willow tops gleamed yellow in the sunlight, and from the brown tufts of grass on the prairie came the clear, cold call of the newly-arrived meadow larks.

Let the cold March winds blow! He would soon be headed for California, land of sunshine!

School was just dismissing when Will arrived at Big Fox Creek. He waited by the door until the last of the girls passed by, giggling shyly. Caroline sat alone, straightening her desk. Will sailed his hat into the room, barely missing her head. Her hands flew to her throat in surprise. Then her eyes crinkled in laughter. "You would frighten one out of a year's growth!" she gasped.

"You've grown plenty to suit me!" Will leaned over and kissed her lightly. "Time for all schoolmarms to close shop."

In a short time the buggy with its two occupants was rolling along between the bare hedgerows toward the Steiner home. "I've got a piece of news for you," announced Will abruptly.

"Well, do tell!"

"In a few weeks I'm leaving with Fritz Zimmerli for all points west of the Missouri."

For a moment Carrie was speechless, unable to comprehend what he had stated as matter of fact.

"Oh, you mean you're going to Kansas with him?"

"No sir-ee, we're stopping at nothing short of California!"

Carrie's mind stiffened. With difficulty she forced it to span the geographic stretches from Iowa to the Pacific which she so adeptly pictured to her classes.

Thinking aloud, she stated, "It would take a couple weeks to make the round trip, by train, with no stopovers."

"Right you are, Honey. But why bar the stopovers?"

"Will, you are joking!"

"Never more serious in my life!"

"But you'd scarcely be back in time for the wedding! We were to be married in June — or had you forgotten?"

"Of course I haven't forgotten! It would mean only a postponement of a few weeks at most. After all, we did postpone it for a year already. Please be reasonable about it. This is the chance of a lifetime to see things outside the county. There's the rest of our lives to settle down."

"Oh I see!" There was a moment of glacial silence. "What do you suppose people around here will say to your going on a cross-country tour and postponing our wedding indefinitely?"

"What difference does it make what folks say? After all, it's our lives we're living."

"Unfortunately, it seems to be only your life that concerns you!" Her eyes blazed green.

They rode on in silence, finally reaching the Steiner gate.

Carrie, in a turmoil, searched in vain for words to bridge the crisis. She hoped desperately that Will would lean over, kiss her and say, "Let's forget about it now and talk it over later." But he sat moodily silent, disappointed that the fulfillment of his long-dreamed-of trip should meet with only scathing rejection.

He opened his mouth – Carrie waited questioningly. "Well, I'd better be getting along."

Carrie's heart sank with a sickening thud. Then fury filled her. "Since you'll be so busy packing these next few weeks, you needn't waste your time coming over." She walked hastily to the house, head held high and eyes brimming with unshed tears.

"Just as you say!" Will's voice was steely. He knew she wasn't going to look back.

He swung Belle out into the road with an angry slap of the reins that caused the startled horse to lunge forward. For several miles Will drove, staring straight ahead. Then the situation seemed to clear. She really hadn't meant what she said. She would get word to him during the week, and they would straighten things out.

The following week, Jacob assigned John and Will to chopping and cording the huge pile of buzzed hickory chunks west of the house. Will was thankful for the job. There was nothing like the swing of an ax and clear ring of splitting wood to wear off the jagged edges of one's temper. Then, too, the woodpile commanded an unobstructed view of the road on which Lew Browning's mail rig could be seen approaching from across the creek. Each morning Will would swing his ax hopefully until mail time, taking pleasure in the flying chips and tautness of his muscles as steel struck wood. Each forenoon as soon as Lew Browning had passed, he would race John to the mailbox and pull out the contents – a seed catalogue, a sample package of liver pills, a notice of a farm sale near Milford . . . That was all and John would tease Will as they returned to their chopping.

On Friday there was an envelope in the mailbox addressed in a woman's handwriting. Will seized it eagerly. It was for John from Miriam Meister. The last of the week turned drizzly. John, declaring the weather was not fit for even a dog to be out, left the woodpile and spent his time in the shelter of the barn mending harnesses. Will, chilled and soaked, finished splitting and piling the wood.

By Sunday morning Will had developed symptoms of the grippe, so he stayed home and did chores while the rest of the family went to church. The afternoon passed slowly with Will torn between two desires. He would go to Carrie that evening. He could feel her in his arms with her head against his shoulder, crying a little and saying it was foolish to have quarreled. In his forgiveness he was even willing to call the trip off – if necessary. But the gentle mood was soon eclipsed by a grimmer thought. She knew that he had only a couple weekends left before the trip, and she had deliberately told him to stay away. All right. He would show her. He wasn't tied to any apron strings – yet!

His restlessness grew toward evening. The grippe symptoms were forgotten. He hitched up Belle, still undecided where to go. His first impulse was to see Fritz.

Accordingly, he drove to the Burrows, Fritz's uncle's place. He tied Belle to the sagging fence and walked through the tall grass to the sunken porch. He was met at the door by Kate Burrows, friendly as always. She brushed her heavy hair back with one hand, as he enquired about Fritz.

No, Fritz wasn't there. He had gone to Memphis for the evening. Was there a message she could give him?

"Well, no – ." Then a sudden inspiration. "How about going to 'Germany' with me tonight?"

Kate gasped, incredulous. "Wait a minute, until I get this straight! You're asking me to go to the Mennonite Meeting House with you?"

"That's what I said."

With an irrepressible laugh and a shrug of her broad shoulders, she said, "Well, I still can't fathom it, but why not? It's fine with me."

Will and Kate found their places beside Joseph Meister and Ruth Bauman in the back pew occupied by young folks.

Hardly were they seated before Carrie entered – alone. She was directly beside the pew before she noticed Will, who was staring piously ahead.

Kate's face had turned a beet red.

A catch of her breath and a raising of her chin — these were the only evidences Carrie gave that she had seen Will and Kate. She swept on by and found a place farther down on the women's side of the aisle.

Joseph reached over and gave Will a vicious nudge. "Man, you ought to be thrashed!"

"Now, what have I done?" parried Will innocently.

"You know doggone well what I mean — treating a girl like that!"

During the next week Will was, by turns, amused and penitent. He never forgot the surprised look on Carrie's face as she passed the seat where he and Kate had been sitting. In a softer mood, Will recalled hearing that a woman's most precious memories centered about her wedding day. Perhaps he had been too hasty putting his trip before their wedding.

There was no need of carrying things too far! The next Sunday he went to church alone, prepared to take Carrie home. He could envision it now: as he held her in his arms, he would tell her that he had canceled his trip west and that their wedding would go on as planned. She would cry softly on his shoulder, and their romance would be renewed.

Carrie appeared a little after the service had begun, poised and attractive in her beige cashmere dress with leg-of-mutton sleeves and high stayed collar. And walking beside her, with his right arm linked to hers, was Steve Bauman! Will's eyes popped in their sockets as he stared in disbelief. His body stiffened. Gradually, he tried to relax his muscles, hoping that brother John and Joe Meister beside him had not noticed his shock.

All right! If that was the way she felt about their engagement, any reconciliation would have to come from her! He would not be the one to eat "humble pie". Never!

The following week flew by with Fritz and Will conferring often on their coming trip. All was now ready.

Anna walked slowly into Will's room with the final armful of shirts, socks and handkerchiefs to be packed into the already full grip. She looked on silently as her son put his knee upon the brown cover of the valise to force its gaping catches together. They closed with a snap. Will reached down and straightened the long leather straps at either end.

"Willard — " she began hesitantly.

Will looked up, momentarily from where he was bending over his valise. "Yes, Mother. What is it?"

"Willard, have you talked to Carrie since you two quarreled?"

Will's jaw set firmly. "She was the one who said to stay away. I'm taking her at her word until she makes the next move."

"Ach, Will! It is not good you should leave without mending your hard feelings."

Will shrugged his shoulders. "Well — "

He turned back to his valise, put his foot on top of it, pulled the straps taut, and buckled them.

"They say absence makes the heart grow fonder."

CHAPTER TEN

Return of the Traveler

The mail carrier was later than usual. For the third time, Anna had left her household duties and walked beneath the pines to the mailbox as if her anxious trips had power to draw him sooner. Shaking her head in disappointment, she was about to return to the house when she finally spied the weathered rig of Lew Browning in the distance. She remained at the mailbox until he drove up.

"Morning, Mrs. Eschman! I'm late today!" he accused himself quickly. "Mrs. Dever on South Road blacked out this morning. The poor kids were nearly scared to death when I got there — till we revived her again."

"Her man — ?" Anna looked inquiringly.

"He's working the road somewhere. Just as well with him drinking — but that boy of theirs, Luke, he's a fine chap! Does most of the work and managing, too, with his paw gone so much."

Anna shook her head. "Poor woman! They say she hasn't the will to live any more. Ever since her Jimmy was killed that night horseback riding, she has been ailing."

"Oh, before I forget it, here's a letter for you!"

Anna's face brightened at the angular writing on the envelope.

"Thank you so much!"

Hardly was the mail rig moving before she had torn open the envelope and scanned its contents. The message was brief, barely covering one side of the sheet. Letter writing was always a tedious

71

task for Will:

"Dear Mother,
    I'll be home on Tuesday, June twenty-second.
Have John meet me at the station, and tell Father to
bring out the fatted calf. Your prodigal son is returning
to become a family man! Will."

Anna wiped her eyes with her apron. "Ach, Willard. You
would joke at such a time!"

Will sat looking out of the train window. A feeling of warmth
and elation surged over him as he watched the unfolding scenery
become more familiar. He had left Fritz Zimmerli at the home of
his parents in Kansas. It seemed good to have time alone with his
thoughts.

In the distance, a group of farm buildings nestled at the foot
of a hill. Now a huge field of corn revolved through the rail-coach
window like a dark green sea, shimmering in the sunlight. Then in
the distance, a narrow road threaded its way through the folds of
a wooded hill. How many times had he and Carrie driven along
just such a road!

Ah, Carrie! How good it would be to see her once more!
Looking back, it had been silly of them to quarrel over such a
trivial thing as the trip. He would make it up to her. There would
be the rest of their lives together.

From ahead came the frequent whistling of the engine as it
plowed between the hills, a furrow that would lead eventually to
the home town of Pulaski. Suddenly there whirled into view the
large barns and white board fences of the Bauman Stock Farm.
Like threads of a bad dream, the thriving Bauman ranch triggered
in Will's memory the scene of Carrie and Steve together in church.
Will brushed the thought aside. They were nearing his destination
now. Will stood up and reached for his grip in the overhead rack.
The train slowed down, past the village cemetery with its white
markers, past the millpond and the water tower.

Then with the grinding of brakes, the locomotive lurched to
a halt before the dull gray depot with its sign PULASKI. Will

picked up his valise and walked briskly down the aisle of the coach. It was good to be home again! He had reached the platform when the train came to a final jolting stop.

"Hi — you!" exclaimed John by way of greeting. "So you're back again I see. Here, let me take your valise."

He reached over and took the suitcase from his brother's hand.

John's face already had a deep tan from the spring work in the fields. His shoulders seemed broader than when Will had last seen him several weeks earlier.

Will took a deep breath as they settled in the spring wagon for the homeward drive. After many hours on the train, it was refreshing to breathe the clean country air.

"M-m-m-m-m-m-m-, smell that clover," he sniffed appreciatively.

"Yep, soon be time to start haying."

"Well, how's everything going?"

"Oh, all right I guess," drawled John.

Will sensed constraint in John's manner and vague uneasiness filled him.

"Is everybody all right?"

"Oh, sure!" John hastily assured him. "How did you like your trip?"

They had now reached the home place. The hillside seemed unusually green as they walked down the grade from the barn to the house. The scent of cooking chicken greeted them from the kitchen. They were met at the door by Minnie, beaming broadly, her dark braids hanging down the back of her blue checked pinafore.

"Something sure smells good!" inhaled Will.

"Ja!" bubbled Minnie. "The fatted calf was too hard to catch for dinner. Anyway, we thought a couple hens would fit better in the kettle!"

Anna entered the kitchen at that moment, smoothing her hands over her apron. Will drank in her features: the round placid face, ruddy from working in the sun and wind, the silver streaks spreading crescent-like through her smooth dark hair and the steady blue-gray eyes that crinkled as she smiled.

"Hello, Mamma, how are you?"

Anna responded by stretching up and planting a firm kiss on Will's cheek. "We're glad you are home again!" Then she added, "Come now, everybody. Get yourselves ready for dinner!"

Jacob, just in from the field, stepped over to the sink by the kitchen pump. He was steamy with perspiration, and his wet shirt clung to his back. After washing his hands and face, he rubbed them vigorously on the coarse towel hanging nearby, then picked up a comb on the sink ledge and ran it through his thinning hair.

He turned, with a broad grin, reached out a sun-browned sinewy arm and gripped Will's hand, "Welcome home, Son! How was your trip?"

"Wonderful!" beamed Will. "I'll tell you all about it once we get to the table. That food smells great!"

The meal was made up of Will's favorite dishes: chicken and dumplings, new green peas, the first of the season, and cabbage slaw. Here, Anna admitted she was really extravagant, for in spite of the advanced season, the cabbage was still so young that it had taken three heads to fill the bowl. Already cut for dessert were two cherry pies with thick, red juice outlining the sixths.

Between passing food and eating, Will related some of the highlights of his trip: picking oranges in the groves, seeing the Grand Canyon and visiting Chinatown.

By now they had finished the dessert, and an awkward silence fell over the table.

"How's everybody around here?" Though Will had already asked the same thing several times before, the question just popped out.

"All right, I guess," answered Jacob.

John pushed back his chair from the table.

"Well, I'd better be getting back to my hoeing."

And Sammy offered to help him with unusual alacrity.

"How's Carrie these days?" Will picked at the few remaining crumbs of pie crust on his plate with his fork as he made the casual query.

Anna hesitated, "All right, I guess!"

Will again sensed the guarded speech, present since his arrival home. Now he knew — it had to do with Carrie!

"Seen her lately?" he asked quickly.

"Why — why — yes, just last Sunday."

"Guess I'll run over there this evening — "

Anna left the room quickly with a choking sound. Minnie hastily carried a couple of plates to the kitchen.

"No, Will, no — " Jacob's voice came thick and low, as he placed a restraining hand on Will's shoulder. "Carrie's married!"

Will's jaw dropped open, unbelieving. "Married — ? But she couldn't be — I wasn't even here!" He stopped short.

"Yes," Jacob nodded slowly. "She married Steve Bauman."

Will sank back into his chair at the table, staring at his father in disbelief. "When did it happen? The wedding, I mean."

"Two weeks ago Saturday," replied Jacob.

"That was to have been our wedding day!"

Jacob did not remind his son that he was not around. He was the one who had asked to postpone it.

Will resumed with a grim hint of humor, "So-o-o, everything went off just as planned with one slight difference — a change in bridegrooms."

Pushing himself back from the dinner table he asked, "Well, what needs to be done in the line of field work?"

"To tell the truth, things are pretty well caught up for now. We finished cultivating the corn a couple days ago. Maybe the last time it will need to be gone over."

With a shrug Will observed, "Looks as though this part of the world is getting along very well without me."

Jacob rubbed his bearded chin slowly, "I can think of one thing to do, if your heart is set on getting a workout. You know the old hog lot down by the creek bottom?"

"You mean the one grown up with tall weeds?"

"Ja! By plowing it now, we could get rid of all those tall weeds before they seed off. Also, we have some left-over clover seed. If that was sown in there, it would make good green pasture for the pigs to root in later."

"Well, I'd better get at it."

"There's time enough to start tomorrow," observed Jacob.

"Guess I'll take Belle out for a drive then."

"Suit yourself! You'll find her in the barn."

Belle raised her head and whinnied as Will opened the barn door. She stretched out her neck and nuzzled the palm of his hand with her nose as he approached. All the adventures of his trip that Will had been saving to tell the family seemed unimportant now — and he preferred the company of his horse to human companionship. Having hitched Belle to the buggy, he trotted her down the road, across the creek bridge and around the corner. But once out of sight of the home place, he allowed the horse to take its own gait as he sank back in the buggy, lost in reverie.

The road led past the old house on the the hill where he and Carrie had stopped beneath the wild cherry tree. It had been in full bloom then, and he recalled its fragrance as the two of them had discussed their future plans together. There were no blossoms now; small fruit had taken over the branches. Then he remembered — that had been over a year before. So long ago! Even the memories had turned to dust and ashes. A shudder passed over him.

The horse traveled on past the Burrows place where Fritz Zimmerli had stayed with his relatives. Only Fritz, his traveling companion, was not there now. He was back home in Kansas. Certainly, Will was in no mood for the laughter and banter of Kate Burrows this afternoon.

In the distance the white Mennonite church gleamed softly neath the elms in the twilight. Will felt like an "outsider" looking at a photograph. "Well," he mused to himself, "the folks at Germany are probably having a field day chuckling over the wedding with the switched bridegrooms." To Will there was only one agony worse than failure; that was ridicule.

Belle instinctively turned in at the church driveway. Will turned her back into the road, slapped the reins lightly and they continued on their way.

It was dark when he returned home, and the Eschman family had retired for the night. That is, all except Anna. She had a lunch prepared for him: a chicken sandwich, potato salad, a piece of pie and a glass of milk. If she wondered where he had been, she never asked.

"It's good to have you home again, Son," she remarked as she moved the lamp to the center of the table for better lighting.

CHAPTER ELEVEN

New Beginnings

 $\mathcal{N}$ ext morning Will woke up to the smell of coffee and the clattering sounds of utensils and dishes in the kitchen below. He realized they had not wakened him at the usual time to help with the morning chores.

As he entered the kitchen, Mary and Minnie were setting the plates and silverware on the red and white checked tablecloth. Anna was stirring the "graham" flour into a saucepan of boiling water with a wire whisk. Cooked graham was a special treat after the usual breakfast of hot oatmeal. The home-cured bacon was already cooked and placed in the warming oven while the frying pan waited for the eggs to be fried last.

By now Jacob and John had entered the house with pails of milk, warm from the cows. They stepped into the summer kitchen where, after straining the milk, they measured out a couple pitchersful for house use then poured the rest into large flat pans. As the milk cooled, the cream would rise to the top and be later skimmed off for churning.

Sam arrived at the table late, breathless from chasing the calves back into the pen from which they had escaped earlier.

Following breakfast, Mary handed the well-worn German Bible to her father. In a guttural voice Jacob began reading a portion of Psalm 103:

> *"Bless the Lord, O my soul; and all that is within me, Bless His holy name.*

> *Bless the Lord, O my soul, and forget not all His benefits.*
> *Who forgiveth all thine iniquities.*
> *Who healeth all thy diseases.*
> *Who redeemeth thy life from destruction,*
> *Who crowneth thee with loving-kindness and tender mercies."*

Then folding his hands on the Bible, Jacob raised his closely cropped, bearded chin and asked God's blessing and guidance for each family member for the day. The words eased their way into Will's distressed mind as oil upon troubled waters.

With devotions over, there was a general shuffling sound as chairs were pushed back from the table.

"Well, I'd better get to those weeds in the hog lot."

Jacob spoke up. "Be sure you let the team rest often. That will be hot, steamy work!"

Will loaded the plow on the stone float and rode it with feet far apart as the team trotted down the hill with their harnesses jangling.

At the edge of the hog lot he unloaded the plow, hitched the horses to it and sank the point of the share into the mucky ground. The soil was the consistency of black cheese thickly interlaced with weeds. The horses leaned forward and strained at collars and tugs as they began to cut the first furrow. With a series of dull ripping sounds, the plow sliced through the tough interlaced roots of pig weed and saw grass that towered up to the horses' shoulders.

With the reins tied together and over his shoulders, Will gripped the plow handles tightly as it lunged through tall weeds. The serrated edges of saw grass lashed across his arms and face, leaving crimson scratches in their wake.

He paused after plowing a complete round of the hog lot, giving the team a chance to rest. The dark coats of the horses were shiny and steaming with sweat. Their nostrils were distended, and they snorted at the rank odors of chopped weeds and muck beneath the hot sun.

Will looked down at the long scratches on his arms as the blood oozed to the surface. Somewhere he had read of early penitents hiring a person to scourge them for their misdeeds. "Flagellation" he thought they called it. "Well," he mused, "if scourging was needed to erase his rash actions, he reckoned that saw grass was as good a punishing agent as any."

"So be it!" he resolved. "God, please help me 'face up' to Carrie's wedding, to take it like a man, and I'll follow you closer."

Will turned the team about and began his second round across the hog lot. It was easier now as he walked in the freshly cut furrow. With the passing hours, gleaming black furrows gradually filled in the space formerly taken over by the tall, noxious weeds. By evening the small field was plowed.

On the following day Will returned to the scene with a spike-tooth harrow and clover seed on the float. The horses walked briskly as he, by turns, harrowed and floated the plot, picking up the weed stalks that rose to the surface. By early evening the soil was soft and crumbly to the touch. With seed bag slung over one shoulder, he walked back and forth, scattering the seed in rhythmical motion. A few more rounds with the horse-drawn harrow and the seed was covered.

Will came in from the field that night footsore and weary but with the satisfaction of a job well done. After stepping out of his grimy work clothes and bathing in the galvanized tub in the summer kitchen, he sank into bed and almost immediately fell asleep. He roused only slightly as a thunderstorm passed over, heralded at first by faint rumbles and shimmering lights, then rising to a crescendo of blinding flashes of lightning and crackling thunder. There followed the staccato beat of raindrops against the window pane, then the steady downpour of rain washing, cooling and reviving the tired, thirsty fields and landscape.

Next morning Jacob beamed at the breakfast table. "Will, your seeding of the hog lot was timed just right. With last night's shower it should sprout immediately."

With Sunday breakfast over, there was the usual scurrying about as the Eschman family prepared and dressed for church. Jacob glanced up quizzically as Will emerged from his room shaved and in his Sunday suit.

"Oh, so you're going to church today?"

"Yep, I usually go."

"Will —" Jacob hesitated as if rethinking his next comment.

"Yes?" Will waited.

"Be careful —" Jacob finished lamely, "what you do and say!"

"I usually am!"

After the family had driven off in the carriage, Will resumed dressing for the church service. He had polished his shoes until they shone. He brushed the unruly lock of hair over his right eye into a partial wave. Then having worked on his tie until it suited him, he fastened it down with the tie clasp Carrie had given him for Christmas.

Hitching up Belle, he took another road to church so as not to overtake the family on the way.

Brother Mueller was already preaching when Will entered the church. Though there was no pause in the sermon, Will was aware of the minister's eyes glancing his way as he sat in the back pew beside John and Joe Meister.

From his seat in the back, Will looked over the congregation. Yes, they were there! Carrie and Steve Bauman sitting half way back from the front, Carrie as neat and dainty as ever, Steve sitting beside her with his arm protectively across the back of the seat.

With the singing of the last hymn, the congregation remained standing for the benediction; the sound of voices rose as members began greeting one another. Joseph reached over to shake Will's hand.

"Didn't know you were back from your trip yet."

"Yep, got back a few days ago. Been pretty busy around home."

Pastor Mueller was leading the way up the aisle and stopped to greet Will. "Good to see you this morning!" as he grasped his hand firmly. By now Carrie and Steve were also making their way toward the back of the church. Those around them fell back quietly, listening expectantly as the couple approached Will. All eyes were upon the three — Carrie, Steve and Will.

Carrie had not seen Will until she was almost even with him in the aisle. She caught her breath softly.

Will reached out his hand toward her, "I wish you much happiness, Carrie!" His voice was low but steady.

"Thank you, Will," Carrie's eyes lowered and did not meet his, her words scarcely audible.

"And congratulations, Steve!" Will raised his voice as he shook hands with the new bridegroom.

"Thank you, sir!"

Steve and Carrie made their way out, stopping here and there to visit with friends as they went.

With shoulders erect, Will walked to his buggy. The crisis was over. It would be easier now. Once out of the church driveway, Belle made her way trotting homeward. It did not matter that Will could not see the road. His eyes were blurred with tears.

CHAPTER TWELVE

Apple Butter Time

Sammy Eschman looked up from his bowl of oatmeal and glanced out of the window. "Who's that coming so early in the morning?"

Jacob, stepping to the door, watched the figure dismount and tie his horse to the hitching post at the edge of the lawn.

"Why, it's Louie!"

"Mary, put another plate on the table!" called Anna as she poured another cup of hot coffee.

By now Louie had sunk down in the spare chair at the table. Jacob's even gaze met his. "Well, Louie, what brings you out so early in the morning? Everything O.K. at home?"

"Well, yes — I guess," the caller answered slowly. "I really came to see if I could get some extra help cutting corn. I seem to be getting behind with my field work."

Jacob set his coffee cup down after taking a sip, "We're pretty well caught up with our corn cutting here; I can spare Will, if he wants to go."

By now Anna had fried a couple more eggs which she brought to the table with thick, crusty slices of homemade bread.

"And how's Annalie?" she asked, looking Louie in the eyes.

Louie's voice trembled as he looked down at the coffee cup he was holding in both hands. He proceeded miserably, "Your — your Annalie, so full of joy and chatter! I have ruined her life! She spends all her time trying to work and keep up with the twins. When I try to talk or ask her something, she doesn't seem

83

to hear me! She just starts crying!"

He looked up, expecting expressions of shock on his listener's faces, but instead there were merely nods of understanding and concern.

Louie continued on. "I don't know what's to become of us when she has still another child to look after! Lord knows I've tried to help, but I'm no good at housework. All I accomplish is to get farther behind in my field work." Tears of frustration threatened to overspill his brimming eyes as he set down his coffee cup.

A wave of guilt swept over Will as he listened with the others. He was sure he had never felt that kind of concern for Carrie, not for anyone else for that matter, such as Louie was now voicing for Annalie.

Anna broke the uncomfortable silence. "Don't fret yourself, Louie. Everything will look brighter after the new baby comes. You will see! Don't worry if Annalie doesn't talk back; just hold her close and tell her you love her."

Minnie stuffed the last of her bread crust in her mouth. "Hey vat you volks need is a cuffle of bloodhounds to track down Timmy and Tommy, den tie 'em up –." She ended her advice abruptly with a coughing spell.

Jacob chuckled, "Not bad advice, Minnie, but next time don't try to talk with your mouth full!"

Anna spoke again. "I heard that Meriel Browning is good at helping about the house. Maybe you could hire her. It would make Annalie more comfortable, at least until she gets into a routine after the baby comes."

Louie responded eagerly, "I'll stop by Browning's this morning and find out if she can come!" He rose to leave at once.

John nudged Will on the way to the barn, "How about taking some buckeyes to Louie's place? Then you and Meriel can make portieres in your spare time."

Will responded with a sharp jab to the ribs, "How would you like to be wrapped around that gate post?"

"Eh, what's going on here?" asked Jacob, catching only the last few words of the exchange between the brothers.

Will shrugged, "Just a little unfinished business between us from nine years ago!"

On the following day, Will, armed with a corn knife, rode horseback to Louie's place. The October morning had dawned, clear and sunny. The leaves on the hickory were a burnished gold and the apple trees were weighted down with their bounty of scarlet fruit.

Will did not go to the house but made directly for the cornfield where he was joined a short time later by Louie. "Well, how is the new hired girl making out?"

"Just great!" beamed Louie, satisfied by a warm, hearty breakfast. "The boys take to her real good. That helps a lot! And Annalie was in good spirits this morning."

"Yep, I would imagine so! Not having to keep up with those two little cyclones, in her condition!"

Will and Louie were well matched as workers. Swinging in unison, they cut the stalks a few inches above the ground. The cornstalks trembled and fell like timber into their arms. Then setting the bunches together with the bottoms spread, the men deftly tied the stalks above the middle, leaving the cornshocks standing like rows of wigwams across the field.

By noon they had worked up ravenous appetites, and at the sound of the dinner bell, they headed promptly for the house. They arrived to find the kitchen floor freshly scrubbed and most of the dinner on the table. Meriel, her face flushed from hustling, was taking the cornbread out of the oven while Annalie sat with an arm about each of the twins.

"Hi, Tommy and Timmy! How are my favorite twins today?"

"Unky Will!" they caroled together. Leaving Annalie's side, they ran to Will, throwing their arms around his two legs.

"Hey, what a greeting!" laughed Will, struggling to keep his balance.

"I eat with Muril," piped up Tommy.

"Me too!" chimed in Timmy.

"Well, O.K. boys," agreed Meriel, "but you'll have to give me time to get things on the table."

The meal was a simple one: beans and cornbread, boiled potatoes and coleslaw, with apple crisp for dessert. Having started the food around the table, Meriel took her place between the highchairs of the two twins.

"Are you sure you don't want one of us to feed them?" queried Annalie. "They have been shadowing you all morning."

"No problem," replied Meriel as she helped first Tommy, then Timmy shove their spoons into their plates of food. Now and then she would manage a bite for herself between theirs. Tommy ate with speed and vigor; Timmy took time between bites to gaze around the table and grin at the grown-ups sitting there.

Looking at his nearly empty plate, Tommy decided the meal was over. "O.K., all gone!" he exclaimed. Turning his plate upside down, he dropped it on the floor and started to get out of his chair.

"Tommy! Sit down!" ordered Louie, staring sternly across the table.

With eyes glued to his father's face, Tommy eased back into his chair. Pulling his forefinger through the leftover food, he began drawing pictures on the tray of his highchair.

"Let me wipe your hands," offered Meriel as she pulled a dish towel from the top band of her apron.

"No! I wipe 'em myself!" Pulling away from Meriel, he ran his gooey fingers through his hair, leaving starchy spikes radiating from his head. Tommy giggled as his hands passed over the stiffened mess. "Look! I've got Beany hair!"

Meanwhile Timmy, playing with both hands in his dish, was squeezing beans and cornbread between his fingers. Delighted with his brother's antics, he thrust both plastered hands through his curly, blond locks.

"See! Me Beany haired, too!"

"Stop it, Timmy!" scolded Louie.

The startled youngster turned quickly toward his father, knocking his half-filled dish off the highchair tray − onto Meriel's blue gingham dress and the floor!

"Oh, no!" exclaimed Meriel as she wiped off her dress with the dish towel. "It's a good thing we didn't have spinach for dinner." She hurried to get a cloth and dust pan to clean the floor.

Across the table, Will was secretly enjoying the drama as he mentally compared Meriel's reactions with what Carrie might have done.

First, Carrie would probably never have placed herself between two little dynamos like Tommy and Timmy at meal time. Secondly, he could not imagine Carrie with beans and cornbread on her immaculate clothing. Though she was a teacher, he had never seen her in action with anyone except adults.

Louie promptly carried the twins off for their afternoon nap, and Meriel, seemingly unperturbed by the incident, cleaned up the floor and returned to her meal as the others were ready to leave the table.

Meriel used each sunny autumn day to help Annalie catch up on some of her housecleaning. The bedding was washed and aired in the brisk autumn breeze. Tommy and Timmy had a great time chasing each other in and out between the sheets billowing on the line.

Later, when Meriel went to gather in the bedding, she suddenly realized the twins were nowhere around.

"Timmy, Tommy!" she called. There was no response.

"Annalie, have you seen the twins?"

Annalie stiffened in alarm. The two women ran to the barn, the hen house, the tool shed, Meriel dashing on ahead, Annalie following at an unwieldy gait, panting from exertion. Meriel hesitated, then wondered aloud if there were any open pits or streams in the area. Annalie assured her she knew of no such places.

Meanwhile, Will and Louie, with swinging corn knives were nearing the edge of the field. Just a few rows of corn remained standing. They had stepped over to the next row when a small tousled head popped out from between the corn leaves.

"Sh-h-h. I'm hiding from Timmy!"

From the next row came another voice. "Not so!! I'm hiding from Tommy!"

Flabbergasted, Louie picked up one boy, Will, the other. "What in tarnation are you two doing out here in the cornfield?"

"No fun at home!" they declared in unison from the men's arms.

"Miss anything around here?" asked Louie as he delivered the twins to their mother.

"Well, thank the Lord!" exclaimed Annalie. "We looked everywhere and were just about frantic! Where on earth did you find them?"

"Oh, they were playing Hide-and-Seek in the corn field."

"Why, that's nearly half a mile away," gasped Annalie. "The very thought of two three-year-olds getting that far from home makes my hair stand on end!"

After the boys were tucked in bed that night, the grownups decided some means had to be devised to keep closer track of them. Meriel had heard of a plan that sounded like it might work. With Louie and Annalie's permission, she started on her project the very next night.

Using strips from worn-out overalls, she fashioned them into shoulder and breast straps, which, in turn, were joined to form a small harness for each of the boys. With red yarn, Meriel outlined the name **TIMMY** on one harness and **TOMMY** on the other.

The next evening Annalie looked up from the baby sweater she was knitting to where Meriel was sewing and Louie was reading. "Do you know what I'd like to do before the baby comes? Make a batch of apple butter!"

Louie stared in astonishment at his wife, who a week earlier had been too exhausted to do the simple kitchen chores.

"That would take a lot of work! Are you sure you're up to it?"

"If our families came for the day, we could enjoy a good visit and end up with enough apple butter for everyone. You know, 'many hands make light work!' Besides, I've had a real hankering for apple butter!"

"If you're sure it won't tax you too much, we'll invite the folks, and I'll see to it that there are plenty of apples picked for the occasion."

Will chopped enough wood for the apple butter festival and tossed it in a pile close to where the fire would be built. Next, the huge kettle, wooden paddles and other large containers were rounded up and washed in preparation for the day. Outdoor tables were improvised from boards on sawhorses to supplement those in the house. On the day of the get-together, each woman was to bring her own paring knife and a large pan for her own use, along with a passing dish of food for the dinner.

The day dawned clear and promised to be unseasonably warm for October. Before any guests arrived, Meriel spent a little time with the twins putting on their denim harnesses, shaking the reins and calling, "Giddy-up, Tom and Timmy," as they raced around the yard. When they paused, Timmy tugged at her skirt.

"Say me first!"

"All right!" obliged Meriel. "Giddy-up, Tim and Tommy," and the trio made one more circle of the yard, galloping together.

"Now it's time to put my horses in the corral!" So saying, Meriel slipped the reins over a broken limb of a tree. For a short time the boys enjoyed their play of being corralled while Meriel went about the preparations for the day.

Aunt Celinda and Uncle Emil were the first to arrive. Immediately, her glance fell upon the twins, who, by now, had wound the reins about the tree and themselves. Timmy was wailing over his lack of freedom to run.

"Oh, those poor little dears!" exclaimed Aunt Celinda, hustling over to them. "What a cruel thing, treating those darling little boys like — like — dumb animals!"

"You're half right, Aunt Celinda," chuckled Will as he walked up behind her. "Little animals, yes! Dumb — by no means!"

Aunt Celinda was finally convinced that the twins, far from being abused, were enjoying the game of being horses; also they were being kept from getting into the fire or wandering away.

She turned her attention to the purpose of the day. "I told Emil to get a move on this morning! I never was one to come dragging in when there was work to be done."

"That's great!" lauded Annalie, approaching slowly and ponderously. "You can start right now on this basket of apples. Take as many as you like. Dump them first in the tub of water to wash, then you can work at your own speed. When they are peeled, quartered and cored, they go into the copper kettle for cooking."

"I know!" interrupted the older woman. "I was doing this back when you were a toddler in diapers!"

Once Celinda's hands got into rapid action, peeling the shining red fruit, her mood softened. Her sympathetic gaze passed over Annalie's bulky figure beside her.

"You poor dear! What can I do to help you?"

Annalie laughed shortly as she passed her hand over her distended abdomen. "Just pray this isn't another set of twins!"

Others were arriving and the place began to hum with activity. A couple quarts of cider were poured into the kettle as starting liquid for the peeled apples, and a delicious, spicy aroma filled the air causing the nostrils and palate to tingle.

When the Eschman family arrived, Anna and Mary took their places beside Celinda and began peeling apples. Minnie hustled over to the twins. Unwinding the reins from the tree, she proceeded to "drive" them around the yard, much to their squealing delight.

Martha and Miriam Meister joined the group somewhat later, chatting and laughing as they reminisced with Anna about the time they peeled apples with them, the summer of the tornado.

Meanwhile the men-folk stoked the fire under the bubbling copper kettle and refilled the tub with clean water for washing apples. Then pulling a couple of benches to one side, they visited with Louie about his crops.

Meriel seemed to be everywhere, her slender body moving about those seated at the tables. She emptied the pans of apple peelings and returned the clean, empty pans to their owners. In between, she set the salads and desserts on the kitchen table and placed dishes of hot food in the oven.

By noon the large kettle of apples and cider had simmered until the apples were tender. The time was right for a break. The group filed into the kitchen where the food was waiting with a stack of plates at one end of the table. Following a blessing by Jacob, each heaped his plate from the bowls of scalloped corn, baked beans, potato salad, and squash with orders from Annalie to go back for seconds and a helping of apple pie.

Carrying their plates outside, they basked in the warm sunshine as they ate at the improvised tables beneath the bright trees.

Following the meal, the group again went into action. With

the dishes washed, Meriel, Miriam and Mary began washing jars for the apple butter and placing them in pans of water on the range to sterilize until time for filling. Anna and Martha stirred white and brown sugar into the smooth apple sauce in the copper kettle. Annalie stood nearby with containers of cinnamon, ginger and cloves.

"Easy on the spices," Louie called over to her, "so we don't have to put out any stomach fires!"

Annalie made a wry face at him. "I'll go easy on the cloves and ginger, but I never saw anything hurt with plenty of cinnamon!" So saying, she dumped in the whole container of cinnamon.

Jacob had banked the glowing embers for a constant heat, and each took his or her turn at stirring the spicy, bubbling mass within the kettle, using a broad, rake-like paddle to prevent sticking and scorching. The huge bulk of apple butter gradually diminished as it thickened to a spreading consistency.

The hot jars were brought out from the kitchen and quickly filled with the appetizing spread. Melted paraffin was poured on top of each jar as a sealer. The thick crustation around the edges of the kettle was scraped into small open containers to be used first.

"M-m-m-m-m, mighty good!" pronounced Louie, smacking his lips, as he licked his sticky fingers.

The visiting neighbors and families prepared to leave as chore time approached. Annalie urged a few jars of the apple butter upon each of the departing guests.

"What a good day this has been!" declared Martha, as she and Miriam left with Dan Meister. "We'll have to do it again next year!"

Tommy and Timmy, exhausted from a day of excitement, lay down on the kitchen floor with their harnesses still on and went to sleep. "Poor, tired little ponies!" soothed Anna as she carried each twin to his bed. Then she and Jacob and the rest of the Eschmans gathered their belongings and left for home. Will volunteered to stay and help clean up.

Annalie wiped off the jars of apple butter, thirty-six of them, and Louie carried them down to the fruit cellar. Will and Meriel worked on the paddles and copper kettle in the yard, Meriel scrubbing the top part with soapy water and a metal scraper while Will used a scrub brush on the bottom.

"Do you have any idea how long you'll be working here?"

"Probably until a week or so after the baby comes."

Meriel paused a moment, brushed a wisp of hair from her eyes, and without warning, toppled over, almost falling into the kettle.

"Whoa there!" Will sprang to his feet and caught her in his arms before she completely fell. "Are you all right?"

Meriel flushed with embarrassment. "Oh, yes, I'm fine! I don't know whatever possessed me to lose my balance."

"You've been overdoing today while you helped everyone else!" Will was surprised; his observation had slipped out before he realized it.

"Well, anyway, I'm fine now and it's time to eat a bite before you leave for home."

The supper was a snack made up of leftovers from the noon picnic with glasses of milk and apple butter on bread for dessert.

It was dark when Will left for home, riding Belle. As his horse jogged along, the episode of the early evening flashed through his mind. Meriel, losing her balance — was it planned? No! She was completely undesigning and lacking in coyness. As he recalled holding her slender, almost frail body in his arms, there was a thrill, but the emotion would pass for protectiveness rather than romance or endearment.

CHAPTER THIRTEEN

Arrival of a Princess

Following Will's departure, the lamps in the Sprenger home were soon extinguished and household members fell into bed. Louie mused as he closed his weary eyes, "It's been a full, rewarding day; but thank goodness there won't be another like it for at least another year." His wife lay beside him, breathing heavily in deep sleep.

Less than two hours later, Annalie shook her husband's shoulder. "Wake up, Louie! I think this is it!"

"Huh," he responded sleepily. Then as he woke fully, he sprang out of bed. "IT IS?? I'll go for Dr. Shelton right away! No, wait! I'd better stop at your folks on the way and let them know."

He strode quickly through the house and knocked on the door of the bedroom where Meriel was sleeping. "Annalie thinks the baby is coming. I'm leaving for the doctor now."

Meriel was up and dressed by the time Louie left the house. She rekindled the fire in the range and put the tea kettle and another pan of water on to heat. She then went into Annalie's bedroom where Annalie, by turns, was either lying still or writhing in pain.

"How can I best help you?"

"Just hold my hand!" Annalie moaned, biting her lips.

Meriel grasped her hand firmly, bending over to wipe her forehead as beads of perspiration gathered upon it.

"Are the pains getting closer?"

"Uh-huh!" panted Annalie, as another contraction seized her. Meriel glanced at the clock. Louie had been gone nearly an hour. The folks should be here by now. "Dear God, let them come soon!" she prayed to herself. She wiped Annalie's forehead again and straightened her pillow.

The front door clicked open and quick steps echoed across the kitchen floor. Then the pleasant round face of Anna appeared at the bedroom doorway. Meriel quickly stepped back to make room for her at the bedside. "Thank God, you're here!" she murmured fervently.

"How close are the contractions?" asked Anna, placing her hand on Annalie's abdomen.

"From three to five minutes." Meriel answered.

"Then I think the little one is about to arrive. I'll be needing some warm water and towels."

Almost before Anna had finished speaking, Meriel was pouring water in a wash basin at the stove and testing its warmth with her elbow.

"Meriel, do you know where Annalie keeps the baby blankets and clothing?" asked Anna, as Meriel placed the basin on the stand by the bed.

"Yes, I'll get them right away." Meriel hurried to the adjoining room. By the time she returned with the needed items, she heard the crying of an infant.

"It's a girl!" exclaimed Anna as she carefully washed off the squirming newborn. Very soon the baby was wrapped in a blanket and placed in its mother's arms.

"Isn't she a little sweetheart?" murmured Annalie, gazing down at the pink bundle in her arms, noting the dark brown hair, the closed eyes and the tiny fists.

"What are you going to call her?" asked Anna.

"Her name is Sara."

"Sara, indeed!" approved Anna. "She is a little princess, every inch and pound."

"Meriel, how about making a pot of coffee?" suggested Anna. "By the time Louie and the doctor get here, we'll all be ready for a snack. Oh, I forgot all about poor Jacob out there! Send him in, too!"

Soon the aroma of hot coffee filled the house, and the apple pie was set on the table. Jacob, beaming, stepped into the bedroom to view his first grand-daughter. "Such a pretty baby!" he chortled as he tickled the baby's cheek with his work-roughened forefinger.

Louie and the doctor finally arrived. Louie hurried over to his wife's side, holding her close, as they looked at the little one in her arms. "She's beautiful!" he exclaimed, "Just like her mother."

After examining mother and child, Dr. Shelton pronounced them both fine. "You have a perfect baby there. You women folk are going to put me out of business, yet," he joked, with a twinkle in his eye.

After the midnight snack of coffee and pie, Dr. Shelton left.

"Can you stay the rest of the night?" asked Annalie wistfully of her parents.

"They can sleep in my room! I'll be fine on the couch," offered Meriel. Once again, in the early hours of the morning, the Sprenger household settled down, with a new princess in their midst.

Will arrived at the Sprenger place, the next morning, to find his parents and Louie eating breakfast together. The fact that they were all in a cheerful mood assured Will that there was no emergency. Frankly, he and the rest of the family had been concerned when Jacob and Anna failed to return home the night before.

"Can I get you something to eat, Will?" asked his mother.

"No, thanks, Mamma. Well, maybe just a cup of coffee. I ate before I left home. Where is everybody else?" he asked looking about curiously.

"Well, Meriel is helping the twins get dressed. And you'll find Annalie in there," replied Anna, nodding her head toward the bedroom.

Will walked slowly toward the bedroom uncertain as to what he might find beyond the door. He opened it cautiously. Annalie was propped up in bed eating her breakfast from a tray. At her side, wrapped like a cocoon, was Sara, her tiny pink face peering out one end of the blanket.

"How come nobody ever tells me when things like this

happen around here?" teased Will.

"How come you didn't bring Mamma over last night? Then you would have known," sparred Annalie.

"What! And be caught up in a birthing? Not me!" Will shook his head vigorously. "It sounds as if you folks had an exciting night. Want to tell me about it?"

"Well, it was so near morning when Dr. Shelton left that Papa and Mamma decided to stay until after breakfast."

"You mean it was just born, then?" Will nodded toward the small bundle lying on the bed beside Annalie.

"It's a she, and her name is Sara. She was born long before Louie and Dr. Shelton got here."

"How did you manage?"

"Oh, Mamma and Meriel were here."

"You mean they delivered the baby?"

"Yep, in fact Mamma arrived just before Sara did."

"Then you and Meriel were here alone most of the night?"

"Yep," Annalie nodded. "I don't know how I would have managed without her."

Meriel knocked gently on the door. "The twins are dressed, if you want them to come in now."

Tommy and Timmy entered, wide-eyed and solemn. Annalie beckoned them over to the bed and slipped her arm around them. "This is your baby sister, Sara!"

"Oh, oh!" Timmy reached a finger toward the baby's eye.

Annalie gently guided the youngster's finger down to the infant's fist. Timmy's face lit up with a delighted grin as Sara's tiny fingers curled around his. Tommy reached over and pushed away Timmy's hand.

"Now it's my turn to shake hands."

"You'll have lots of turns to play with her," put in Annalie. "Sara is your little sister, and she's living with us from now on."

Tommy turned to Meriel. "Can you make her a harness, too, so she can play horse with us?"

"I promise!" agreed Meriel solemnly. "When your Mommy thinks she's big enough to play horse, I'll make a harness for her."

"Time for breakfast, Timmy and Tommy," called Anna from

the doorway where she had been watching with amused interest.

A short time later, Will paused where Meriel was hanging the washing on the clothesline. "Annalie was telling me what a help you were last night."

"That's kind of her, but I didn't do much, just sat and waited with her. You know, I was really scared."

"Scared?" queried Will. "You're always so calm and quiet, I can't imagine you scared."

"Perhaps 'concerned' would be a better term," reflected Meriel, as she finished pinning a billowing sheet in the brisk October breeze. "Bringing a new life into the world is an awesome responsibility, and that was my first experience watching a baby being born. I was so thankful when your mother arrived. From the moment she entered the room, she had everything under control. The baby is such a beautiful little girl; I'm just happy for everyone it's all over."

Annalie's strength and energy returned so quickly that Meriel's services were needed only a couple weeks after Sara's arrival.

"She's been great with the twins and so much company for Annalie, we're going to miss her a lot," Louie confided to Will. "I'll be taking her home this coming Saturday evening."

"I could bring Belle and the buggy and take her home, if it would save you a trip. After all, she lives out my way." The offer had popped out of Will's mouth before he gave it a thought. "Now, why did I say that?" he wondered to himself.

Louie took him up on the offer.

Will appeared at the Sprenger place on Saturday, as he had promised. The ride to Meriel's home was a quiet one. She was unusually shy. Perhaps, it was the letdown after the busy days of work. She felt she was imposing to have accepted the ride so readily.

They were approaching the Lew Browning place on the edge of Pulaski. The mail rig stood in the open shed. Old Flory, the gray horse so well known along the mail route, was grazing in the lot by the road.

Will carried Meriel's suitcase up the path to the weathered house. Meriel smiled. "Thank you so much for the ride home. I really appreciate it."

Will thought of asking to call again. Then he remembered the many calls on Carrie at the neat, white Steiner house and the broken relationship. He wasn't ready to take another plunge – not yet. He tipped his hat. "I was glad to do it."

Inside the house, Meriel closed the door and leaned her head against the door frame. Unshed tears stung her eyelids and tasted salty as she swallowed hard. What had she said or done that was wrong? When Will offered to take her home from the Sprengers, she had assumed that he was at least a little interested in her. His abrupt leaving proved how foolish she had been to even imagine such a thing. If only she possessed a little of her sister Eadie's "gift of gab", she might have made a better impression. She dismissed the thought almost angrily. "I'm not Eadie; why should I pretend to be like her?"

"Meriel?" her mother's voice broke into her troubled thoughts, "How did you get home so soon?"

"Will Eschman brought me."

"Now, isn't that nice!" beamed her mother.

Meriel groaned silently to herself.

As Belle trotted homeward, Will's thoughts shifted between Carrie and Meriel. Carrie, always radiating self-assurance and perfection; Meriel, so caring and unassuming as to keep herself vulnerable to those about her. So slightly built she appeared fragile, yet with amazing endurance as she worked at Annalie's and kept up with the twins. She had completely won the hearts of his sister and family.

"Why am I comparing those two, anyway?" he spoke half aloud to Belle and himself. "Carrie is out of the picture, and I've delivered Meriel and her luggage safely to her doorstep. So that's that!"

With a snap of the horse reins, he dismissed both Carrie and Meriel from his thoughts.

CHAPTER FOURTEEN

Friend in Need

The mid-weeks of November were miserable, cold and rainy. The country roads, which a short time before were hard as stone, had softened into quagmires with the steady rain. The horses' hoofs slithered as they sank into the ooze and came out with a "plop" caused by the suction of the gumbo clay. The wagon wheels slid erratically about until they found tracking in a rut.

Farmers stayed off the roads if possible, repairing equipment in their machine sheds or barns. If travel was necessary, they aimed to make the round trip early in the morning when the ground was frozen enough to at least partially support the weight of horse and rig.

Lew Browning, though, faithfully made the rounds with his mail rig. He was over an hour late when he arrived at the Eschman place. The rig was encrusted with mud, and even Lew's face and beard were splotched with mud kicked up by Flory's hind hoofs.

Lew was accustomed to taking the whims of weather and roads in his stride, whether the heat and dust of summer or the snow and bad roads of winter. The deep furrows in his mud-splotched face bespoke deeper concern.

Jacob met him at the mailbox with a letter "to go". Seeing the frown on his face, Jacob commiserated, "Roads mighty bad today, eh!"

"Well, they're aggravating! Making it so I can't get home before dark!" He paused to spit out a mouthful of tobacco juice.

"After I get home, I have to hustle up enough chopped wood for the next day."

"Ja, is that so?"

"We have enough logs hauled up for our winter supply of wood. Harold was starting on the job of chopping it, when his ax slipped and he chopped his ankle — a nasty break! Doc Shelton fixed it up for him, but he's laid up on crutches, goodness knows how long! Meriel has been chopping wood to keep the range going, but that's no woman's job. Beside, we're needing our winter supply laid by."

"Is Harold your only man at home?"

"Well, there's Ted and Cleo, but they're just small tads. Good at piling wood, but I'd hate to trust them with an ax."

"Sounds like you're needing a couple of hands to help out!"

"Yep, appears so! Know of anyone I could hire?"

"Well, there's Will and John — course they'd have to do the deciding. I'll put it to them!"

By the following morning it had turned cold enough to form a frozen crust on the road. Will and John rode over to Brownings on horseback. Tying their horses in the barn, they walked up the path to the house. The bright-hued flowers once bordering it were now reduced to brown stalks by the frost and heavy rains.

Harold had seen them coming and was leaning on one crutch at the open door. "Come in! It's good to see you!"

"Looks like you struck the wrong limb there!" Will nodded at the bandaged ankle.

"Yep, it's amazing how one slip of the ax can change your whole life."

"Heard you could use some help!" broke in John. "If you direct us to the woodpile, we'll work awhile before coming in."

"It's right behind the house. You'll find all the tools you need; axes and cross-cut saw in the woodshed there, too."

John and Will began by cutting up a pile of old barn siding into kindling which Ted and Cleo promptly carried and placed in the woodbox at the end of the kitchen range.

They next proceeded to chop small chunks of cherry and oak for use in the range and the big sections of oak and hickory into larger pieces for the heating stove in the living room.

The two men worked steadily, stopping only long enough to eat the chicken and dumpling dinner prepared by Meriel and her mother. Ted and Cleo prided themselves on keeping up with the "men choppers" and banked the wood along the walls behind the kitchen range and living room stove.

By mid-afternoon, the leaden skies dropped their burden in a drenching rain. With caps and jackets dripping, Will, John and the two boys hurried inside.

"At least we've cut enough wood to last you over the weekend," John reassured Mrs. Browning. "Hopefully, the weather will clear by then so we can finish the sawing and splitting before Thanksgiving."

"You two men can't ride home in all this rain!" Ma Browning responded. "Sit a spell 'til it clears up; then we can find a couple dry coats to keep you warm while you travel."

While the rain pelted down outside, Will and John sat with the boys at the table in the warm kitchen. The Brownings' rooms were much smaller than those at the Eschman house, crowded but cozy. Through the archway was the living room, likewise crowded with furniture. Will noted that the portiere from Brome's Dell school days was missing from the archway — probably a casualty of years of wear and tear. A heating stove filled the center of the room, and in one corner was a small round table, topped with a fringed shawl. A mirror on the wall behind it, and an assortment of combs, brushes and cosmetics gave evidence that it was an improvised dressing table. Each window of the room was filled with blooming geraniums and impatiens.

A deep, rich aroma filled the kitchen, intensifying as Meriel took a pan of molasses cookies from the oven.

"These might help warm you up!" she said, as she set a plate of them on the table before Will, John and the boys.

"M-m-m-m, mighty good!" commented John, chewing as he spoke.

"Glad you like them," Meriel smiled. "They are Eadie's favorites."

"Eadie!" recalled Will. "Now, wasn't she your curly-topped, little sister in the first grade?"

"You're right!" agreed Meriel. "But she's grown some since

then. She goes to high school at Bloomfield, now. She'll be home for Thanksgiving."

Disappearing for a moment, Cleo returned with a battered-looking box. "Would you guys like to play dominoes while you're waiting for the rain to quit?"

"Now don't bother the men with your childish games!" frowned Luella Browning as she paused and wiped her hands on her apron.

"Oh, we might as well play!" answered Will indulgently. "Meriel, are you free to join the game?"

"Don't mind if I do, thank you!" Blushing a bit, she took her place at the table.

Time passed quickly as the players visited and plopped down their dominoes, forming trails that looked like miniature railroad tracks. By the time the "boneyard" was depleted and the winner had matched dots on his last domino, the rain was over. Will and John made their way homeward.

"Well, what do you think of her?" queried Will as their horses splashed their way over the miry roads.

"Think of whom?" parried John, innocently.

"You know who! Meriel!"

"She makes good molasses cookies!"

"Is that all you have to say about her?"

"Well, if I wasn't marrying Miriam, I could find her quite attractive!"

"You marrying Miriam?!! How come you never told me before?"

"Must have slipped my mind. Miriam and I announced our engagement while you were on your western trip, but no wedding date has been set."

The brothers rode awhile in silence. Will had never thought of a daily routine without his younger brother at his side. Again, he sensed a vague uneasiness that life was passing him by.

CHAPTER FIFTEEN

The Blizzard

Early Monday morning, Will and John returned to the Brownings and began sawing the pile of logs into chunks for firewood.

Using the crosscut saw, they swung into action, their strong muscles pushing and pulling in unison. With each stroke the saw teeth bit deeper into the resistant log, until, with a final whine, the chunk broke loose and fell with a thud onto the frozen ground. In one sweeping motion, the fellows then tossed it aside onto a nearby pile.

By Monday night the log pile had disappeared. In its place was an enormous heap of chunks waiting to be split. All day Tuesday, axes rang as Will and John worked at reducing the chunks to firewood. Smaller chunks were chopped into sticks for the kitchen range; the big chunks were reduced in size enough to go through the door of the heating stove.

Ted and Cleo, arms piled high with wood, made regular trips to the woodshed, cording the wood into one of two piles, depending upon which stove it was to feed.

"We can easily finish the job by tomorrow noon," declared Will at the supper table.

Luella paused as she refilled the dishes with stew and biscuits. "That will be a real cause for thanksgiving, to have our winter supply of wood in the dry shed and ready to use." She then added, "Now, I don't mean to hurry you at eating, but you two had better be on your way home before dark. It's getting cold and windy outside!"

Meriel had hung the men's coats and caps on nails behind the range. "They'll be warmer for the ride home," she explained. Then, as if thinking aloud, she continued, "Pa should be home by now. He gets so cold when he's out late like this."

Meriel handed the coats to the men as they rose from the table. In doing so, her hand brushed over Will's wrist.

"Oh, I'm so sorry!" she apologized, blushing.

"No need to be!" Will assured her quickly. The touch had sent a warm glow up his arm.

Will opened the kitchen door, letting in a gust of cold air as he and John stepped out into the gathering dusk. Lew Browning drove in with his mail rig as the Eschman brothers reached the barn. As they helped him unhitch his horse, Lew expressed his gratitude for their promptness in working up the wood supply and promised their money would be waiting for them when they finished the job the next day.

They were interrupted as another rig pulled into the yard. A high lilting voice called to them from the buggy, "Hi! We're home!"

"That's my daughter, Eadie, and her friend, Richard Hadley, from Bloomfield," Lew announced proudly. Eadie's escort was a stranger to Will and John. He helped Eadie out of the buggy and the two of them ran quickly to the house.

Will and John mounted their horses and rode home at a gallop through the cold night air.

The day before Thanksgiving had dawned cold with a leaden sky. The Eschman brothers, with shoulders hunched beneath turned-up coat collars, guided their horses close together to help conserve heat for man and beast. "We should be able to finish cutting wood in a couple hours this morning." Will's words issued forth like wisps of smoke on the frigid air as their horses trotted over the frozen ground.

"That suits me fine!" responded John, dropping his reins momentarily to slap his numb fingers on his thighs. "That will give us longer to thaw out before eating Mom's Thanksgiving dinner."

They passed harvested cornfields where a few remaining

cornstalks waved tattered leaves of truce to the oncoming winter; then they quickened their pace as the Browning home came into view. The light smoke rising from the chimney gave the weathered house an air of peace and tranquility.

As soon as they had put their horses in the barn, John and Will went immediately to a chopping attack upon the woodpile. Moments later, Ted and Cleo, drawn by the sound of ringing axes, were out to carry in the split wood.

A few enormous snowflakes drifted lazily down. "Wow! Look at the size of those flakes!" exclaimed Cleo. "Maybe we can get our sleds out tomorrow!"

"One robin doesn't make a spring nor one snowflake a coasting party," quipped John.

"Just you wait and see!" persisted Cleo.

They didn't wait too long before the snow began whirling faster. Will and John chopped with greater speed, and the woodpile began to grow with a mantle of snow settling upon it.

Soon, Meriel made her appearance, wearing a man's denim chore jacket over her heavy sweater and a scarf about her head and shoulders.

"The boys said they were getting behind carrying in wood. Just thought maybe I could help, too."

"The more, the merrier," grinned Will. He picked up a large chunk of wood and thumped it on the ground to remove the wet snow, then proceeded to split it.

By now the snow was swirling about them dizzily, until the group by the woodpile seemed to be caught up in the middle of a giant snow-scene paperweight. Will glanced at Meriel, rosy faced, with snow fast settling on her red scarf and shoulders and a few errant flakes lighting on her nose and eyelashes as she gathered an armload of wood. He had never seen her more beautiful and vibrant than at that moment.

The spell was broken by Luella's call from the kitchen door. "Better come in for some hot coffee and a snack before you all freeze out there!"

Each of the group picked up an armful of wood to carry as they went. "Don't forget your ax," John reminded Will, as he put his under his arm, "or you'll never find it again 'til next spring!"

They stamped their way into the woodshed where Harold, leaning on one crutch, was placing wood on top of the pile.

"Never felt more useless in my life," he fretted.

"You're doing just fine!" encouraged Will. "And you've got two great helpers here." Will nodded at Ted and Cleo. "By the way, how old are you fellows?"

"Eleven". "Twelve!" they answered in unison and then laughed as they took Will and John's soggy gloves and placed them in the warming oven to dry.

"This should help warm you!" Luella motioned them to the kitchen table, centered with a heaping plate of freshly baked doughnuts and mugs of steaming coffee.

"Will it ever!" exclaimed John, his eyes beaming. Within seconds the cold, hungry crew were feasting on Ma Browning's doughnuts and washing them down with sips of hot coffee.

Eadie spoke through the archway as she sat at the improvised dressing table and brushed her newly washed hair. "I should have been out there helping, too, but I didn't want Richard to see me tonight with stringy hair."

Harold responded dryly, "I doubt very much that Richard will be seeing you or your hair tonight, period!"

"But he always keeps his word," persisted Eadie, peevishly.

"Be that as it may." Harold turned away with a shrug.

"Hey, look out the window! Isn't that Paw coming in the driveway?" Meriel pulled back the curtain and peered out intently as the snow-covered horse and rig approached slowly, almost ghost-like, through the blinding snowstorm.

"We'd better get out there!" exclaimed Will and John in one breath. They gulped down the last of their coffee and reached for their coats behind the kitchen stove. As they pulled open the door, a gale of snow and frigid air swept into the room.

Covered with a layer of snow, Lew resembled a grotesque snowman more than a human being. Will and John lifted the older man out of the buggy and steadied him as they made their way slowly to the house.

Lew spoke haltingly, his teeth chattering, "I only made half the route today. Those folks beyond the meeting house will be mighty disappointed, not getting their mail and paper before the holiday."

"They'll get by all right without their news," reassured John. "Main thing is to get you inside and thawed out."

Luella held the door open for the men. "Don't get near the stove too soon!" she cautioned with wisdom born of past experiences with snowstorms. She placed a basin of cold water before her husband as the fellows eased him into a chair by the table. Lew submerged his hands into the water and winced with pain as he slowly opened and closed his red fingers.

Luella gradually raised the water temperature, pouring in a few sips of warm water at a time from the tea kettle.

With a whiskbroom, Meriel brushed the snow from her father's shaggy fur coat, changing his appearance from a polar bear to a grizzly one. "Let me take this heavy thing off," she offered.

"No, leave it be. I'm freezing!" Lew protested. His teeth chattered as he clutched the coat close to his shivering body.

"You can warm up here," Meriel comforted, easing her father into a huge leather chair behind the stove in the living room. Lew gave a deep contented sigh and immediately fell asleep.

John and Will returned to the barn long enough to rub down Lew's gray mare and give her a generous pile of hay. Their horses stretched out their noses and whinnied for attention. "All right, we won't forget you!" John pitched a small forkful of hay to each of them.

Bracing themselves against the shrieking wind, the brothers made their way back to the warm kitchen. Harold looked up as they entered.

"Looks as though you're going to be stuck here with us until the storm blows itself out."

"Of course," asserted Luella. "Your folks won't be expecting you home in this weather. We can bed you down in the boys' room, come night."

Lunch was simple — a huge kettle of vegetable soup and homemade bread. Lew continued to sleep, undisturbed, behind the stove while the family ate. Eadie wrinkled up her nose at the table. "I don't know why Paw has to keep on that smelly fur coat while he heats up behind the stove!"

"Let him alone!" defended Harold. "He's earned the right to rest as he pleases after being out in this storm."

The afternoon passed quickly as Harold pulled out a worn deck of AUTHOR cards and began dealing them out. Eadie and her partner, John, easily won all rounds.

Meriel looked up at Will as Eadie laughingly scooped the "books" toward herself. "Guess I'm not too great as an AUTHOR'S partner." She rose to add another chunk of wood to the stove.

"Here! Let me help with that," Will offered. He eased a large chunk of wood through the heater door and using a poker, settled it into place as sparks flew up the chimney.

Lew stirred behind the stove, "You can take my coat now if you like."

Meriel called to him as she hung it behind the range, "Mamma has some hot soup waiting for you! Better come and eat it!"

Darkness fell early as the blustering wind continued to assail the shuddering windowpanes with gusts of snow. Luella had placed an extra straw tick in the boys' upstairs room near the place where the stove pipe went through the ceiling. "You fellows can decide who takes the bed or the floor."

"The floor sounds great to me," offered Will.

As bedtime approached, Ted and Cleo led the way up the narrow wooden stairs, Ted holding high the small kerosene lamp that cast dark, grotesque shadows on the papered walls of the stairway. Harold followed, holding his lamp in one hand as he hitched himself up backwards, one step at a time.

John had already started up the stairs when Meriel appeared with an armload of comforters. "You'll be needing these to keep warm tonight."

Will held her wrist firmly as she transferred the bedclothes to his arms. "I have never seen you when you weren't taking off to wait on someone. It gives me the feeling you are about to fly away like a bird. Do you suppose we could find a time when we could just talk together?"

Meriel's cheeks flushed. She could feel her pulse beating beneath Will's firm grasp on her wrist. "Oh, I think so."

"How about my picking you up some evening, when the weather isn't as wild as tonight, say for the Christmas program at Bromes Dell?"

"That would be fine with me!" Her eyes twinkled as she smiled up at him.

"Then it's a date."

John and Will spread one comforter over the straw-tick and used the rest of the bedding for cover. Then, removing only their shoes, they crawled into their improvised bed.

The rustle and dust from the straw-tick during Will's fitful sleep caused him to dream he was out in a strawstack, and as his feet moved too near the edge of the warm comforters, he envisioned himself running barefoot through the snow trying to catch up to Meriel. Rhythmic snores, coming from the beds where the Browning brothers were sleeping snug and warm, brought Will back to the reality that he and John were holding down a straw-tick in Browning's upstairs bedroom.

The wind outside finally subsided and toward morning Will drifted into a deep sleep. He was roused as Luella shook the stove grates and replenished the fires downstairs. Soon the stovepipe near the straw pallet was radiating heat and the bracing aroma of freshly brewed coffee wafted upward through the stovepipe hole.

The table was already set when Will, John and the Browning boys came downstairs into the welcome warmth of the kitchen.

"Happy Thanksgiving," greeted Luella. "Breakfast's ready. Just find a place at the table."

There was some chair scraping and confusion as each settled into place, then an awkward moment of silence as Luella was aware that her guests were accustomed to a blessing before eating.

Undaunted, she turned to her older daughter, "Meriel, will you pray for us?"

Meriel bowed her head and began speaking simply. "Dear heavenly Father, on this special day we just want to say 'thank you' for all Your goodness to us. Thank you for our family, our home and this food. Thank you for these friends who have helped us in our time of need. Bless them and give them a safe trip home. In Jesus' name, Amen."

Following breakfast, Lew met the Eschman brothers by the range as they were buttoning their jackets for the ride home. His eyes were watery with emotion as he pressed several silver dollars into their hands. "Thank you for working against such great odds to supply us with wood for the winter. I wish I could give you more!"

"That's just fine," responded Will. "Thank you folks for your hospitality and putting us up for the night."

"I'll help you get your horses ready, as soon as I get a shovel from the woodshed," offered Lew. The three men picked their way around the snowdrifts in the yard, then took turns shoveling the drifted snow from the barn door.

As the barn door creaked open, the horses reached their heads toward the light and whinnied expectantly.

"I don't envy you guys your ride home," commented Lew. "You know, you're welcome to stay over 'til the roads are broken through."

"It's best we get on our way," John paused as he tightened the girth strap of his horse's saddle. "They are probably wondering about us at home."

The way stretched before Will and John in undulating white drifts with only the shaggy rows of osage hedge on either side to suggest that there might be a road between. Giving their horses plenty of rein, the fellows let them pick their way homeward. Occasionally a horse would lose its footing and flounder up to its belly in the enveloping white softness until its hoof struck solid ground beneath.

As the sun climbed higher, its rays shone warm and pleasant on the riders' backs. However, the same rays reflected from the unbroken whiteness about them became almost unbearable to their eyes. Dark spots danced before them as they squinted to shut out the intense light.

Finally the homestead appeared in the distance, nestled at the foot of the hill. Light smoke curled lazily from the chimney. Two figures, probably Sam and Minnie, were shoveling a path to the outbuilding.

"I can't remember a more beautiful sight!" exclaimed Will as the horses quickened their pace homeward.

CHAPTER SIXTEEN

Christmas at Bromes Dell

With the weather moderating after Thanksgiving, the huge drifts gradually settled. Farmers welcomed the occasional snow flurries and night freezing which kept a solid snow base on the roads, good for travel with sleighs.

On the evening of the Bromes Dell Christmas program, Will drove to the Browning's in the cutter to pick up Meriel. After tucking the robe snugly about Meriel's feet, he climbed into the cutter, and the mare started off at a brisk trot with sleighbells jingling.

Meriel responded comfortably to Will's questions. Harold's leg was definitely on the mend, and he was getting around the house quite easily without his crutch. Ted and Cleo must have found a cache of Christmas Spirit. Besides doing their chores at home, they were practicing for the program and cutting evergreens for decorating the school. Eadie felt too sophisticated to appear with the family at a school program. She had gone with Richard to a pre-Christmas party in Bloomfield.

Will turned suddenly to Meriel, "You can tell me if I'm being too nosey, but do you always do the praying at your house?"

Meriel, taken aback, hesitated before answering. "No, I'm not usually asked to pray. I'm the only one in the family who goes to church — the little Methodist church in Pulaski. Well, Harold had been taking me lately until he hurt his foot. But about the morning you and John were at our house: Mamma knew that you folks, being Mennonites, expected a blessing before meals, so she asked me."

The thought struck Will ironically. In a Mennonite family, where a show of faith was expected by outsiders, he had left all worship activities to his parents, except his attending church. He slipped his hand over Meriel's. "Well, I just hope when a praying matter comes up, that we're both praying on the same side of the issue. Otherwise, mine won't have a chance of being heard."

Meriel chuckled softly. "Well, I guess when we get to heaven there'll be no partitions between our churches. What do you think?"

Will grinned as he shrugged, "Just so we're on the same side of the partition."

By now they had reached the schoolyard where other rigs were beginning to assemble. Lights were glowing softly from the windows. Will helped Meriel from the cutter, then drove on as Meriel entered the door and waited for him. Within the building, the air was spicy with the scents of evergreen boughs and candles on the window sills.

As Will and Meriel made their way toward empty desks, they were almost bowled over by Tommy and Timmy Sprenger, exuberant with joy in their new blue suits, white shirts and huge red bows tied beneath their chins.

"Whoa there!" exclaimed Will, catching the boys in his arms. "How are my favorite twins tonight?"

The twins grinned up proudly into Will and Meriel's faces. "We're in the program!"

Will and Meriel found seats next to Louis and Annalie. Little Sara, on the desk in front of Annalie, raised her arms as she eyed Meriel soberly from her ruffled bonnet. "What a sweetheart you are!" exclaimed Meriel as she picked the baby up and cuddled her.

The seats behind them were soon filled with Will and Meriel's parents. Later John, accompanied by Miriam Meister took the seats to their left. John reached over and tugged Will's coat sleeve. "Hey, know what? I'm pretty sure they'll be taking me on at the meat-packing plant in Ottumwa right after Christmas."

Will eyed his younger brother proudly as he offered his hand. "Put'er there!" Then in an apprehensive tone, "Does that mean you'll be forgetting your land-tilling family when you're rolling in money?"

Miriam looked up, smiling into John's face. "You'll come home often for your Mom's cooking, won't you?"

Steve and Carrie Bauman entered the schoolroom shortly before the program began. Even with specially fashioned clothes, Carrie was noticeably plump and squeezed with difficulty into one of the back seats. With Meriel at his side, Will found he could face even Steve and Carrie in a friendly manner. They were just another couple, and Carrie was evidently far along in her pregnancy.

The schoolroom grew silent as the stage curtains were closed. When they slowly reopened, the twins, Tommy and Timmy, stood in the center of the spacious area clutching hands, motionless for a moment; then with faces almost as red as the bows beneath their chins, they began chanting in high pitched voices:

"We are both quite little
With a man-sized job to do;
To wish you a Merry Christmas
And a Happy New Year, too."

They bowed deeply and solemnly, then amid loud applause, they scampered off the platform to the arms of their parents in the audience.

Groups of girls in bright, new dresses sang carols heralding the birth of the Lord Jesus. Boys with long, crooked staffs and towels about their heads, pantomimed the awe-struck shepherds in the field at night. Ted and Cleo Browning, along with Sammy Eschman, clad in colorful bathrobes, made their way slowly down the center aisle of the school as they carried gifts to the Christ Child in a crude manger overflowing with straw.

Then came a moment of hushed expectation. Tom Burrows from the School Board, partially concealed by the stage curtain, held a bucket of water and a dipper as a precaution against fire. The teacher, Rebecca Schillig, in a navy dress with a touch of white lace at the neck line, moved slowly across the stage with a lighted candle. Approaching the fir tree decorated with strung popcorn and apples, she very carefully lit the small white candles fastened to the tree with metal clamps. A soft crescendo of "Ohs and Ahs" rose from the audience as the tree took on a lustrous glow from the many tiny flames.

The children assembled on the stage and began to sing, "O Christmas Tree! O Christmas Tree! How lovely are your branches". Later, the audience joined them in singing "Silent Night".

There was another moment of silence as the teacher snuffed out the burning candles. Then a flurry of excitement broke loose as Jacob Eschman, school director, distributed popcorn balls and pencils stamped with Christmas greetings to each child. Scurrying "Elves" carried gifts from a previous name drawing to their rightful owners. As the "blizzard" of gift wrappings and popcorn settled down, the celebrants began to make their way home.

"I can't remember a finer Christmas program!" exclaimed Will as the horse trotted briskly homeward with the cutter. Meriel heartily assented.

Will's arm slipped caressingly around Meriel and she snuggled close in its embrace. They rode awhile in relaxed silence.

"We'll have to get together on a regular basis," decided Will audibly, speaking to both Meriel and himself.

"M-m-m-h-m-m," agreed Meriel cozily from the warm circle of Will's arm. "That would be nice."

CHAPTER SEVENTEEN

The Box Social

"Just forget about me," Fritz Zimmerli reassured the solicitous saleslady in Wagler's General Store. He eased himself into the large armed chair behind the base burner at the rear of the room. "I'll do my shopping after I've thawed out a bit."

Lizzie Wagler was not only an efficient clerk; she was adept at asking questions to pump a steady flow of news and gossip from her rural customers. She also knew it was useless to try to pump Fritz Zimmerli when he was not in a talkative mood.

Settling back, Fritz drank in the leathery tang of harness parts and bridles suspended from the beams, the dull sheen of galvanized milk strainers hung on wooden pegs and the acrid scent of salt blocks along the back wall. Blending with the other smells were those of sulphur in a tin canister and a wooden keg of black-strap molasses. He hoped there would be no shoppers for any of those items today. He was enjoying his private listening place too much to be discovered.

On his first day back with his aunt and uncle, the Burrows, he was bored. His cousins, Kate and Carl, had both married and were gone. Fritz found the old couple's repetition of farm events and family history stale. However, he was not ready to look up his younger friends until he had caught up on some village news. He had learned long before that listening, unobserved, paid better dividends than prying folks with questions.

The soft crackling of coals in the base burner was interrupted by the jangling of a bell as the store door was opened. Anna

Eschman entered, her full woolen skirt barely clearing the gray slushy snow.

"Glory be! I see you're bringing us more of your nice, fresh eggs," greeted Lizzie as she eyed the basket on Anna's arm. "I sold our last egg yesterday."

"Just a few," answered Anna. "Jacob has been babying the hens to get these — fresh straw in the nests and hot mash every morning. These should help out on our groceries."

Lizzie Wagler talked constantly as she counted the large brown eggs — five dozen of them.

"What do you hear from John and his new job?"

"Oh, he's getting along fine at the meat packing plant. Things are sure quiet at home with him in Ottumwa. I guess Will misses him the most."

"I would guess so," agreed Lizzie. "Those two were always together, at work or wherever. Well, what can I get for you?"

"We'll need some lard," Anna announced, almost apologetically. "We've run out, and it will be at least another week before we butcher again."

"I can imagine, with all those good pies you bake. Your family's lucky to have a good cook like you." Lizzie dug her spatula into the tin container by the counter and sliced out a hunk of lard, which she slid onto a boat-like cardboard container. She tapped it gently with her forefinger as she peered at the numbers on the scales. Then topping it with a square of wax paper, she wrapped the package in heavy brown paper.

"And a couple pounds of coffee," added Anna.

Scooping into a burlap-lined wooden barrel, Lizzie filled a paper bag, which she weighed, then emptied into the coffee grinder. A loud grinding sound erupted as she turned the handle and the aromatic fragrance of fresh coffee beans filled the air.

Anna sighed when Lizzie informed her that would about equal the price of her eggs. The bolt of outing flannel she had hoped to buy for Annalie's baby clothes would have to wait for another trip to town.

As Anna left, Emil Meyers entered the store, stomping the slush from his heavy boots. He ordered a twenty-five-pound sack of flour for his wife and a pouch of chewing tobacco.

"How is your telephone business coming, Mr. Meyers?"

"We're just biding our time 'til the frost goes out of the ground so we can set more poles and hook up new customers on our line."

"I hope that will be soon." Lizzie nodded at the box-like phone mounted on the wall near the cash register. "It will be a real boost for our business when all the folks in the community can call ahead about their groceries and other supplies."

Fritz's eyes lit up as Meriel entered the store. He was about to stand up and make his presence known, then thought better of it and remained seated, hidden behind the stove. Making her way to the counter, Meriel asked for crepe paper.

Mrs. Wagler's high-pitched voice carried across the store. "Oh, so you're going to decorate a box for the Box Social, yes?"

Meriel selected a bolt of white and one of shell-pink paper. "I think these will do. And do you happen to have a large man's-sized shoe box?"

Lizzie chattered on. "Isn't it exciting – the Bauman's sponsoring a Box Social to raise money for painting Bromes Dell School? And so romantic, having it on Valentine's Day, too!" Meriel murmured something in reply and soon left the store with her purchases.

When Meriel was out of sight, Fritz rose from his corner behind the stove and walked to the counter. "Guess I'd better get my things and go home – to Uncle Tom's that is. I'll take some boiling beef for stew and some of those eggs. Aunt Addie promised to make noodles when she got some eggs." While Lizzie was wrapping the beef, Fritz walked over to a small keg and fished a dill pickle from the brine. "Just put this in with the beef." He then sauntered across the store and picked out a bolt of white and one of shell-pink crepe paper.

"Why, Mr. Zimmerli, fancy you getting trimmings for the Box Social," teased the storekeeper, "and just like Meriel's too."

"Oh, is that a fact? Then she's got good taste," he added with a chuckle. "I just want to help my Aunt Addie out, since she's crippled with rheumatism. Could you show me how you women make those fancy doo-dads to trim the boxes?"

Lizzie Wagler painstakingly fashioned a rosette from a small piece of the crepe paper and made a short strip of ruching for trimming the edge of the box.

"You are so artistic!" lauded Fritz, "You should add an Art Department to your establishment, here."

Mrs. Wagler flushed deeply. "Why, Mr. Zimmerli! You always say the nicest things!"

"Oh, by the way, would you happen to have another large shoe box? I'm sure my aunt has used all of hers for storage."

Obligingly, the clerk handed Fritz another empty box.

"And good luck helping your aunt!" she giggled lightly.

Will turned to Meriel as the cutter pulled out of the Browning driveway. "Now, how am I to know I'm paying my money for the right box?" he asked.

"You can take a peek — just to satisfy your curiosity. I guess I'd prefer eating with you instead of — maybe old Eli Traschel."

Will picked up the brown paper bag in the deepening dusk and peered inside at the white box, festooned with shell-pink flowers and ruching.

"M-m-m pretty neat, if I do say so! I'm sure I would remember that dainty creation anywhere."

As the rigs arrived at the Bauman place, the guests were met at the door by young "ushers" who took the paper bags containing the decorated boxes, so no one was seen carrying his or her own box.

By the time all guests had arrived at the "heart and streamer" decked mansion, the massive table in the dining room was piled with boxes of every shape and color of the rainbow; additional ones covered the buffet.

Cyrus Heath, auctioneer of the evening, rose to his feet and cleared his throat. He brushed his black mustache with his forefinger, then picked up a small box covered with forget-me-nots. "Now, what am I offered for this pretty little item?" He held it up in his right hand for display. A teenager, turning a deep shade of crimson, waved his dollar bill in the air as he bid.

"Sold!! To Sammy Eschman!" Heath brought down his gavel with a flourish. Sammy, box under his arm, scurried off to find his date for the evening.

It was followed by a round yellow box with yellow streamers like sun rays surrounding it, next , a green box topped with huge poppies. The bidding was lively.

Cyrus Heath paused as he was handed a large white box, festooned with shell-pink rosettes and ruching. "Now what am I bid for this beautiful work of art?"

A gasp of admiration floated over the room , followed by a stir of expectancy.

Lizzie Wagler sucked in her breath, then placed her hands over her mouth.

"Four dollars!" bid Will.

"That looks like something Meriel would make! I'll bid five!" called a voice from the back of the room.

Folks turning around were surprised to see Fritz Zimmerli.

"When did you get into town?" asked Emil Meyers.

"Oh, just the other day. Lucky to make it for this occasion."

"I'll pay six!" countered Will.

"Seven dollars!" announced Fritz.

The rest of the men settled back in their chairs to watch the fun. Meriel glanced from one bidder to the other with a perplexed frown on her face.

"Eight dollars!" raised Will. . . . There was a pause.

"Nine!" bid Fritz with an air of finality.

"Ten dollars!" called Will.

Fritz raised his hands, palms up. "I'm out of money!"

"Sold!" boomed Cyrus, banging his gavel. "To the lucky man over there."

Will stood up and collected his trophy. Turning to Meriel, he was surprised to see so little pleasure on her face. "Didn't I pay enough for it?" he asked, puzzled.

"It's all right," soothed Meriel with a faint smile.

Heath's voice was droning in the background as he auctioned off a blue and white item, then a lavender box.

"Well, Shades of Caesar! What have we here?" exclaimed Heath, suddenly, as he held up another pink and white box almost identical to the one Will had in his hands.

"What am I to bid for it?"

Meriel's eyes opened wide in disbelief.

"Five dollars!" called three voices in unison.

"Make it six!" called Fritz.

"Six fifty!" called another voice.

"Seven!" bid Fritz.

"Seven," repeated the auctioneer. "Going once, going twice, going three times to Fritz Zimmerli. Well, folks , this closes our auction. Gentlemen, open your boxes."

As Will carefully opened the ruffled edges of the large box in his hands, he was assailed by the pungent odor of dills and pickled bologna. Lying between the sandwiches were hard-boiled eggs and a couple pieces of unfrosted cakes.

Will glanced questioningly at Meriel who was blushing with embarrassment. "I'm sorry, but that's not my box."

Opening the envelope on the inside, he made out the scratchily written name of Addie Burrows. Taking a deep breath, he left the distressed Meriel and strode over to the aging Mrs. Burrows. She brushed back her graying hair as he approached her. Summoning up all the gallantry he could muster, he bowed, "I believe I have the honor of eating with you."

"Oh my!" she replied, as flustered as a school girl. "I never dreamed my box would bring so much. Fritz decorated it for me. Didn't he do a nice job? I have a favor to ask. Would you mind if my husband ate with us? He didn't have enough money to buy my box."

"The more, the merrier," answered Will, secretly relieved for a man to share the conversation with him and Mrs. Burrows.

Meanwhile, Fritz joined Meriel, who was still confused by the whole affair. "May I share this beautiful box with you?"

Relieved to have a companion for conversation and yet suspicious of some trickery, Meriel responded slowly, "This is a surprise, seeing you here tonight. Have you been back long?"

"Just a couple days. I wouldn't have missed this evening for the world." He lifted the cover to the box, revealing the chicken salad sandwiches and pastel frosted tea cakes.

While Fritz consumed the delicacies in the box with gusto, Meriel finally managed to down half a sandwich. From the corner of her eye she caught glimpses of Will carrying on a lively conversation with Mr. Burrows while they ate.

"May I see you home?" asked Fritz when the party finally ended.

"Thank you, but I came with Will and I'll return with him." She looked pleadingly at Will, not knowing what his reaction would be.

Will and Meriel, along with the other departing guests, thanked their host and hostess, the Baumans, by the broad oak stairs in the spacious entryway.

Will silently helped Meriel into the cutter. Across the yard, Fritz tipped his hat and, grinning broadly, drove to the Burrows place.

The young couple rode in silence, broken only by Belle's trotting hoofs. Will cleared his throat. "That was a neat bit of 'chicanery' between you and Fritz. When did you two get together to work it out?"

Meriel hesitated, distressed and uncertain. "I didn't even know he was in these parts, until he showed up at Bauman's tonight."

"Oh, come now! The exchange of boxes I can accept as a neat prank, but to lie about it — that's another matter."

Barely audible, in a shocked voice she asked, "Will, have I ever lied to you?"

"Well, no, but there's always a first time."

The slender body drew away and huddled at the far side of the seat.

"How about letting me in on the secret?" Will cajoled as they reached her door at home.

"I-I can't, when I don't know the answer myself!"

"Very well, then, goodnight!" With an air of finality, he turned and left.

A feeble "Goodnight" echoed as the door clicked shut between them.

Through his mind flashed the replay of another broken relationship two years earlier, as an angry Carrie had slammed the door shut. This time it was over so gently. Yet all he could see was trickery and deceit on Meriel's part.

"**WOMEN!!**" he muttered, "I thought I could trust Meriel at least!"

CHAPTER EIGHTEEN

Telephone Poles

The spring of 1900 danced coquettishly over the Iowa countryside. Fields of winter wheat suddenly rolled out their green carpets, and wild cherry trees spilled their lacy blossoms over the fence rows. Swallows twittered busily as they replastered their nests on the barn rafters.

Though two months had passed since Valentine's Day, Will's frigid emotions refused to yield to spring's softening influence. Recurring thoughts of the Box Social galled him as he followed the team along the furrows of mellow soil. "Why had Meriel tricked him with her box that night? And why had she denied scheming with Fritz Zimmerli when all evidence so clearly implicated her? Why would she stoop to action so unlike her usual self?"

Spurred on by annoyance and frustration, Will threw himself into the field work. Even with his brother John away, working in Ottumwa, Will was the first in the neighborhood to finish sowing oats.

During his many circuits around the field, one positive facet from the night of the Box Social glimmered in Will's mind. It was the new-fangled telephone on the wall of the host's dining room. Charles Bauman was enthusiastic as he cited the many benefits of instant communication across the miles. Of course, with his money and high position in the telephone company, Bauman could be partial in his interests.

But then, Will's mother, returning from Wagler's store, had told how a call on the "talking box" had saved Meister a trip to

123

town when he learned that the bridle he ordered had not yet arrived at the store.

It was hearing his brother-in-law, Louie, declare that a couple rings on his phone could save him a cross-country ride to deliver a message that sold Will on the idea he needed a telephone.

"If Louie can afford one of those contraptions, then I can, too."

With spring planting finished, Will rode Belle over to the Bauman place on the following Saturday. Bauman sauntered out the kitchen door, coffee cup in hand, "Have you had breakfast, yet? Coffee's still hot. Just had a phone call from Steve and Carrie. They have a fine seven-pound baby girl, named Cherri."

Will congratulated Bauman on the birth of his grandchild and thanked him for the offer of coffee; then he came to the point of his visit. "I understand you are heading up the telephone company. Can you tell me how to get a line past my place?"

Bauman set his coffee cup down. "I'll be glad to tell you what I can about it. Our telephone company is expanding so fast that we have divided the territory into several districts. I believe young Snellinger is the man with whom you'll be dealing."

If Bauman had struck him across the face, Will could not have been more taken back. He looked at the older man, incredulously. "You don't mean Oscar Snellinger is in charge of setting poles past my place?"

"Well yes, I guess so," Bauman answered in an easy tone. "Jim Snellinger is a man of means and owns a fair-sized portion of stock in the company. He's in charge of your district. However, he's getting up in years, so his son, whatever his name, does the line work for his father."

A dry, bitter taste filled Will's mouth. "How long do you think it would take to set the line past my place?"

"Probably not more than a week or so. You could save half the cost by working along with them."

"All right," Will decided. "I'll do it. Where will I find Snellinger?"

"They're working this week on the Schillig place."

Will steadied himself to the point of civility as he approached the pole-setting crew at work and enquired if they would be able to set poles on his place.

Oscar had changed little over the years. He was short and stocky built with eyes bleary from drinking. He answered without pausing in his work, "I reckon so, when this job's done."

"And am I right," asked Will, "that by working with the crew, I can cut down on the cost of labor?"

Oscar answered Will with a sneer on his face. "So you want to work with my men, eh? Well, O.K., if you think you can keep up with them. I'll tell you one thing—they don't sit around on their hind ends all day reading books!"

Fury filled Will, equal to the day he and Oscar had slugged it out on the school ground over Meriel. His fists clenched in his trouser pockets, then opened again. This wasn't a schoolboy affair to be settled with fists.

With steely eyes, Will answered curtly, "I'll keep up! When will you be setting poles on my land?"

"A week from Monday."

As the days of the week passed slowly on the calendar, Will steeled himself for his encounter with Oscar and his crew. At last the appointed day for pole setting arrived.

"Gid-dap, you dad-blasted jackasses!"

The coarse shouted command alerted Will that the telephone linemen had arrived. He looked down the road to see the four-man crew sitting astride a wagon load of poles drawn by a team of mules. Jake, stubbly-faced with a thatch of gray hair, laid down his rawhide whip and drew up reins as they approached Will. Cosmo, dismounting, spit out a cud of tobacco and took a flask from his pocket. After a couple of gulps from the bottle, he wiped his handle bar mustache on his shirt sleeve. "Here, Boy." He passed the flask on to Alec, the largest and youngest of the group. "This will make you work like a man!"

Alec grinned vacuously. His black, greasy hair slid back from his bloated face as he tipped his head back to drink.

"Hah!" he snorted. "Hah, good!" and handed the bottle back to Cosmo. Seeing Will nearby, Cosmo offered the bottle to him.

"No thanks!" returned Will. Cosmo shrugged his shoulders.

Oscar cut in sharply, "Come on, you guys! Let's get with it so we can get this job over with!"

The men followed Will a few rods up the road to the southeast corner of his property and prepared to set the first pole. Turning the oversized augur, Jake loosened a core of soil the diameter of a telephone pole. Cosmo helped him pull it out. "OK, Alec, get digging!" yelled Oscar, the boss. Alec picked up the long-handled post hole digger and walked unsteadily to the next location. Bending over it, he lost his balance and fell flat on his face.

"You'd better sit a spell," grunted Cosmo as he picked him up. "I think you got too much of that likker energizer."

By noon the remaining two workers were red-faced and sweating. Will finished digging the last hole by himself. Two of the men used long poles with forks at the end to raise the smaller end of the pole while the others lifted and guided the larger end into the hole. The remaining space in the hole was filled with dirt, which was packed in by tamping.

The sound of the dinner bell called them to the house. Will took the lead with the others following. With a loud scraping of chairs, the crew fell into their places at the table. Alec loaded his plate with meat and potatoes, lowered his head and began eating. At the far end of the table Jacob began praying in German as he blessed the food. "Hey, I need the salt and pepper!" bellowed Alec without looking up. Jacob finished his blessing just in time to respond with a guttural "Amen!"

As the food was passed, the workers helped themselves silently and ate hastily, then rose from the table and shuffled out as soon as they were finished. The work progressed somewhat faster through the afternoon hours.

On the following day, Will hurried through the morning chores and then waited. By turns, he watched the road, then did odds and ends of jobs, checking his watch frequently. At 11:30 he entered the house from which emanated the rich aroma of roast beef. Anna was thickening the dark beef stock for gravy, while Mary beat the mashed potatoes and Minnie filled the water glasses on the table.

"Mamma, I don't think they are coming today."

Anna shook her head, vexed and troubled. "They what??
Now what am I going to do with all this food?"

"You might share it with Annalie. There are plenty of mouths
there to feed, and with another one on the way, she'll probably
welcome a vacation from cooking."

Anna ladled the left-over food into containers and drove with
the girls to Louie and Annalie's place. The twins pranced about
them excitedly as they carried the food into the house. Annalie
hugged her mother in appreciation. "It's too bad you had all that
work for nothing," she consoled Anna. "But I'm sure glad you
didn't throw it out!" she added with a grin.

Next morning the crew showed up at the expected time. "We
missed you yesterday," Will said. "What happened?"

Oscar spoke for the group. "My men all felt rotten yesterday
with belly aches and the heaves; it must have been something they
ate for dinner the day before."

Will's eyes grew flinty at the slur on his mother's cooking.
Struggling to keep from punching Oscar in the mouth, Will
decided to keep his mouth shut. He figured the less he riled Oscar
and the workers, the sooner they'd be off his property.

The work progressed fairly well as they took turns digging
holes and setting poles.

When the dinner bell rang, Will started for the house. Then
realizing he was walking alone, he called back, "Coming with
me?"

Oscar spoke up, "Naw, just go ahead and eat. We brought
our own sandwiches and drink. We like it better that way."

"Yah!" chimed in Jake. "We'll even bless our own food." He
put his hands together and gazed piously skyward.

"Hah! Hah! Hah!" roared Alec, throwing his head back.

When Will entered the house alone, Anna glanced up in
surprise from dishing the mashed potatoes. "Where are the others?"

With a shrug of his shoulders and a wry smile Will replied,
"I guess we won't be having guests for dinner any more. They all
brought their own lunches."

Anna threw up her hands in exasperation. "Well I never! This
is the first time I ever had anyone turn down my cooking!"

"Now Mamma, don't feel hurt about it. They're just a bunch

of clods who don't know a good thing when they see or taste it. At least you won't have to cook for them anymore. And judging from the reception your meal got yesterday, Annalie's family won't let this one go to waste, either."

Jacob delivered the second meal to his daughter's house. He was greeted by Louie with a broad grin. "So, is this going to be the usual procedure? It must be hard on Mom, but much obliged, just the same!"

Jacob's pale blue eyes grew flinty. "Ach, those scoundrels! The way they've treated my Anna!" He threw up his hands. "They're just no goot! No goot!"

By the end of the week, the pole-setting job was nearing completion. The digging also got messier as the land sloped to the creek bottom. The augur stirred the sediment at the bottom of the post hole to the consistency of thick pea soup. The only way to remove it was with a long-handled dipper.

As Will returned from dinner on Friday, the four crew men lay sprawled on the green sod, soaking up the warm sunshine. The cattle grazing in the nearby meadow raised their heads and lowed softly as Will rejoined the group.

Oscar was in an unusually genial mood. "Looks like two more post holes will finish the strip across your land, Eschman."

"All you'll need is for Emil to string his wire and hook up your phone. Then you'll be set to talk to your sweetie. Is it still Meriel?"

Will tried not to show his revulsion at Oscar's conversation. Meriel's name on Oscar's lips was blasphemy.

Oscar wheedled on. "By the way, Will, suppose you could dig the last two holes? My men have sore backs. We'll do the pole setting."

Will marveled at himself for allowing Oscar to push the rest of the digging on him. Maybe it was relief at being so near the end of the job — just to be rid of Oscar and his crew. If he did the digging, it would be over sooner than waiting on the others.

Will bored the post holes with the augur, plied the digger and ladled out the soupy mud. It caked on the legs of his overalls and splattered onto his face and hair.

Finally, the last pole was set and tamped into place. The crew clambered onto the wagon. Oscar leaned over and whispered something into Cosmo's ear. Cosmo exploded into an ugly laugh, "Why you old bastard!" With a crack of the rawhide whip, the mules lunged into action with the wagon rattling after them.

Will, soggy from the afternoon's digging, forced his weary legs to carry him up the hill to the house. He could hear the crewmen laughing loudly in the distance as the mule-drawn wagon disappeared down the road and wondered vaguely what the joking was about.

Never was he so glad to have a job finished as the week stint of pole setting. He bathed in the summer kitchen and changed into clean clothes before eating supper. Then early in the evening he turned into bed, exhausted.

CHAPTER NINETEEN

Treachery on the Creek Bottom

When Will came down to breakfast on Saturday morning, every joint in his body ached. He slowly eased himself into a chair at the breakfast table. However, in spite of his sore joints and muscles, a great weight was lifted from his mind. The shiftless tactics of the road crew and the sludge of obscene language were now in the past. He relaxed over the hot cereal and sipped his steaming coffee as he answered Jacob's questions about the installation of the new telephone.

The peaceful mood was shattered when Minnie exclaimed, "Hey! Whose cows are those by our mailbox?"

Will stared at the cattle eating the new grass along the yard fence. Others were wandering farther down the road.

"They're our cattle! And they're all out! Now, how in thunder did that happen?"

Leaving the rest of his breakfast, Will strode down to the gate. As he followed the fence toward the creek bottom, he came across a break in the barbed wire — no it wasn't a break! The ends of the wire were bright and shiny, freshly cut by wire nippers. A short ways farther down was a second cut — and still a third.

It suddenly dawned on him. The wire cutting had been done while he was in the house eating dinner. That's why they had insisted on eating their own lunches in the wagon instead of the food his mother had prepared. Under pretext of lame backs, the crew kept him so occupied digging those last post holes that he hadn't noticed anything amiss, and the fellows along the fence had kept the cattle at a distance within the field. That explained their laughing and joking as they drove home the night before.

In a surge of anger all the profanity of Oscar's crew from the past week splattered his mind like a fall in a pig pen.

"Those low-down polecats! Those bastards!" he kept repeating, as he strode back to the house.

"Willard!" shouted his shocked father. "What's come over you?"

"The dirty bastards! They cut the fence in three places so our cattle could get out!"

With Will almost immobilized by anger, Jacob took command of the situation. "Sam, help Will saddle the horses and round up the cattle. Mamma and the girls can help head them off so they will go back through the open gaps in the fence. And bring along the pliers to mend the wire, once the cattle are in."

Will saddled Belle with a trembling hand while he muttered to himself, "John would have to be away at a time like this!"

With Will and Sam yelling as they rode and the rest of the family flailing the air with brooms and branches, the nearby cattle soon found their way back through the broken fence and into the field. The more obstinate critters had wandered across the creek bottom and were reluctant about returning to captivity. Will and Sam, galloping across the bridge, headed them off. Three heifers and a young bull refused to cross the bridge and took to the marshland. The brothers followed, their horses wading in water up to their bellies.

They were almost to the top of the creek bank when the young bull put his head down belligerently and bolted back toward the marsh. Will dug his heels viciously into Belle's flanks. The startled mare whirled suddenly, sending the bull back up the creek bank where Sam took over, driving him back toward the pasture lot. Again Will kicked the mare's flank, shouting "Git up there!" in an effort to overtake his brother and the retreating animal. Belle, in response to her master's unaccustomed harsh treatment, lunged forward and stumbled. One of her feet slipped into a muskrat hole in the bank. With her hoof still in the hole, the mare plunged downward, head-first and landed on Will, pinning him to the bank beneath.

Will's first sensation was a sickening thud, then darkness as the horse above him shut out all light. Agonizing pain shot through his rib cage and left leg as the mare twitched spasmodically and tried to right herself.

"Easy, Belle, easy!" Will groaned hoarsely, then passed out.

Sometime later he became conscious of galloping hoofs and loud, excited voices, then his father bending over him.

"Ach Mein Gott! Are you all right, Will? – Sam, help me get him out! – Whoa there! Steady Belle!" With extraordinary strength, born of urgency, Jacob lifted the mare's belly while Sam pulled the groaning Will out by his shoulders. Will again passed out in a cold sweat.

By now, Anna and the girls, shaken and pale, had joined the group. They covered Will with their jackets, and Anna wiped the sweat from his forehead with her apron which she then folded and put under his head.

The horse continued to flounder and whinny. Jacob and Sam finally managed to free her leg from the hole, only to find it broken at both knee and ankle joints. Jacob shook his head sadly, "She'll have to be put out of her misery."

"Sam and Minnie," he ordered, "ride to the barn, and hitch the team to the wagon. Throw a batch of hay on the wagon bed and get a couple of comforters so we can get Will to the doctor." Then lowering his voice, "And bring back the gun with you."

The passing of time for Will was measured by stabbing chest pains with every breath, the chilling dampness of the spring sod gradually permeating the back of his clothing and the soothing hand of his mother periodically wiping his sweaty brow as she crooned solicitously, "Ach, my Willy! You are going to be all right!"

Suddenly, he was aware of the rattling of wagon wheels as Sam and Minnie veered the trotting team off the road onto the creek bank near him. Soberly, Minnie handed the gun to her father.

Will roused again as Jacob was raising the gun into shooting position. "No!" he called hoarsely.

"It has to be done, Son."

"Then give me the gun!" demanded Will. "And hold me up."

Jacob slowly handed the gun to his son and supported his shoulder. With every muscle steeled, Will raised the gun and called Belle's name. The mare raised her head and looked at her master pleadingly. "I'm sorry, Belle!" he apologized as he pulled the trigger.

At the report of the gun, Belle's head dropped to the ground. There was a final tremor and the faithful horse lay motionless. With blurred eyes, Will handed the gun back to his father.

Jacob was again in charge. "Before we load you in the wagon, can you tell us where you hurt the most?" Will motioned to his chest and left leg. The two brooms, improvised for splints, were bound on his leg with strips of cloth, torn from the bottom of Anna's petticoat. When Will had been eased onto the hay in the wagon and covered with the comforter, Jacob began the trip to the doctor's office in Pulaski.

The late afternoon sun was streaming through the window when Dr. Shelton glanced at his patient lying on the office couch. Will's chest was firmly taped and his left leg was bandaged and wrapped with cotton strips.

"All I can say, Will, is you are one lucky guy! You have two things in your favor — a tough constitution and the fact that it's early spring instead of summer or fall. A few weeks later, the clay banks would be hard, in which case your chance of survival would have been slim.

"As it is, you have several broken ribs. They'll be painful but will heal eventually. Also, the leg is badly bruised and sprained but not broken. Use these crutches to keep the weight off, and it should be all right in a few weeks.

"By the way, you never did tell me how the horse came to fall on you."

Jacob stated briefly that the fence had been cut and the cattle got out.

Dr. Shelton shook his head vigorously, "I don't know what this country's coming to with all the vandalism."

A few days after the accident, Emil Meyers drove out to the Eschman farm with a huge coil of wire on his wagon. After stringing the wire and nailing wooden pegs with sea-green insulators to the poles, he pulled the lead-in wires into the house and anchored the box-like telephone to the wall.

"Now, you're in business!" he announced proudly. "Your call will be three short rings; this booklet has the signals for other parties on your line. How about you being first to try it, Will?"

Will shook his head, "No, I'll save my phoning for when I have business to transact."

"Well then, who wants to be first?" pressed Emil.

"I will!" offered Mary, and she cranked a long and two short rings for Annalie's place.

"You wouldn't believe the change in my wife, Celinda," confided Emil to the others while Mary was talking on the phone. "She's so contented since we have our phone. In fact, I fixed a special strap to fit around the back of her neck, so she can listen while she sews or peels potatoes."

Ironically, the telephone, which was a contributing factor in Will's accident and loss of his mare, Belle, was also the means of heralding the incident over the countryside. Phone calls began to flood the Eschman household inquiring about Will's progress and recovery, much to Will's chagrin.

The following Sunday afternoon found the Eschman household buzzing with activity as friends and relatives stopped by to see Will. Anna, Mary and Minnie were kept busy passing coffee, cake and lemonade to the guests.

"Now, mind you, don't get too close to Uncle Will's leg!" cautioned Annalie, as the twins tried out the crutches.

Meanwhile, Sara had cuddled up to Will. "This is to show how much I 'wuv you'," she cooed as she pressed a fist full of violets into his hand.

Dan Meister and daughter, Miriam, emerged from the group. Meister grasped Will's hand firmly. "Just want you to know, I share your grief over the loss of your horse. She was a fine mare!"

"Thank you, sir." Emotion choked Will from saying more, but deep within was gratitude for a friend who understood him.

Miriam's eyes lit up as Will's brother, John, joined the group. "I didn't know you were home. How are things going in Ottumwa?"

"O.K.!" grinned John, taking her hand. "But I thought I'd better get home before things fell apart, completely." He nodded toward Will and his crutches.

"All right, little brother, that will do from you." Will waved them off as the couple made for the door.

Will winced as he noticed Aunt Celinda approaching. Her high-pitched voice jarred him, even from a distance. "I was just telling Emil how providential it was you had the telephone to while away your time while you were laid up."

"I wouldn't know," Will shrugged. "I haven't used it yet."

"You mean you haven't even talked on it after all the effort Emil and the road crew spent to get it here?"

"That's right! I enjoy peace and quiet more than talking over a telephone."

Celinda shook her head as she stalked away. "I just don't understand that fellow!" she muttered. "Here all of us bend over backward to cheer him up and he goes out of his way to be ornery!"

As the other guests were departing, Fritz Zimmerli entered the house. For the first time in the afternoon, Will's eyes lit up with enthusiasm.

"You old buzzard!" exclaimed Will, as Fritz held out his hand. "Whose bones did you come to pick this afternoon?"

"Not yours!" countered Fritz. "They're too stale and dry. Just stopped by to see if you're as cantankerous as folks say!"

"A fine friend you are! Wait till a guy's down to heap insults on him. I'm surprised you didn't bring Meriel along to help hatch up some new shenanigans."

"Now before you get too high and pious, let me remind you that you knew how to 'dish' it out to others back in your younger days. Like when you took my cousin, Kate, to the Meeting House to tease Carrie, or have you grown too old to remember that?"

"So, you came all the way over here to dig muck out of my past?"

"Well, no. Just to pass the time of day, but if you're going to be so blame defensive, I might as well be on my way."

"Sit down," motioned Will. "At least you're one up on Aunt Celinda. You old scalawag! I don't put any prank past you, but how did you get Meriel involved in that Box Social affair?"

"I didn't! You're going to find this hard to believe, but she had no idea I was in the store – nor in town for that matter. I was sitting back in the dark corner behind the stove, thawing out."

So that was it! Meriel had been telling him the truth! A flood of relief swept over Will. "Well, on with your story."

"You know the storekeeper's tongue for gossip and her piercing voice. When Meriel came into the store for crepe paper and a shoe box, Lizzie gushed all over the place about the coming Box Social. She held up the crepe paper, so I couldn't help noticing the colors and the size of the box."

"So after Meriel left, you came out of the woodwork," put in Will.

"Exactly! I did a little shopping first for Aunt Addie. Then I described her arthritis and how I wanted to help her decorate a box for the social. With a little 'buttering up', Lizzie gave me a full course on decorating boxes for socials."

"Using Meriel's colors, of course."

"Of course. I just happened to pick the same colors."

"I should have guessed!" exclaimed Will as the light dawned.

"No, you were too busy being the suspicious suitor and blaming Meriel for everything that happened."

"And how does she feel about me now?"

"Any other girl would have cut you down and tossed you out to the buzzards long ago, but not her. Believe me, if I could find a girl like her, I'd know better than to let her slip through my fingers over some petty misunderstanding."

"O.K. You've made your point!" said Will, closing the subject.

CHAPTER TWENTY

Out of the Pit

After Fritz left, Will wavered between relief that Meriel had remained faithful to him and feelings of remorse for the cutting things he had said to her and his part in breaking off their relationship. But how could he let her know he wanted to renew it? Though he was fluent in communication with others, he had never learned how to say "I'm sorry".

A solution came to him in the morning. He would send her a birthday card. Come to think of it, he had never heard her mention when her birthday was, but the card would let her know he was thinking of her and would be a good ice-breaker whether it arrived before or after her birthday.

He asked Minnie if there were any birthday cards around the house.

"Now, just what would you want with a birthday card?"

"Never mind; do you have one?"

"Well, I think I could find one. But I'd have to know whom it was for, so as to get the right kind."

"Any kind will do — oh yes, and bring an envelope."

Minnie snorted, "Whoever heard of sending a postcard in an envelope? It will go cheaper by itself."

Minnie returned in a short time with a birthday card covered with roses; however, the card was too big for the envelope.

"Now, with your steady hand, can you trim off the edges so it will fit?"

"Oh sure! And I'll even write the message for you. What

139

shall I say?" she asked with an impish grin.

"Don't bother. I'll write my own message."

Sometime later, Will walked painfully on his crutches down to the road and placed the sealed letter inside the mailbox. He had finally made a move. The next step was up to Meriel. Would she ignore the letter or respond to it? He would have to wait and see.

"Are you sure you don't want to go with us to town?" asked Anna a few days later. "It will do you good to get away from the place for awhile."

"No — just go along without me. I'll soak up the sunshine, here by the front door." With a sigh, Anna made her way to the rig where the other members of the family were waiting for her.

Shortly after the family left, a buggy pulled up to the front yard gate. "Oh no!" groaned Will as Jim Snellinger, Oscar's father, strode up the walk with a determined gait. "Yes — ?" greeted Will as Snellinger, panting for breath, stopped before him.

"I'll come right to the point," he began in staccato syllables. "Rumors are flying all over the neighborhood that my son caused your accident and the death of your horse."

"Well, the fence was cut, letting the cattle out on the afternoon your son's crew was on my place."

"Did you see them cut it?"

"No sir, but they were the only ones here all day."

"What about it being cut at night by rustlers?"

"Not likely, since none of the cattle were missing."

Snellinger's conversation took a sudden turn. "I've talked this over with Oscar and the crew. Alec's owned up to cutting the wire. He's not too bright, you know, and shouldn't have been hired on the crew in the first place. So I fired him."

Will looked directly at Snellinger. "I don't believe Alec had it in him to cut the wire — not unless he was put up to it."

"Well, anyway, he won't be with us anymore. I'm a just man!" continued Snellinger. "And we have a telephone line to put through. Nothing could be proven in court, connecting the accident to the cutting of the fence. However, to stop wagging tongues and to let our work go on smoothly, I'm writing this check for a hundred dollars to cover the loss of your horse."

The pen in Snellinger's pudgy hand scratched across the checkbook in wide flourishes.

Will stared at him coldly, without raising a hand to take the proffered check. "That may buy another horse, but it will never replace my mare, Belle."

"Well, anyway, I'm leaving it." Snellinger laid the check in Will's lap, turned and began walking toward the gate.

Will called after the departing man, "You might pass the word on to your son and his crew. If any of them put foot on this property without permission, I'm using the same gun on them as I did on my horse."

Snellinger quickened his pace, and without looking back, he climbed into the buggy and drove off.

Will sunk into a stupor of depression, sick of the world and sick of himself.

He was roused some time later by quick, light steps on the walk. "Oh no, not more callers!" he muttered, still rankling from his encounter with Snellinger. Opening his eyes fully, he saw it was Meriel approaching with a pail in her hand.

Conflicting emotions surged through him. Relief that she had responded to his letter, disappointment that she had caught him in such a low frame of mind.

"Well, hello there!" he forced a tone of enthusiasm. "And what might you be carrying in your pail?"

"I've been picking strawberries over on the Heath place to make jam, and I thought your folks might like a few for shortcake."

Will began to rise slowly. "I'll get something to put them in."

"Never mind – I can put them in one of your Mom's pans in the kitchen."

In a moment she emerged with her half-filled pail. In her fingers was a large strawberry which she held up to Will's lips. "How have you been?" she asked as he proceeded to eat the berry.

Will groaned slightly, "Do you want a blow-by-blow account?"

Meriel's eyes crinkled, "Well, at least you're still alive, and you didn't commit murder on Oscar or his crew!"

She slipped her warm suntanned hand gently into his. "It's been mighty rough, hasn't it – putting up with Oscar's crew, the accident and losing Belle – everything together."

"That's not the worst of it," confessed Will. "I can't understand how I let Oscar and his bunch stir up so much anger in me. After listening to their profanity for a week, I found myself rehearsing their language – even to swearing when I found the cut places in the fence." Will paused, then resumed in a husky voice, "If – if I hadn't been so furious, I might have been more gentle with Belle – and she might be alive today." His voice broke.

Meriel placed her hand on his shoulder. "Don't blame yourself. You had nothing to do with the muskrat hole in the bank; horses do sometimes step in them, you know. As for swearing – other men have failed the same way – Peter, for example, and he was restored."

Will's arms went around her and he buried his face in her hair. "Oh Meriel, I love you so much! And I've done everything wrong to prove it – my suspicions, my anger. Can you forgive me?" He paused a moment, then continued, "These last weeks have been a torment – thinking I had lost you for good. I don't dare ask if you love me. I don't see how even God could love or forgive me!"

Meriel's hand slipped caressingly over his face. Raising her head, she kissed him lightly on the cheek.

"I think I have always loved you, Will – ever since that day when we were children and I watched you walking up the road to Bromes Dell School, toting that enormous sack of buckeyes for me."

"If it would make you feel any better toward God, I'd be glad to pray with you about it."

Will gripped her hand tightly as she began: "Father, we love You because You first loved us. We are a sinful bunch of folks and don't deserve Your love or forgiveness. But we come anyway because Your Son Jesus said 'Whosoever comes to Me, I will in no wise cast out.' Will needs You. Please give him Your peace! In Jesus' name, Amen."

There was a moment of silence before Will spoke: "Lord, I've done everything my way, and it has fizzled out! My life's pretty much of a mess. It's all Yours, if You want it. I'm sick of trying any more. Just make me what You want me to be! Thank You for Jesus and thank You for Meriel. Amen."

As he finished praying, Will's eyes met with Meriel's. He held her close, their cheeks wet with mingled tears. "Oh Meriel — if you can put up with this stormy nature of mine, I promise to do all I can to make you happy. Will you marry me?"

"Yes", she murmured as he continued to hold her close.

Finally, Meriel drew her head back, looked at him through brimming eyes and smiled. "I almost forgot to thank you for the lovely birthday card."

"You did get it then. I hope it wasn't too late."

"No, in fact it was a little early."

Will grinned sheepishly, "Do you mind telling me just when your birthday is?"

"Not at all," she answered mischievously. "It's November 25th."

"Oh my! I sure missed that one! All I can see to do is to set our wedding date for November 25th. That should help keep it on my mind."

Meriel looked at him quizzically. "Are you serious or joking?"

"The more I think of it, it sounds like an excellent idea! Harvesting would be over. We could settle in for the winter and be ready for spring planting."

"Where?" asked Meriel, surprised at his swift planning.

"Well, you and I together will come up with the right place."

"If you really mean it, I'm willing!"

Will looked at her long, took a deep breath and engulfed her in his arms again. "Darling, you'll never be sorry!"

CHAPTER TWENTY ONE

To Find a Nest

The approaching wedding of Will and Meriel was hailed with enthusiasm by both their families. Lew Browning's eyes would grow misty as he shared the news with the patrons on his mail route.

"Have you heard? Will Eschman is planning to marry my Meriel. He's a right smart young man and will make a fine husband for my girl."

Luella expressed her approval in a practical way. Undaunted by the lack of money, she saw to it that all the flour sacks in the house were bleached and hemmed to make dish towels, and every unused article of clothing was torn into strips for braided rugs.

Eadie quipped to her high school friends, "I don't even dare drop one of my skirts on a chair. If so, I'll see it next day in a braided rug."

Quilt frames were set up in the Eschman parlor, and every spare moment was spent either tying comforters or making quilts.

Will's leg was healed to the point that he was able to carry his share of the farm work. Though it irked him to be assigned to the riding jobs while his father and brother did the walking, still he was grateful for their consideration as he rested with his swollen leg elevated at night.

Jacob called up to him on the wagon as he and Sammy pitched the haycocks onto the towering load, "Will, have you thought of using Snellinger's check toward buying a team, now that you'll be working your own place?"

"I don't know," reflected Will. "Seems a lot like taking blood money."

"Nonsense!" retorted Jacob. "Just plain restitution! Even the Bible says, 'For all manner of trespass, the neighbor shall pay double for the loss.' And surely cutting a fence, maliciously, would come under that heading. Snellinger is lucky that you didn't press charges in court for all the trouble he caused you!"

"Well," agreed Will finally, "the way you put it does make sense. Maybe, I'd better spend the money on a horse or team before Snellinger changes his mind and stops payment on the check."

Accordingly, Will called Meister on the phone that evening, and the next day he drove over in the horse and buggy.

Meister was graying noticeably about the temples. However, his smile was as warm as ever and his handclasp firm as, again, he expressed sympathy over the loss of Will's mare, Belle.

Will explained briefly about the hundred dollars Snellinger had paid for the loss of his mare and added that he was willing to add enough to pay for a team.

"Tell you what!" began Meister. "I have a couple horses that should make you a good team – one is a gelding, the other a mare. They don't have the lines or grace of your mare, Belle; however, they are well matched and good workers. But let me prepare you before you see them. The mare is blind in one eye.

"It's like this: A stray cat came to the barn and decided to have her kittens in the horse manger. When Nell reached down for a bite of hay, the cat lashed out and scratched her eyeball and infection set in. We had the vet out, but he was unable to save the eye. It doesn't affect her working ability. She works perfectly when hitched with Nick."

As the men entered the barn, the two chestnut-colored horses raised their heads and nickered. Will noticed with a jolt that the mare's right eye was pale blue and opaque.

"Doesn't she stumble all over the place?"

"No, it's surprising how steady she is on her feet. And when she is hitched with her blind side next to Nick, she seems to take her cue from him and pulls perfectly. Now don't be rushed into taking them. You can try them out or talk it over with your father.

I have other matched horses in the pasture. However, I can let you have this pair, harness and all, for one hundred dollars, which would be about half the price of another team."

Will thought for a moment. Surely, these two horses were a far cry from his beautiful mare, Belle. But they would serve the purpose as he got started in farming, and Nick would look fairly presentable hitched to a buggy.

"I'll take them. Do you want me to cash this check at the bank, or will you accept it in payment?"

"It's fine as long as you endorse it."

As Will was tying the team to the back of the buggy, Meister laid a hand on his shoulder, "Just want to congratulate you on your coming marriage. You could never find a finer mate than Meriel."

"Thank you," Will answered, simply and humbly.

Summer shuttled swiftly into fall. The haymow bulged with its store of new mown clover and timothy. With shorter days and cooler nights, the corn ears matured early, and the men began their autumnal ritual of setting up corn shocks.

On evenings and weekends Will would pick up Meriel and together they would drive through the countryside following each real estate ad for a prospective home. What had begun as a joyous adventure was now becoming routine and fraught with urgency as each lead turned out beyond their means or unfit for farming purposes.

It was the last Saturday in September when Will once again stopped to pick up Meriel. "Here, I'll carry your basket," he offered as she appeared with a heavy sweater over her house dress to ward off the chill of the day. Will pulled the horse to the side of the road as they reached the hilltop. "That boulder will make a good place to eat our lunch. One good thing about these trips are the picnics."

While Meriel arranged herself on the boulder beside the basket, Will set out a basin of oats for Nick. "Somewhere out there has to be our dream home," she mused as she gazed over the panorama of yellow aspens and burgundy oaks beneath an azure dome. "Have you a special place in mind, today?"

Will evaded her question and began investigating the contents of the basket: the egg salad sandwiches, ripe peaches and oatmeal cookies. He carefully unwrapped the fruit jar of hot coffee. "With your knack, honey, you can make any place or meal fit for a king!"

Meriel studied his face soberly. "I have a feeling this place is going to take a lot of fixing before it's fit for a king."

Will waited to answer until they had finished eating and were on their way down the road.

"That's it," he pointed as they neared the Ben Traschel place.

"O-o-o-o-oh," her voice fell as she surveyed the ramshackle buildings.

"Don't be so sad!" pleaded Will. "We've exhausted our list of places. This one will be cheap. Maybe we're supposed to show how we can rejuvenate a run-down place."

Meriel mustered a faint smile as Will helped her from the buggy and they passed through a battered gate, sagging on one hinge. Together, they waded the tall grass and weeds in the front yard and were met at the front door by Ben Traschel with a wide, toothless grin.

Ben nodded toward his wife as he hitched on his sagging suspenders. "Maw 'n me ain't doing so good at keeping things up in our old age. But take a fine, young couple like yourselves, this would be a perfect place to start out."

Meriel cringed inwardly as Ben addressed her directly, "You and the Missus can visit a spell and look about the house while I show Will around the farm."

As the men folk left, Meriel glanced about the dim interior, reeking with the odors of burnt potatoes, onions, and stale hog fat. She took in the dark, sooty curtains hanging askew at smudged windows, patches of wallpaper waiting to fall from the ceiling, and greasy, splotched floor boards, undulating like a tipsy sailor.

Through her mind flashed the nuptial phrase — *for better or for worse*. "Dear Lord," she breathed, "please don't let the worst come so soon!"

She forced herself to visualize how fresh wallpaper, crisp curtains and a scrubbing brush with lye-water on the floor could change the appearance of the room.

After what seemed like an eternity of listening to Mrs.

Traschel's dull recital of physical woes, Meriel felt relieved to hear Will's voice outside the screen door.

"Thank you for taking the time to show me the place. We'll let you know next week if we take it or not."

Meriel waited until they were driving home to ask what he had decided.

"Well, it might have possibilities. But every fence would have to be replaced to keep the stock in. The barn would have to be almost rebuilt to keep it from collapsing, and the fields have lain fallow so long, it would take years to restore them to productivity. It would take more money to make the place livable than to buy a newer farm."

Meriel laid her head on his shoulder and began to sob softly. Will drew her back and looked into her face, "Are you sorry we didn't take it?"

"Oh no! Just so relieved I won't have to start scrubbing that house!!"

"Honey, you would have been willing to clean up that mess of a house if I had decided to buy the farm?"

"Well, you know it says — for better or for worse!"

Will clasped her tightly in his arms, "Pray God, we find a place soon before putting you through something like that!"

Sunday morning, Josef Schillig, with his usual stern expression, approached Will and Meriel as they were leaving the Mennonite service. "I hear you two are looking for a place to live once you are married."

"Why, yes sir, we are!"

"My wife and I plan to leave the farm and move to town this winter. Farm work's getting too much for us. Mind, I don't want to sell, as I aim to turn it over to my son in a few years. I need someone to take care of it now. I was looking for a church member." He eyed Will sharply.

"Sir! I consider myself a Christian, even though I may not be a member of the Mennonite church."

"Well, be that as it may, I know your reputation for good work and honesty — still I was hoping for a church member."

"Sir, I don't believe in joining a church to better myself in business. But if you would consider me as a tenant on your place, you won't regret it."

"I believe I can trust you. Come around tomorrow."

On Monday, Will and Meriel drove to the Schillig place known as Golden Acres. A yellow-turreted house crowned the hilltop surrounded with well-kept barn and sheds. Cornfields radiated from the farmyard, waiting to be harvested.

Will and Meriel sat a few moments in the buggy by the roadside, drinking in the view. Like children on Christmas morning, they found it difficult to believe their good fortune.

They were met at the door by Mrs. Schillig, dressed in a gray house dress with a white collar. Her hair was combed back severely from the face. She stretched out her work-worn hand in greeting. "I'm so glad to have someone who will keep up the place for us. After years of working, it would break my heart to see it run down."

"You have a beautiful place here," answered Will. "And we'll do our best to keep it that way."

"We'd never have enough furniture for such a large place. You might want to use the upstairs for storage," suggested Meriel.

"How much furniture do you have?" asked Mr. Schillig entering the room.

"To tell the truth, none so far," answered Meriel, blushing.

"Then, we'll leave the dining table and chairs, also one bedroom of furniture. It will save us storing and you buying," Schillig declared.

Overcome with gratitude, Meriel murmured her thanks with misty eyes.

The terms were drawn up for a three-year lease, subject to review at the end of each year. Will agreed to help Schillig harvest his corn so he could move sooner into his town place. The time of occupation for Will and Meriel was set for the last of October.

CHAPTER TWENTY TWO

I Do — I Do

*O*nce the housing situation was settled, wedding plans moved swiftly for Will and Meriel. They decided to be married in the Schillig place, their future home. Will's sister, Mary, helped Meriel make a simple lace-trimmed white dress for the ceremony and a second burgundy-colored dress of the same pattern for traveling.

On Thanksgiving Day, the families of the bride and groom gathered for the ceremony. The wedding table was covered with a snowy white linen tablecloth. Its hand-drawn border had been hem-stitched by Meriel. Clusters of yellow mums and russet oak leaves, along with Mrs. Schillig's Boston ferns, filled the area before the bay windows where the bridal party would stand.

Jacob and Anna sat in the front row of chairs, smiling in remembrance of their own good years together. The Brownings were seated to their right. Luella, petite in a navy blue dress, sat for once with her hands folded quietly in her lap. Her husband, Lew, wearing his best black suit and a freshly trimmed mustache, occasionally brushed the back of his hand across misty eyes.

The Browning and Eschman offspring, all in their Sunday best, mingled in a happy group behind their parents. Louie and Annalie proudly displayed their own little clan: the twins, now school age and dressed in their first long navy blue pants, sat solemnly beside their father, imitating him. Three year old Sara, dainty as a princess in her red velvet dress, folded her hands demurely and fixed her eyes on the wedding alcove, waiting for the bride and groom to appear. Baby Emma alone seemed unimpressed by the occasion. She cooed happily as she swayed back and forth on her mother's lap. Placing a finger on Emma's lips, Annalie whispered "Sh-h-h" and proceeded to straighten the infant's white knitted outfit. A few close friends and neighbors mingled with the family.

The room hushed as Rev. Mueller took his place in the wedding alcove and the bridal party joined him. The groom stood tall in his new black suit and white bow tie. His shoulders were thrown back and his jaw firmly set. The bride at his side bespoke gentleness as she waited demurely in her lace-edged wedding gown. Behind them stood their attendants. John, attired like his brother, served as best man. Eadie, in a pink version of the bride's gown, smiled radiantly as she held Meriel's bouquet.

"Dearly beloved," Pastor Mueller beamed kindly upon the wedding group and all present, "we are gathered here in the presence of God and these witnesses to unite this couple in holy matrimony. Willard, do you take Meriel to be your lawfully wedded wife?"

"I do!" responded Will in an earnest voice for all to hear.

"And do you, Meriel take Willard for your husband to love, honor and cherish as long as you both shall live?"

"I do!" Meriel responded in a voice audible only to Will and the pastor.

The pastor's voice grew more serious as he held up the gold wedding ring handed to him by the groom.

"Dear friends, let us think a moment about this golden band that I am holding in my hand. It has never been worn before, and represents a new circle of love between the Lord and Will and Meriel. It is meant to remain so until the Lord grants them children to add to the circle. Secondly, (as the pastor turned the ring slowly) it is a perfect circle with no beginning or end. It will not end tomorrow, next week or next year. It speaks of a perfect, unending relationship. And finally, notice its gleaming gold color. That did not just happen, but it was heated and tried in a furnace. Trials and testings are bound to come your way. May you both allow God to guide you through them, so that your marriage may be a shining example of love and commitment."

(Then turning to the groom,) "You may now place the ring on Meriel's hand." With smiling lips and glistening eyes, she looked up into Will's face as he slipped the wedding ring onto her finger.

"You may now kiss the bride," said Rev. Mueller, smiling as he watched.

Only then did Will's reserve break. Gathering his wife into his arms, he planted a long, lingering kiss on her lips, amid the applause of the onlookers. A reception line beginning with Pastor Mueller and the parents quickly formed to congratulate the newlyweds. Dan Meister wished them many happy years together. Fritz grasped Will's hand. "Congratulations! You finally got yourself together! May I kiss the bride?"

"Permission granted!" grinned Will.

After kissing Meriel lightly on the cheek, Fritz turned to Will. "Be good to her. She's one in a million!"

Later, as the wedding guests sat eating and visiting, Will and Meriel left their place of honor at the table and mingled with the different groups about the room.

Suddenly someone exclaimed that the bride and groom had disappeared. Meriel's brother, Harold, explained shyly that the newlyweds had a long drive ahead of them — Ottumwa, to be exact. They had left him in charge of the house and chores.

Meriel had slipped into her burgundy dress just prior to leaving the Schillig place. Now, bundled in a warm coat, close-fitting hat and muff, she snuggled close to her husband for warmth. Suddenly, she realized how little she really knew about him. The lines of an old Negro spiritual ran through her mind. "No turning back! No turning back!"

As if reading her thoughts, Will asked suddenly, "Well, honey, how do you feel about being Mrs. Eschman?"

She quickly slipped one hand from her muff and nestled it inside his warm, gloved hand. "Whither thou goest, I will go!" she whispered softly. "Even to the ends of the earth."

Dropping the reins momentarily, Will enveloped her in both arms. "Darling, you're precious!"

It was dark when they reached Ottumwa. Gas street lights

twinkled, giving a fairyland glow to the city. After studying the address in his hand as he stopped the horse under a street light, Will drew up to a colonial-type house with pillars in the front. "This must be the place we're looking for," he announced.

Meriel murmured her admiration.

The large hallway within glowed with two gas lights in cut glass globes. Beneath a beveled mirror on one side of the hall was a mahogany lowboy with a guest register on its polished top. Will introduced Meriel and himself to the landlady, a neat middle-aged woman in a soft gray dress with white collar and cuffs. Then, in a business-like way, he signed the register: Mr. and Mrs. Willard Eschman, Pulaski, Iowa.

"So you're from Pulaski," the landlady commented, reading the signature upon the register. "You must be chilled after such a long drive. If you like, I'll bring some hot coffee and cookies to your room, later."

Will and Meriel murmured their thanks as she led them up the polished oak stairs and down a carpeted hall. "This is your room," their hostess announced, opening a heavy oak door. Inside, two hobnail lamps on the dresser cast a soft glow over the pink and white-flowered bedspread and draperies.

In a few minutes the landlady knocked and delivered a tray with a complete china coffee service and a plate of cookies. The couple were then left on their own. For a while they sat on the edge of the bed relaxing as they consumed the cookies and sipped hot coffee from the fine Dresden china cups. Checking his watch, Will noticed it was nearly midnight.

He also sensed Meriel's growing shyness. "I'm going to take the tray back down stairs," he said, "and I'll check up on the horse once more before we turn in. You can get ready for bed while I'm gone."

As the door closed behind Will, Meriel slipped into her beige nainsook gown with lace trim, hung her clothes in the closet and climbed into bed.

A short time later, Will re-entered the room and turned out the lamps. Meriel's heart raced as he moved about the darkened room and began to get into the bed with her. Again, she realized that in many ways they were still strangers.

He slipped one arm under her head and drew her close to himself. "Darling!" he murmured, as his lips hungrily sought hers. "At last, you're all mine!"

Meriel slowly yielded her lips, her body, her future into Will's keeping.

The following morning they were awakened by church bells ringing. Meriel, resting on Will's arm, drank in the chimes as a benediction on their marriage.

The two dressed leisurely, then drove through the Sunday deserted streets in search of an eating place. From the residential part of Ottumwa, where they had spent the night, the street dropped abruptly into a basin area leading into the business section of town. They finally located a German bakery and restaurant. After a hearty breakfast of bacon, eggs, hash-browned potatoes and toast, they looked over a showcase filled with German pastries, cookies and bread.

"Look Will!" exclaimed Meriel. "Have you ever seen such an array of luscious cakes and cookies?"

Will could not resist teasing. "Here I bring you to the city to show you the sights, and your eyes are glued on something to eat. Besides, you can probably bake better tasting things at home."

"On this occasion," persisted Meriel, "it would be nice to take home something special as a souvenir." They bought a couple dozen decorated cookies, a German chocolate cake and a loaf of bread. After a leisurely afternoon of sight-seeing, they returned to the rooming house for a second night.

On Monday they browsed through a large department store. "How about buying something you can't eat?" suggested Will with a grin. Each section of the store offered a new wonderland of gifts and treasures: luxurious rugs and furniture, fine china and silverware, expensive jewelry, and imported clocks and knick-knacks.

"Now that would make a nice souvenir!" Meriel pointed to a copper teakettle on the shelf. "It would remind me of our wedding weekend every time I fix a meal!"

The copper teakettle was purchased, and after eating another meal at the German restaurant, the two started for home.

A few miles out of Ottumwa, the sunshine became enveloped in heavy clouds, and a penetrating wind blew head-on. The couple turned up their coat collars, wrapped the blanket about the two of them and snuggled tightly together for warmth. Nick, the horse, shook his head and trotted doggedly into the wind.

"Remember a year ago?" mused Meriel.

"I was thinking about the same thing — chopping wood for your paw, the sudden blizzard and staying overnight at your place."

"That was the beginning of quite a year," resumed Meriel. "The Box Social, the telephone crew and your accident."

"Never in my wildest dreams did I fancy it turning out like this! Especially as I was lying under Belle on the creek bottom."

"Makes me think of the hymn we sometimes sing — " Meriel added, "God leads His dear children along." In answer, Will merely pressed his bride closer to himself.

Dusk was falling as they turned into the driveway of "Golden Acres". Will unlocked the door, then gathering Meriel in his arms, he carried her over the threshold. "Welcome home, Mrs. Eschman!"

The house was all in order, and Harold had left the woodbox well-filled with kindling and stovewood.

After kindling a fire in the range, Will left to put away the horse. When he returned, Meriel had cut thick slices of the fresh store bread and brought out butter and left over chicken from the pantry.

The copper teakettle had been filled and was singing on the stove. The coffee pot was simmering and the aroma of fresh coffee filled the air.

The evening snack thawed the chill from their bones and lifted their spirits. Then with Will carrying the lamp, they made a brief tour of the other rooms before turning in.

"Did you ever see a finer place to start housekeeping?" exulted Meriel.

Will agreed that he hadn't.

Will glanced toward the window as they reached the bedroom. "Maybe we'd better just climb into bed with our clothes on. I have a feeling we won't be alone for long!" He drew the shades and blew out the light.

As he climbed into bed, there was a sudden lurch, and the springs, mattress and bedding all dropped to the floor.

"Oh, oh! Somebody's already been here and taken out the bedslats!" exclaimed Meriel.

After a few minutes of giggling and looking up at the bedstead, they decided to spend the night on the floor. "We can't fall any lower!" they agreed.

A short time later, there were two shotgun blasts outside the window followed by an earsplitting din as practically every pot and pan in the neighborhood was banged to add to the tumult.

"What in the world is that?" exclaimed Meriel.

"That, Mrs. Eschman, is a 'shivaree' and I think we had better get out to them before they break down the door and pull us out."

In a short time, the noisy visitors were in the kitchen, wolfing down the cookies and enjoying the German chocolate cake along with hot coffee served to them by Will and Meriel. When the last of the refreshments had disappeared, the merry-makers also melted away, calling out their thanks and good wishes as they left.

CHAPTER TWENTY THREE

Their First Year

*S*ince Christmas seemed to trip over the heels of their wedding, Will and Meriel gave orders to the family — no more gifts. Their two families had already showered them with wedding presents. They, in turn, had wedding pictures made as Christmas gifts, one for each family group.

Christmas Eve found them with Meriel's folks. Luella Browning had fixed her traditional Christmas Eve supper. As the tureen of potato soup (rich with carrots, ham and onions) made its way around the table, Louella filled Will and Meriel in on the latest family developments.

"Have you heard? Harold has a new girl friend — Reah Zimmerman, Fritz's sister from Kansas. She lives with her uncle and aunt, the Burrows."

"Yah!" added Ted with his mouth full of sausage and hot biscuit, "She talks enough for both of them."

"Has she proposed yet?" chimed in Cleo as he helped himself to the cabbage salad.

Lew Browning's mild eyes grew stormy. "All right, boys, time to lay off Harold! They make a real good couple, Harold and Reah."

Harold, at the end of the table, turned red as he ladled soup from the tureen. "Shucks!" he answered slowly. "I figure there's no need wasting words when I can learn all I need to know just by listening."

Eadie, in a new holiday jacket, glared at her younger

159

brothers. "Will you fellows stop bickering at the table?"

Her friend, Richard, was enjoying the banter. Finally, to change the subject, he turned to Will. "How are you making out in married life?"

"Just fine!" Will and Meriel beamed together. "We've been wondering when you folks were planning to tie the knot?" asked Will.

To break the strained silence Meriel put in, "I think we're ready for dessert now, Mom. Will was asking if you were having your special apple pie tonight."

Luella smiled broadly as she handed the pie to her son-in-law.

As soon as supper was finished, Richard rose, and pulling back Eadie's chair, stated that they hated to eat and run, but his folks were also expecting them at their Christmas party.

Meriel helped her mother clear the dishes from the table, then presented her parents with the wedding picture. With "oohs" and "a-ahs" the family declared it was the finest looking bridal couple they had ever seen.

A short time later, Will and Meriel were celebrating Christmas in their own house. A small fir tree which Will had cut was mounted on a stand in the corner of the living room. Meriel had decorated it with small red bows and tiny hawthorne apples. It contained but two gifts: a small box tied securely in the branches and a larger rectangular package on the stand beneath the tree.

"I guess the head of the house comes first," said Meriel as she handed the larger package to her husband. "Since you were wishing for some way to keep your bills, receipts and papers in order, I thought this might help."

As Will quickly untied the ribbon ties, his package opened into an expanding file with labeling tabs on the top. The two outer covers were covered with burgundy challis left over from Meriel's traveling outfit and monogrammed with the initials **W.T.E.**

"Just what I need!" beamed Will in appreciation. "And what a beautiful job you did with the gold embroidery!"

"I'm so glad you like it," Meriel smiled as she traced the gold monogram, **W.T.E.** (Willard Todd Eschman). "Some day we'll be seeing that name in all kinds of important places."

"And this is for the heart of the home!" Will untied the tiny box from the fir tree and handed it to his wife.

As Meriel opened the box, a golden chain slipped through her fingers until an oval shaped locket lodged in the palm of her hand. Upon its face was a small white cloisonne oval, centered with a sprig of exquisite pink roses.

"Oh, my! Does it open?"

"Here, let me show you!" Within the small golden case he had written in tiny letters, "Meriel, I love you — Forever, Will." He fastened the chain about her neck and held her tightly.

With the coming of cold weather after Christmas, the family gathered at Jacob Eschman's homestead for butchering. White wisps of smoke curled up around the large metal barrel filled with steaming water. Hiram Heath, a neighbor and expert butcher, joined the Eschman men folk waiting in the snow-covered farm yard for the action to begin.

At a given signal, Sam, inside the pigpen, opened the chute door allowing one hog to escape. As it dashed down the chute, Heath, his mustached mouth firm and feet braced for balance, struck its head with a hammer, then cut its throat.

Scarcely had the hog quit squealing before John and Will, grabbing the animal by the hind legs, plunged it into the scalding water, then onto the improvised table of planks where Louie scrubbed and scraped off its hair until it lay in state — cold, stiff and clean.

Meanwhile, Jacob had thrust a wooden peg through the tendons of the hog's back legs. Will and John then hung the animal on the bare limb of a tree near the summer kitchen.

Mary brought out a dishpan for the heart and liver when the hog had been slit open, while Jacob stoked the fire beneath the barrel and added more water for the next three hogs to be butchered.

The carcasses would be chilled overnight, then divided into hams, shoulders and side meat to be salted and smoked. The whole process of curing meat, grinding sausage and rendering lard would extend through most of the remaining winter days. It would also furnish the Eschman family with much of their meat supply through the rest of the year.

Spring breezed in gently, showering the landscape with blossoms of wild plum and cherry trees. True to Meister's prediction, the partially blind Nell not only did her share of the field work but made an excellent teammate for Nick. With his faithful horses, Will finished planting in record time. The cornfields flourished. Then he took time out to prepare a garden plot for Meriel.

"Guess that's the least I can do," he teased, "if I'm expecting grub on the table."

Meriel handled the chickens and churning in superb farm-wife style. She delivered butter and eggs to the Schilligs and her folks, then traded the rest for groceries at the store.

Through the summer days she picked and canned green beans and transformed buckets of cucumbers into crunchy pickles. She spent her spare time peeling pans of transparent apples which she later cooked into sauce and canned.

The golden glow of autumn flooded the acres of cornshocks and pumpkins and revealed more apples and pears on sagging boughs, waiting to be harvested and preserved.

A wave of guilt swept over Meriel as she felt her zest for conserving the year's bounty waning. Frequent nausea plagued her as she stooped to pick the last of the tomatoes. Still, she was determined not to complain. Will was putting all his energy into getting the abundant crops harvested.

He broached the matter at the supper table as she wiped the perspiration from her forehead. "Seems to me you're looking mighty 'peaked' these days. Aren't you feeling well?"

"I get so aggravated with myself," she apologized. "There's all this good produce on hand — and I feel just 'do-less' lately."

"I say it's time to see Dr. Shelton. Either he has some tonic for you, or else, you let up on the work."

The next Saturday found them in the doctor's office. Following his examination, the doctor addressed the couple with a kindly twinkle in his eye. "Well, Meriel, I'd say, about next July you should be presenting your husband with a fine son or daughter."

Will broke into a wide grin as he hugged his wife. "Wow! Did you hear that, Meriel?! A son of our own!"

Dr. Shelton chuckled at Will's excitement. "Well, at least there's a fifty-fifty chance of it being a boy."

"All right!" persisted Will on the way home. "You are taking it easier from now on."

"Women have been having babies ever since Eve, and it hasn't been any great deal to stop work over," countered Meriel.

"Well, since this baby of ours is someone special, there'll be no more picking vegetables or toting baskets for you this fall!" Again he gathered her tenderly into his arms.

The end of the year found their ledger definitely on the credit side. Schillig grinned delightedly as he viewed the haymow and granaries bulging with their store of hay and grain.

"You've done a beautiful job working the farm, Will! Can I sign you up for three more years?"

"The weather conditions have been favorable," stated Will modestly. "Let's take it a year at a time — next year, yes."

Meriel welcomed the winter months that brought an end to canning and time to stitch tiny nightgowns and kimonos for the coming baby. With loving care, she added a colorful touch of edging or smocking to each garment before laying it aside.

John and Miriam had planned a July wedding, so excitement in the family ran high over two red letter days coming in the same month.

CHAPTER TWENTY FOUR

A Son is Born

Spring burst forth, unusually early, with its harbingers of birds and flowers. Will reveled in following his faithful team as day after day of sunshine allowed him to finish his planting in record time. He helped Meriel plant a small garden near the house, insisting on limiting the size, as she would not be in condition for much outside work.

"Now all we need is a good shower," he enthused, "and the crops will really boom!"

He watched hopefully as flickers of lightning lit up the night sky. However, it proved to be only heat lightning, foretelling another hot day.

A few brave corn plants poked their heads through the parched soil. Will painstakingly cultivated the meager rows, hoping by destroying all weeds and loosening the soil to coax more growth from the stunted plants. Eventually, the stand had germinated but the stalks were short and anemic in color. Will stood in the center of his parched cornfield as he waited for his steaming team to cool off.

Looking up into the intense blue, he prayed, "Lord, can You hear me? If not for my sake, well, for Meriel's sake, please let enough rain fall to give us a decent crop." His words seemed to bounce back from the shimmering sky. He resumed cultivating with a dull, aching heart.

Meriel had foregone watering her precious flowers, and instead, used the rinse water from her washing on the vegetables.

She was rewarded with a fair turn-out of green beans and cabbage. The new potatoes remained few and no larger than marbles.

When Will came in from his day's work, he found Meriel had supper on the table. In the absence of meat there were hard boiled eggs, cabbage salad and the last of the old year's shriveled potatoes, fried crisp in bacon fryings.

"Not a very hearty meal for a hard-working man," she apologized, "but there is fresh bread pudding for dessert."

Will gathered his full-figured wife into his arms, laying his head against her faded, freshly laundered dress. "Have I told you lately that you're the sweetest gal this side of the Mississippi?"

"You're a flatterer!" she teased back. "But at this stage, I'll take all the compliments I can get from anyone."

Mid-July brought John and Miriam's wedding day. It dawned, hot and sultry. "Do you feel like making the effort to go?" asked Will as Meriel moved ponderously about the kitchen, wiping sweat from her face.

"Why don't you join them!" suggested Meriel. "No need of us both missing the ceremony."

"And leave you alone? By no means! Why don't we just have our own celebration by taking it easy today?"

Meriel smiled, relieved as she prepared a light lunch for the two of them.

Will glanced up quickly as she caught her breath. "What is it?"

"Maybe you'd better call the doctor. This may be it!"

Will sprang to the phone, thankful that a ring could save the time of a long ride. After talking to the doctor, he also called Meriel's mother, Luella. She responded, "Yes, I'll try to get a ride over, right away."

The doctor arrived shortly after, bringing Luella with him.

As the sultry afternoon ebbed away, Meriel's gown became soaked with perspiration. Her lips were swollen as she bit them to hold in cries of pain from the severe contractions. At intervals, Luella wiped the beads of sweat from her daughter's forehead.

The clock in the adjoining room struck five. Will reminded the group that by now the bride and groom had boarded the train and were on their way to St. Louis for their honeymoon.

The sky darkened earlier than usual, and the muttering of thunder was heard in the west. Soon flashes of lightning split the sky, followed by rolls of thunder and sudden dashes of rain. Then a heavy downpour set in, bringing new birth to the drought-stricken countryside.

Within the house, a brisk breeze, laden with the scent of rain, fluttered the curtains and brought a new surge of vitality to those about Meriel's bed.

"Now one more time!" encouraged the doctor.

Summoning all her strength, Meriel gave a final push. A baby's cry was heard, then the happy reassurance from the doctor, "You have a fine baby boy here. What are you going to call him?"

Meriel, exhausted but happy, looked down at the small bundle in her arms trying to suck his fist. "We decided to call him Everett, didn't we Will?"

"Yes," corroborated Will proudly as he leaned over the mother and child and patted the baby's small hand. "Everett Eschman. Someday, you'll be hearing great things about this young fellow."

John and Miriam Eschman stopped at Golden Acres Farm a couple of weeks after Everett's birth. They tripped into the house as bubbly as two school children. "We missed you at our wedding!" they exclaimed as soon as the first embraces were exchanged.

"We thought of coming," responded Will, "then decided a wedding and a birthing might be a little too much for one occasion."

"Let's see this child wonder!" demanded John.

Meriel took the baby from the crib and placed him in Miriam's arms. Everett opened his round blue eyes and puckered his mouth in response to Miriam's cooing.

"Wow! He's just as cute as the folks said he was!" admired Miriam as she handed the baby back.

"Now tell us about the big city," put in Will. "How did you like St. Louis and the World's Fair?"

"You wouldn't believe it!" enthused John. "A pavilion for

every country, with scenery and people in costumes. It made you feel you were actually there."

"And we ate ice cream," Miriam added, "without a spoon or dish." She waited a moment for her statement to sink in. "They served it in a cone-shaped container made out of something like a cookie. You ate the whole thing as you walked about, the ice cream and the cookie container. They called them 'ice cream cones'."

"Oh yes," John added, "we had a chance to ride in one of those new-fangled horseless carriages – but I couldn't get Miriam into it."

"Not on your life!" Miriam shook her dark, curly hair emphatically. "You couldn't stop it by saying 'whoa' or pulling on a line. I want to live long enough to raise a family!"

John and Miriam took up housekeeping on the Meister farm which Dan had turned over to his daughter and son-in-law. He and Aunt Martha moved into the smaller house they had prepared after the tornado.

The thunderstorm and heavy rain which had ushered the Eschman's son, Everett, into the world, revived the languishing crops in the Pulaski area. The struggling corn plants burgeoned into lustrous emerald seas, waving and tasseling in the summer breeze. That fall Schillig was again delighted with the abundant yield and cash value of the corn on his place. His wizened face crinkled into a broad grin as he counted and folded the four crisp fifty dollar bills that Will placed in his hands. "You know Will, you have a knack for raising corn. Why don't we sign a new three-year lease? That will give you and your family the security of not having to leave a good farm."

"Thank you, sir," Will answered modestly. "I simply do my best at tilling the soil. The rains and the harvest are in the hands of the Lord."

After talking the matter over with Meriel, Will agreed to stay on the Schillig farm another year. "Maybe, this year," he confided to his wife, "we can get enough money ahead for a down payment on a place of our own."

No sooner had the fall crops been harvested than snow

flurries from the west began to sift across the stubbly fields, reminding the prairie farmers that winter would soon be a reality.

Everett was now old enough to scoot across the floor like an oversized bug. The elfin, supercharged dynamo kept Meriel on the jump retrieving pans and utensils he had raided from the lower cupboards and keeping breakables out of his reach.

Christmas was viewed at the Eschman's through the eyes of their young son. Their small fir tree was trimmed with tiny, bright, indestructible ribbon bows. Beneath the branches were a rubber ball and an outing flannel rabbit with shoe button eyes, also a set of wooden blocks embossed with the letters of the alphabet.

Will had built a child's rocking chair with horse-shaped panels on each side. Meriel painted the horse a deep shade of brown with carousel touches of red, blue and gold harness and bridle. The horse's bit was fashioned from an old broomstick. Everett would shout excitedly holding onto the horse's bit as he moved back and forth in the rocking chair.

The new year brought its mystery package of hopes, suspense and surprises, done up in monthly installments.

Will seized the first balmy days in March to begin working the ground for his crops. "Are you sure you're not pushing things too hard?" asked Meriel, as he sank wearily at the supper table after a long day in the field.

"Nope!" he responded. "I figure if I do all in my power to plant a crop properly, the Lord will do His share!"

Meriel prayed in her heart that Will would not become bitter should the Lord choose not to bless with a huge harvest.

The oat crop had already spread its green carpet by the time Will had finished his corn planting the last of April. A light shower sprouted the corn and pushed the oats into a thick green thatch.

"You sure jumped the gun in getting your crops planted!" Schillig nodded approvingly to Will. "You should have a bumper crop this year!"

"It's still too early to tell," Will replied. Personally, he hoped Schillig was right. Most of the older farmers were still in the planting process.

For the second year in a row, the forces of nature toyed cat-like with the midwestern farmers. Nightly flashes of heat lightning and gathering clouds with a promise of rain gave way to another scorching day with the sun's rays licking all the moisture from plants and soil.

"Guess we'll just have to replant later." Louie shook his head in discouragement when his first corn crop failed to germinate. "At least we can turn our pigs and cattle into the green corn later, even if it doesn't make ears."

Will kept on doggedly cultivating his corn fields into mid-July even though the leaves on the short stalks were curling badly, and the task was becoming increasingly tedious. He climbed slowly up the back veranda steps for dinner. As he entered the kitchen door, he saw Everett playing with his blocks on the floor.

"How's my birthday boy?" asked Will as he swept his son up in his arms.

"Cake!" Everett said, pointing to the table. "Mine!"

"Everett got a birthday card from each of his grandmothers!" beamed Meriel. "And before I forget, there's a letter for you, too."

"It's from Fritz," Will replied as he opened the envelope. "And he's in Michigan. I wonder what mischief he's up to now?"

"You'll have to begin speaking more kindly of him," reminded Meriel with a sly grin. "Remember, his sister, Reah, and Harold are getting married in a few months."

"Do you have to remind me? Let's see what he has on his mind! M-m-m-m-m-m!" Will's eyes lightened as he scanned the contents.

Rhodes, Michigan
July 12, 1901

Dear Will,
 No doubt you are amazed to hear from me; and from another part of the world. How are you and your lovely wife Meriel? And how is your young son that my sister, Reah, wrote about?

I just wanted you to know that I've arrived in Utopia. There's plenty of rain and everything is lush and green.

Land here is cheap. You can buy a whole section for what a few acres would cost in Iowa. I've bought a farm with a shanty on it. Just say the word and I'll hold a section or more of land in case any of you folks want to join me.

Regards, Fritz

P.S.
I'm shipping you a few bags of Michigan potatoes by freight. You can sell them or share them with your friends and family.

After lunch, Will continued tilling his reluctant fields, but now, as he walked the long corn rows, new plans began stirring within him. He had always admired Fritz for his adventuresome spirit.

Even now, Will chuckled as he recalled the western trip Fritz had inveigled him into taking, years earlier, and how his whole life had been changed by that one decision. This new offer of Fritz sounded like a real opportunity. "By gracious, I'll take it!" he spoke aloud to both himself and his team. When he returned to the house at suppertime, Meriel could detect a new faraway look in his eyes.

CHAPTER TWENTY FIVE

Greener Pastures

The horseless carriage had become a reality in the quiet midwest countryside. Members of the Bauman family, including Steve and Carrie, were among the first to buy the new contraption. The drought conditions had baked the clay roads into perfect highways for motor travel. On Sunday afternoons the Baumans, clad in dusters with duckbill caps and scarves on their heads, would cruise sedately past the farms, leaving behind a light cloud of dust.

Five-year-old Cherri Bauman in a pale blue pinafore with a matching headband over her curly auburn hair was an exact image of her mother as she waved blithely at Will and his family on the front porch of the Eschman house.

A twinge of envy swept over Will's mind. He supposed that Carrie must be very happy, now that she had everything that money could buy — a fine home with expensive furnishings, even a new-fangled car.

However, the cloud quickly vanished when he realized that nothing could replace the peace and contentment that his wife, Meriel, and their son had brought him.

The motorized buggies also made a hit with those who enjoyed thrill riding. Oscar Snellinger and his cronies from below the Missouri line would tear by the houses with their bulb horn honking and the throttle wide open. Some folks guessed they were going thirty-five or forty miles per hour!

The neighborhood was up in arms as geese and chickens were

killed and horse and buggies forced off the road. Petitions were nailed up in the post-office and Wagler's store:

"Whereas, our livestock are being killed and the lives of our children threatened; and whereas, it is no longer safe for law-abiding citizens to travel, due to reckless car-drivers on the road, we petition that all motor vehicles be banned from public highways."

The names of Schillig and Traschel headed the list of petitioners. The following week, an editorial appeared in the Bloomfield paper.

NEW MODES — NEW CODES

We are all aware the farmer has legitimate cause for concern, with the coming of the motor vehicle to the area. To quote an old adage: "For every evil under the sun, there is a remedy — " May I suggest a few remedies that may help solve our problems.

Common Courtesy on the Road —
Even stopping, when necessary, to help a fellow-traveler lead or quiet his frightened horse, will help the motorist win friends.

Proper Laws —
With strict enforcement, to judge and punish those who jeopardize the lives and property of others with excessive speed and recklessness.

Caution —
On the part of the farmer in keeping his livestock and children off the road. Those driving horse-drawn vehicles should keep well to the right of the road and use lanterns at night to warn others

of their presence on the roadway.

Meanwhile, let us all keep a positive attitude. Motorized travel is a form of progress with an unlimited future; and like it or not, the 'Horseless Carriage' is here to stay."

Schillig tied the horse to the fence post, left his horse and rig in the Golden Acres yard and strode to the house as Will and Meriel were finishing their lunch.

"Don't know what this country's coming to!" he stormed as Will met him at the door.

"So, you met Oscar as you drove out," grinned Will. "I saw him drive by here a few minutes ago in a cloud of dust."

"He nearly ran me into the ditch with that infernal machine of his."

"Mr. Schillig," broke in Meriel, "how would you like a piece of custard pie before I put it away?"

"Don't mind if I do."

His face brightened for a moment as the tasty forkfuls of pie melted in his mouth.

"You can take home a piece for Mrs. Schillig, too."

"Much obliged," he mumbled with his mouth full.

When he had finished eating the pie, Schillig pushed his chair back from the table and turned to Will with a frown.

"Eschman, your crops sure don't come up to what they were last year. I notice the corn has fired at the base and the leaves are curling badly."

Stung by the inference of poor farm management, Will clenched his fists in his faded overall pockets, then pulled them out.

"As you can see, sir, your fields are thoroughly tilled. The ground is soft and there's not a weed to be seen. But I'm not God! Until we get rain, there's not a thing more I can do to make your corn grow."

Schillig's face grew stern. "Don't be blasphemous, Eschman!"

"Sir, I meant that in reverence. Simply, that it's in God's

hands and not in mine!"

"Well," Schillig continued churlishly, "I was just wondering how the Missus and I were going to make it through the winter with no corn money coming in."

"There'll be some income," Will spoke defensively, "and I'll see that you get your fair share!"

Will scowled as he and Meriel later watched Schillig drive out of the driveway. "One thing sure," he declared emphatically, "this is my last year working for that man!" He then turned critically to Meriel, "And you had to waste good custard pie on him!"

The frustrations of the summer drought were temporarily subdued when the shipment of potatoes arrived, as Fritz had promised. Will felt like a prairie Santa as he, with Meriel and Everett at his side, drove to the homes of friends and relatives with his Michigan bounty.

"Bless you!" quavered Mrs. Traschel as Will filled a container of hers from a potato bag.

Louie and Annalie beamed as they opened a fifty-pound burlap sack, took out several large, uniform Catahdin potatoes and fondled them. "Did you ever see anything so beautiful?" exclaimed Annalie. "All these weeks I've been trying to make do with last year's shriveled spuds."

"We'll keep a supply of these potatoes coming to you, once we get settled in Michigan!" boasted Will exuberantly.

Meriel arched her eyebrows in surprise. "We will?"

"I'd like to have a chance to raise beauties like these, myself," put in Louie as he weighed a large potato in his hand.

Will turned to Meriel, penitently, as she sat silent on the way home. "I'm sorry, honey! I guess I got carried away and jumped the gun again at Annalie's. I forgot we hadn't even talked about going to Michigan."

Meriel looked up with a slight smile on her lips. "I knew you had it on your mind. You've been going around with that far-away look in your eyes ever since getting Fritz's letter."

"Then you wouldn't mind going to Michigan? It would mean pulling up roots here."

"Will, I'd rather face the unknown with you than to watch you fretting yourself like a bird beating against the bars of a cage."

A second letter arrived the following week. Fritz welcomed the news that Will and Meriel were planning to join him. "But," he added, "I should warn you that the fields are cut-over pine land. That means they are full of pine stumps. Also, there are no modern houses available, only deserted log cabins and shanties left over from lumbering days. However, the land is still a good buy and has great possibilities."

The thought was a sobering one, especially with a little one to care for. Will felt he couldn't press the matter with Meriel; he would hold his peace. Later, he stopped by the door of their bedroom, thinking he heard the sound of the rocker. He was not mistaken. Meriel was holding Everett tightly as she rocked, with the Bible open in her lap and her eyes closed in prayer. Will longed to join her but felt awkward about it and passed by with a lump in his throat.

That night in the darkness of their bedroom Meriel gave her answer. "I guess there have always been little ones growing up in the wilderness. Besides, Everett will no longer be a baby when we get there. You know, God has promised to go before and make the crooked places straight. So, I'm ready."

Will held her tightly. "Darling, you won't be sorry! Have I told you lately how much I love you?"

CHAPTER TWENTY SIX

Goodbye Iowa

The news soon spread over the community that Will and Meriel were leaving for Michigan in the early spring. Schillig was loud and vehement in denouncing Will for the move. "Like a rolling stone, he never was too dependable! When the going gets tough, he leaves and makes his decision based on a few potatoes."

Their own families were more charitable. Though saddened to think of them moving so far away, they bent their efforts to help speed them on their way.

Articles were designated for shipping, including the table and four chairs from the summer kitchen. Sturdy crates were used for holding household items. They could later be knocked down and built into cupboards or benches.

Will chose his tools carefully: hammers, screwdrivers, saws and T-square; also a generous supply of assorted nails, screws and bolts.

He also decided to take his faithful team, Nick and Nell. It would take a lot of money to replace them. "Besides," he observed, "not to take them would be like leaving part of the family behind."

The family added their spare blankets and bedding to the growing stack of necessities, plus jackets, assorted overalls and boots. Luella offered her sewing machine. "You'll have more time than money once you get there, and you were always good at whipping up something out of 'thin air'!"

However, instead of "thin air", the two mothers accumulated

lengths of gingham, calico and denim, to which Luella added yards and yards of colorful flowered ticking, bought on sale. "It will be easier to stitch up ticks and fill them with straw when you get there than to lug all such stuff with you."

By the first of March, most of the packing was done. The wheat and corn had matured better than expected in spite of the drought. Will stopped at Schillig's to pay him off after selling the grain.

Schillig's eyes gleamed as he received the substantial payment. "You know, I could use you if you decided to stay on."

Will could not resist a final touch of sarcasm: "Thank you, sir, but it's time for this stone to get rolling along."

The nearly empty rooms reverberated with footsteps of friends and neighbors coming to wish Will and Meriel well as the time of their departure neared. Everett, now a toddler, was kept busy as he greeted each visitor with a hug.

Aunt Celinda sobbed loudly as she gathered Everett into her arms. "Poor little fellow! Being taken to that wild land full of bears and Indians!"

Everett's blue eyes widened and his mouth puckered in concern, not sure what she was talking about. However, he patted her sympathetically on the shoulder to comfort her, "It's OK!"

Pastor Mueller assured them of his prayers. "God bless you both and make you a blessing wherever you go!"

Meister, white-haired and slow of gait, grasped Will's hand. "Godspeed, my friend. This takes me back to when I left Switzerland and arrived here, alone, in the Midwest."

Will found it difficult to keep his voice steady. "Thanks for your confidence in me through the years. I'll remember you every time I work Nick and Nell."

Meister's weather-lined face broke into a smile. "So Nick and Nell are making the move with you. They're a good team. They won't let you down."

With crates and furniture loaded in the freight car, the days at Golden Acres were over. Will, Meriel and Everett spent the last weekend with their folks. They sat around Anna's table loaded with favorite foods and desserts and reminisced about the days they were growing up.

"Did we ever tell you, Papa, about the time Will and I were cultivating in the field by the creek?" A sly grin wreathed John's face. "We drove the team through the water so Pa would think they were sweating. That way, we had more time to play around while the team dried off."

"No wonder Will is leaving the country now, since the truth is out!" quipped Jacob.

It was a bittersweet time of laughter, with tears often near the surface, as golden memories mingled with the uncertainty of the future and the realization that at the next gathering there would be new faces, and perhaps some missing.

On the last Sunday evening they stayed with Meriel's family so as to be near the depot for their departure next day. Harold would keep the team and see that they were loaded in a stock car at the proper time.

"Sorry you're not going to be here for our wedding," Harold addressed Will shyly. Will turned to the prospective bride and groom seated together on the couch.

"How about you and Reah spending your honeymoon in Michigan?"

"If you're still out there in a year or so, we might consider joining you then."

Luella kept up a line of constant chatter, dispensing practical advice, as she packed fried chicken, sandwiches and cake into a shoebox for their lunch on the train. She cautioned them to keep a close watch on Everett's health. She also reminded them that turpentine and lard was a good home remedy to rub on the chest for colds. Much to her consternation, she discovered that the yards of flowered ticking she bought for Meriel had been overlooked in the packing.

Will objected as he watched her rolling the material into another bulky package to be carried. "We already have all the carry-on luggage we can handle. Why not just mail it to us later?"

Meriel, noting the crushed look on her mother's face, touched Will's arm lightly and whispered, "Honey, can't we humor her, just this one last time? We'll manage, somehow."

"Well, all right then," he relented with a shrug.

Only as the train ground to a panting halt in front of the depot did Luella find herself at a loss for words.

"Good-bye!" she half sobbed as she embraced each of her departing family.

Lew grasped Will's hand. Nodding at Meriel, he advised, "Take good care of her!" Then with misty eyes, he clasped his daughter silently for a moment.

Scarcely had the Eschmans settled into the red plush seats of the coach, when the train started with a lurch, then slowly puffed and slid into motion as it eased out of town and into the countryside.

The locomotive began to pick up speed as it passed the well-kept barns on the Bauman ranch. Familiar scenes reeled into the horizon as the train sped eastward toward the Mississippi River.

It seemed that spring had flung her laciest apparel over the prairie landscape, as if enticing Will and Meriel to stay in their home state. Wild cherry blossoms spilled over every hilltop, clumps of lilacs embraced old homesteads and osage orange trees edged the winding roads. Their drooping clusters of flowers would soon burgeon into yellowish, green orange-like fruit, filled with milky sap.

The clackety-clack of turning wheels seemed to echo Will's thoughts as they sped along.

"Good-bye, old pasture lots, good-bye.
Good-bye, black cattle on the hills.
Brown muddy creeks and winding roads.
Good-bye, old friend, good-bye!"

CHAPTER TWENTY SEVEN

Michigan

There was a short stop at the Burlington depot, then the locomotive edged its way slowly across the bridge spanning the mighty Mississippi. On the Illinois side of the river, broad expanses of bottom land spread out like mammoth brown comforters of rich loam tied with young green corn sprouts.

Gradually, the farm lands gave way to urban developments. The buildings compacted into city blocks. Within the heart of the metropolis, the buildings stretched upward into skyscrapers. All railroad tracks converged into Chicago's Union Station, the hub of a gigantic transportation system.

Inside the spacious waiting room, the Eschmans found a section of seats that was not too crowded. Meriel sank wearily onto a bench, and Will piled their luggage on the floor around her. He then left to check their tickets. Everett, eager for activity after hours of being confined in parental arms, toddled back and forth rubbing his hands over the smooth oak surface of the bench.

People passed by, singly and in groups. Uniformed porters pushed carts piled high with luggage and shepherded travelers to the proper waiting areas. They nodded their red-capped heads and smiled broadly as they were tipped for their services.

Meriel's head nodded and her eyes blurred. Only the determination to watch Everett kept her from sound sleep. Occasionally, she spoke his name, then he would return and climb up on her lap.

Finally, Will returned with a fistful of paper slips and a

183

satisfied smile on his face. "This should get us to our destination — Rhodes, Michigan. Besides, I have the check claims for our belongings, once we get there."

Meriel sighed in relief.

"Say, you look exhausted! Maybe you can catch some sleep when we get settled on the next train. It's almost boarding time, now."

Once they found places on the waiting train and stashed their things on the luggage rack above, Will took Everett, and Meriel sank almost immediately into oblivion. Not until the train door opened, hours later, letting in a cold draft and the conductor calling a station, did she rouse from deep sleep.

"Where are we now?" she murmured drowsily.

"Battle Creek, almost to Jackson where we change for Bay City."

Everett, stretched on the seat opposite them, was sleeping as soundly as if he were in his own bed.

As they entered the long brick depot at Jackson, the scent of coffee from the lunchroom reminded them how famished they were. After they made their way to the counter in the lunchroom and chose doughnuts to go with the coffee, they felt somewhat revived for the second day of their journey.

It was four in the morning as they boarded the north-bound train. It had only three coaches and the upholstered seats were dingy compared to their previous coach. The sun had risen as the train neared Bay City.

After stopping momentarily at the west side depot, the train backed across the Saginaw River to the east side depot and their coach was shunted onto a sidetrack. Most of the passengers left the coach. A few new ones entered and found seats. A sudden jolt alerted them that they had been coupled onto another train.

The coach door opened, framing the conductor, tall and wiry, in a blue uniform and conductor's cap. With watch in hand, he began chanting the towns on route, including Pinconning, Mt. Forest, and Rhodes.

As the conductor reached for Will's ticket, he sized him up with keen eyes. "New in these parts, aren't you?"

"Yes sir, a friend of mine bought a tract of land for us near

Rhodes, and we aim to farm it."

"Reckon you can make a go of it if you don't mind hard work."

"Just what kind of train are we riding now?" questioned Will.

The conductor gave a sly grin. "Some folks refer to it as the 'Jack Rabbit Special'. This coach is tacked to the end of a freight train. Back in lumbering days, this was a pretty busy line, running both freight and passenger trains. I've been with them some twenty years and there's been a lot of change in that time. Most of the big timber is gone, leaving only pine stumps. The logging trains and lumbermen are a thing of the past. Now it's pretty much farmers and small town people riding back and forth. They took off the passenger run but kept a coach on the freight line to accommodate folks."

As the train ground to a halt at Mt. Forest, the conductor informed Will and Meriel that their stop would be next.

"Indians!" someone announced, "From Saganing Creek!"

Meriel caught her breath and wondered if Aunt Celinda's dire prediction about bears and wild Indians had materialized. Glancing out the coach window, she noticed a couple nondescript men leaning against the gray building by the track. Their only distinguishing features were headbands over shoulder-length hair.

A couple swarthy-skinned women, wearing heavy, coarse skirts and the same type of headbands, approached the conductor at the coach door. Talking rapidly, they held their baskets up to his face.

"Oh, so it's Arbutus time again!" he smiled at them amiably. "We'll be here about ten minutes while they switch off a freight car. Can you get your selling done in that time?"

The women passed down both sides of the aisle, holding their baskets close to the passengers' faces. As they approached, a delightful, heady fragrance filled the air.

"What are they?" asked Meriel as she pressed her nose close to a cluster of tiny pink, waxy blooms.

"Arbutus," responded the young Indian woman, rolling her tongue musically over the name. "We pick in the woods near here." She waved her hand in the general direction of the coach window.

"How much?" asked Meriel as she held a small compact clump of blossoms, framed with dark green leaves.

"Ten cents!" smiled the Indian.

"Oh, Will, let's get them!"

Will obligingly fished into his pants pocket and came up with two nickels. "It's worth it to see you so sold on a Michigan product."

Will caught the attention of Matthews, the conductor, shortly before reaching Rhodes. He was assured that their consignment of goods was due the next day; also, there was a good rooming place, Ma Webber's, across the tracks from the general store.

The sky was overcast when the Eschmans arrived at Rhodes. Meriel braced herself against the brisk wind and pulled the edge of her coat about Everett to shield him from the snow flurries. Will led the way with all the luggage tucked under his two arms. Entering the general store, they were impressed by how much it resembled Wagler's store back in Pulaski. Besides the general grocery supplies, there was a window that served as both postal and ticket office.

Bill Kettering, the middle-aged storekeeper, greeted them cordially. He wiped his hands on his white apron, then shook hands with Will. Yes, he knew who Fritz Zimmerli was. He would probably be coming to town today. The Eschman team was due to arrive tomorrow, and their furniture would be all right in the box car a few days till they could haul it home.

"Martha, how about a stick of candy for the little guy?"

The storekeeper's wife, a petite, neatly dressed woman took the brass top from a tall glass container and handed a striped peppermint stick to Everett. Beaming, the boy said thank you and retreated to his father's arms.

"That's a bright little fellow you have there!" she exclaimed.

As Kettering had stated, Fritz made his appearance in a short time. After a round of handshakes, Will confronted Fritz.

"I thought you told me it would be beautiful spring weather when we arrived. Do you call this spring?" Will motioned to the snow flurries outside the store window.

"You came on the wrong day!" retorted Fritz. "Now, yesterday was a nice day, and tomorrow probably will be, too.

You have to expect variety in Michigan weather. I see Meriel has found spring already." He pointed to the small bunch of arbutus in her hand.

"Have you folks eaten yet?" asked Fritz. "You'll feel better when you do, and this meal is on me." He loaded the family and their luggage into his wagon and drove over to Ma Webber's square two-story house.

They were met at the door by Ma herself, as sturdy and as amply built as her house. "Come in out of the cold," she urged, concern for them written on her placid face, flushed from cooking.

Fritz introduced the group as his friends from Iowa. "They will be staying with you a few days till they get settled on their farm north of town."

Ma led them to a table already set and proceeded to dish up dinner. The aroma of roast beef, potatoes, and gravy smelled heavenly after snacking on doughnuts and coffee. The Eschmans ate the meal with gusto.

"When do you want to look over the place?" asked Fritz as they were finishing their generous pieces of apple pie.

"Just as soon as we're through eating," answered Will.

"Sure you don't want to rest over night first?"

"Looking over the place is what we traveled 600 miles for."

"If you insist, we'll get started right away," agreed Fritz.

"Oh my!" exclaimed Ma Webber in distress. "You can't take that little fellow out without more protection from the wind." She disappeared from the room and returned with two warm blankets.

With eyes close to tears, Meriel thanked Ma for her concern. She then followed the men to the wagon. There she chose to sit on a pile of straw in the wagon bed rather than the seat to be sheltered from the wind. With Everett on her lap, she wrapped one blanket around them both, making a huge cocoon.

On the two and a half mile stretch of sandy road to their farm, they passed several weathered frame houses covered with tarpaper.

"I suppose our house is similar to these," ventured Meriel, bracing herself for what she would find.

"Yes," answered Fritz hesitantly. "This is your typical house around here."

Some of the fields were enclosed with tiers of uprooted pine roots, reaching skyward with long, gaunt fingers; other fields had a huge pile of stump roots in the center; still other untilled areas were dotted with stumps like mushrooms.

"Well this is it!" announced Fritz as they crested the last hill. Before them lay a level stretch of partially cleared land with a huge pile of uprooted stumps in the middle. The inevitable tarpapered house near the road and a dilapidated shed made up the farm buildings.

Entering the house, they found the door sagging on its hinges and several broken windows. They would have to be replaced, Will concluded, before they could move in. A rusty range stood in the kitchen.

"One good thing; we're heading for warmer weather instead of cold," assured Fritz. "I have lumber you can use for window frames and anything else you may need. You should have it shipshape within a week."

Will glanced at Meriel, dreading to see her reaction. "Well, dear, what do you think? Any suggestions?"

She seemed lost in thought as she stood in the middle of a bare, dingy room clutching in her arms, Everett, wrapped in the blanket. "I was wondering how we could measure a window for curtains."

"Well, I don't have any measuring tape or yardstick with me, but we can use this −." He reached over and pulled off a loose board from the side of a window frame.

CHAPTER TWENTY EIGHT

A Home in the Wilderness

"I'm so glad my mom insisted on sending this ticking material in a carry-on package," Meriel confided to Ma Webber as the men left to work on the house. "I can make it into a straw tick that will be ready to use when we move into our home. Now, all I need is for Will to find the crate with the sewing machine in it when he gets back."

"No need for that," put in Ma Webber. "You can just use mine. It will save the bother of unpacking yours."

In less than an hour, Meriel had the bright tick casing finished and ready to be filled with straw.

"Very pretty!" admired the older woman. "Now, what do you intend to do with all your left over material?"

Meriel brought the piece of window casing from the clothes closet. "Will tore this loose yesterday to help me measure our windows. Now, if you could loan me a yard stick or tape measure, I'll find its length. Then I can make curtains for each of the windows. They'll help brighten the rooms. Also they can be closed at night for shades and help keep out the drafts in cold weather."

"Well, I never!" exclaimed Ma Webber. "Now, who else would have thought of that?"

"Me sew too!" Everett called eagerly, as he gathered bits of the colorful material from the floor.

"We'll fix you up with some bracelets," humored his mother as she tied a strip of ticking on each of his wrists. She then gave him an additional piece of material with which to play.

189

By the end of the week, Will reported the repairs had been finished, and the house was ready to be scrubbed and occupied. The team had arrived, he had located a wagon, and he was ready to get settled as soon as possible. He didn't mention that Fritz and he had whitewashed the walls and ceilings of the house. That would be a surprise for his wife.

Will and Meriel discussed their plans leisurely over Ma Webber's breakfast of pancakes, bacon, and eggs. This day being Sunday, they decided to take a ride and become better acquainted with their surroundings.

"Do you have any church services here?" asked Meriel.

Ma Webber shook her head negatively.

"A circuit preacher stops in to eat, once in a while. But so far, there have been no meetings. Folks around here just don't seem to be a 'churchy' type of people."

After breakfast, Will hitched the team to the wagon and the Eschmans began their exploratory jaunt over the countryside. Caressed by soft breezes and sunshine, they relaxed into the contentment of their earlier married days. Everett nestled between them on the wagon seat and slipped a chubby fist into the hand of his parents on either side. Nick and Nell stepped along briskly, seeming to share in the family's togetherness.

At the first corner, Will left the regular road for a little used trail that meandered into the shaggy terrain ahead. He stopped the team on a crude wooden bridge over a small gurgling stream. "This must be the 'Little Molasses' that Fritz was talking about."

"I can see why," Meriel commented, as they looked down into the dark brown water. It was the color of molasses, yet so clear they could see the many minnows darting about and even pebbles and tiny shells on the bottom. "How come it's not muddy like our creeks in Iowa?"

"Must be a difference in the soil; humus, moss, and sand, instead of clay bottom like back home – I mean in Iowa," Will caught himself.

Beyond the stream, the trail rose sharply, and the ruts became soft and sandy as they led through unfenced lands known as the huckleberry marshes. Scrub oaks and jack pines staggered across the landscape with brush covered hummocks between.

"Let's drive in and take a closer look," coaxed Meriel.

Will turned the team and followed a set of wagon tracks past bushes covered with tiny white, bell-shaped blossoms, which they took to be huckleberries. They left the wagon when they reached a wooded area and walked into a thicket. There they were greeted by scents of pine, new leaves and burgeoning buds. Rays of sunlight filtered through catkins on the poplar trees and etched lacy patterns on the needled carpet below.

Meriel dropped to her knees to better examine the vegetation on the woodland floor. She collected sprigs of a trailing vine and a tiny plant with glossy leaves and miniature white flowers with hopes of having someone identify them later.

Everett plopped down in front of her and leaned back against her knees. She gave him a hug, then playfully pushed him over. "You little cubby bear! How am I to see anything with you right under my nose?"

Laughing, he ran off to pull leaves on his own. Soon he returned with an assortment of vegetation in his fist.

"See, Mommy, mine are pretty, too."

A familiar shaped leaf caught her eye.

"Where did you find this one?" she asked, slipping a rough oval-shaped leaf from his hand. He proudly marched back and pointed to the creeping plant from which he had pulled it. True to her expectations, she found a few clusters of pink blossoms on the tough, hairy vines creeping over the ground.

"Look, Will!" she cried with the thrill of one making a great discovery. "Everett's found my trailing arbutus!"

Reluctantly, Meriel left the marshes and rode with Will to their tarpapered house. Will unlocked the door and waited for her response.

"Oh, you've painted the walls and ceilings!" exclaimed Meriel in delight, as she gazed at the light interior of the rooms.

That, along with the new window frames, was a transformation from the week before. "Now if you can just find something for rods for my curtains, we'll be all ready to set up housekeeping."

Will was sure he could find the right thing on the way back to town. He stopped at a culvert where cattails were growing. With his pocket knife he cut a dozen or so dried stalks. The dry fluff drifted away on the wind as he topped them.

"And we might try these also, to make sure we have something that will work." As he spoke, he cut another armful of various-sized willow wands that grew nearby.

They arrived back at Ma Webber's in time for Sunday evening lunch. Everett had already fallen asleep. Will carried the sleeping youngster into the house and placed him on the bed in their room.

"I can plainly see you folks found your way around today," Ma observed as the windblown and sunburnt couple sat down at the table to eat.

"I believe Meriel prefers the marshes to our farm," Will teased. "I could hardly get her out of them."

Meriel smiled in agreement, "I never knew there could be so many fascinating plants to investigate!" She spread her collection of wild specimens on the table for Ma Webber to identify.

"This one," said Ma Webber, holding up the piece of vine, "is trailing pine. And that tiny plant is wintergreen. When you see it later this summer, it will have red berries on it."

"If you'll excuse us," Will nodded to the landlady, "I think we'd better be getting our rest if we're to get our place ready for occupancy tomorrow. By the way, Meriel, did you think of what we'd need for cleaning out there?"

"That wife of yours is a whiz. She has everything collected to make your place spotless. That includes soap, rags, brush, and bucket."

The following morning was misty and cold. Ma Webber had fixed sack lunches for the Eschmans to take along when they went to clean.

"You're so good to us!" Meriel exclaimed gratefully.

"I just feel like you're my family," declared Ma Webber. She glanced out at the fog and mist as the Eschmans were finishing their oatmeal and toast. "You know, I've been thinking; this is not fitten weather for little tykes like him to be out in." She nodded her head toward Everett. "Besides, your house will be damp and drafty from your scrubbing. Why not leave him here with me?"

"What do you think, Will?" Meriel looked inquiringly at her

husband. "We could also get more done, if we went alone."

Will chewed his last piece of toast slowly and took a long sip of coffee. Meriel could see his jaw muscles tightening.

"I'll go get the team. Be ready in twenty minutes."

Meriel began gathering cleaning materials and her wraps.

Everett quickly took his coat and cap from the closet and ran to his mother. "We go clean now, Mamma!"

Laying her wraps to one side, Meriel bent over and gathered the youngster into her arms. "Mamma and Papa go clean house and make it nice for you. But it's too cold for Everett. Can you be a big boy and stay with Grandma Webber today?"

"But I go, too!" insisted the toddler with apprehension filling his face.

"Not today, honey! You must stay here so you don't get sick."

"But I go, so YOU don't get sick. I gotta go! I gotta go!"

Proceeding to put on her wraps, Meriel ignored the fretting child. By now he was in his coat with his knitted cap pulled askew over one eye. Meriel picked him up and placed him firmly in Ma Webber's arms as he wailed and thrashed about. Disengaging herself from the boy, she walked away with his cries ringing in her ears.

Will had driven the team up to the porch steps and waited with stern features as she loaded cleaning materials and curtains into the wagon and finally climbed in herself.

"Seems that Ma Webber has taken over our family! How could you leave Everett with a complete stranger?"

"But I thought he would be better off in a warm house with her."

"Yes, YOU thought! You seem to think anything that woman says is gospel truth!"

"This will be the last time I leave him," Meriel stated dryly as she slid to the outer edge of the wagon seat.

Her throat and shoulders ached with self pity as they rode to the farm in silence.

Once at the farm, Meriel went immediately to sweeping floors throughout the house while Will built a fire in the rusty range. She stopped only long enough to put a pail of water on the stove to heat for cleaning.

By noon, the bare pine floors and woodwork had been scrubbed. A fresh, clean smell pervaded the house, and a pot of coffee was simmering on the stove. After wiping off a makeshift table with a damp rag, Meriel set out the lunch Mrs. Webber had prepared for them, along with a couple mugs of hot coffee.

"It's sure beginning to look a lot more like home," Will ventured as he munched on a sandwich. He glanced at his silent wife.

Meriel smiled wanly. "Once I get the windows washed and the curtains up, it should be quite cozy." She sipped her coffee without looking up.

"Don't overdo this first day," offered Will, trying to sound magnanimous. "There's always another day to wash windows."

"It's just that seeing those curtains at the windowsill make it all seem worthwhile." Her eyes brimmed with tears as she toyed with the gold chain about her neck.

Will regarded her more closely. "Are you wearing your good locket to clean house?"

"It seems to be the one thing left that makes me feel special these days."

Will slipped a hand over hers and lifted the pink-flowered locket. Opening it, he read the tiny words he had inscribed in it, four Christmases earlier. "Meriel, I love you forever, Will." He gently closed the locket and enveloped his wife in his arms.

"Darling, can you forgive me for flying off the handle this morning? I've been a real heel! I don't deserve a wife like you, but I love you with all my heart." He held her tightly, while her tears dampened his shirt on the shoulder.

He finally released her with a chuckle. "Here we are, two lovebirds perched on the only good chair in the house. I guess if we want to see what those curtains look like, we'd better get to work on the windows."

He drove the nails into the upper window frames and cut the dried cattail stalks to length while Meriel washed the window panes. With the curtains mounted, they stepped back to admire their work.

"Did you ever see anything more beautiful?" beamed Meriel.

"Once our furniture is moved in, we'll have the coziest home in Michigan."

Having locked the door of the tarpaper house, Will gave the team free rein, and they trotted briskly back to Rhodes. Meriel accompanied her husband to put away the horses. Then, hand in hand, the couple walked to the house, feeling closer than they had in days.

Once inside, they inquired in unison, "How is Everett?"

"He finally went to sleep, and now he's doing fine."

They sat quietly beside the boy on the couch. His face was still flushed and tearstained. He opened his eyes, then sprang up, throwing his arm around the closest neck. "Don't leave me!" he pleaded clinging tightly to Meriel.

"We won't," she promised. "Tomorrow, we're all going home together."

CHAPTER TWENTY NINE

A Stump in the Garden

*W*ill referred to the auction flyer in his hand as the wagon creaked over the sandy road north of his farm.

"It says here that this Guy Sauter is selling off his entire inventory of stock and machinery. Any idea why?"

Fritz Zimmerli drew long on his pipe before answering. "I understand his wife died, not too long ago. His health hasn't been too good, lately. Guess farming's gotten too much for him. See anything on that sheet that might interest you?"

Will shrugged, "At this point, I'm in the market for most anything that walks or grows on a farm. However, I'll have to see how my cash holds out." He turned to Meriel and Everett on the back seat. "What can we get for you today?"

"Well, I'll settle for a few laying hens," his wife responded.

"Will they lay in bed with us?" asked Everett as he looked up and tugged on her sleeve.

"No, honey!" Meriel answered her son with a quick little squeeze. they'll live in a henhouse and lay eggs in a nest.

"Oh, and I can go get the eggs!" Everett recalled being carried to the henhouse on one such occasion.

"Indeed you can!" exclaimed his mother. "At first we'll both go to get the eggs, but after a while you can go all by yourself to gather them."

Everett straightened his shoulders and sat up tall on the wagon seat beside his mother.

By now, they had turned into a lane, leading back to a log

house shaded by huge cottonwoods. Many vehicles were already parked in the yard and barnlot. Groups of men congregated about machinery and pens of stock. Will's group gravitated over to the sheep pens.

Brown-faced ewes stared passively at the spectators around them and bleated to keep contact with their lambs.

"They're a nice-looking flock," Fritz commented. "They should do well in your back pasture."

The two men were interrupted by the high, chanting voice of the auctioneer. "If you don't mind, Fritz, I'll let you do the bidding," said Will. "You know these folks, and they'd probably prefer doing business with you rather than me, a stranger."

"Here's the owner," interrupted Fritz, as a graying, lean-faced man joined them. Then, by way of introduction, "Will Eschman is a friend of mine; just moved from Iowa, along with his wife and son." A nod of his head included them all.

Meriel's attention was drawn away from the group by a large, florid-complexioned woman who tapped her on the back.

"Are you the new woman I've been hearing about?" she asked in a penetrating voice.

Meriel glanced up puzzled, not sure whether it was a simple greeting or a criticism. "We've been in Michigan for a few weeks."

"Where did you come from?" the woman persisted.

"From Iowa; I'm sorry, but I don't believe I heard your name."

"I'm Clothilda Grant. You probably noticed our house in Rhodes. It's the big white one across from the school. I notice you've already met Mr. Sauter, the owner here. That's his girl, Della, over there." Clothilda waved a thumb across the yard, where a slender, dark-haired young woman stood with a boy at her side. "If she was half the daughter she should have been, she would have stayed home and helped her folks; then her mother might be alive today!"

Meriel's interest and concern were aroused for the young woman and the child she assumed to be her son. However, she refrained from asking any questions that would draw more criticism from Mrs. Grant.

When the auction was over, the Eschmans returned home with a crate of Plymouth Rock hens, a plow, harrow and cultivator in the wagon bed. A red Durham cow, tied to the back of the wagon, followed reluctantly.

On the following day, Will and Fritz helped Sauter, along with his daughter and grandson, drive the hundred Shropshire sheep over to the Eschman pasture. Meriel and Everett followed them in the wagon.

One small lamb that had a hard time keeping up was placed in the wagon bed, much to Everett's delight. He cuddled the soft, woolly creature in his arms and talked to it. The mother ewe followed close behind, bleating and holding her brown nose up to the wagon bed. Sauter's dog, Gerty, dashed about keeping each straggling sheep in line.

Once the sheep were enclosed in the pasture, Meriel invited the group into the house for lunch. Della gazed in awe at the cheerful interior – a remarkable contrast to the tarpaper on the outside. Her eyes rested on the bright twill fabric curtains covered with roses that hung at the windows.

"Where did you find such beautiful curtains?" she asked.

Meriel smiled, "They were left over after I made a straw tick from the same material."

"It's so kind of you to ask us in to eat," Della murmured with tears of gratitude close to brimming over.

"We're the ones who should be grateful," responded Meriel. "I don't know how we would have managed without your help. Your boy is a real herdsman. What's his name?"

"Joey!" responded his mother, proudly. "He's going to miss taking care of the sheep."

"With so many things to get organized around here, I'm sure Will could use him, and Everett would love to have him for a companion."

"I was wondering if you folks liked mushrooms," ventured Della, growing a bit bolder.

"I really don't know. Where do you find them?"

"Your sheep pasture is the best place I know. We came here every spring to pick them when I was growing up. This is mushroom season, you know."

When Meriel mentioned the matter to Will, he surmised the following day would be as good as any for mushrooming. "You gals and the boys can take an outing and get acquainted while I get the garden ready for planting and get rid of that stump in the middle."

Della and Joey arrived early the next morning. Clad in a faded gingham dress with a man's bandanna tied over her dark hair, she and Joey sat patiently on the front steps with their buckets and dog.

Meriel and Everett soon joined them. "Just thought you might like these," said Meriel, as she reached into her bucket and took out warm biscuits, each spread with strawberry jam. The group followed the lane to the pasture, taking pains to shut the gate after them.

A few ewes took steps toward them, raising their brown noses and bleating softly. In the background, young lambs frolicked on the hillside, taking short running steps and leaping high in the air with the pure exuberance of being alive in the warm sunshine.

"Now, you'll have to show me what we're picking," declared Meriel. "I haven't the faintest idea what these mushrooms look like, and I sure don't want to pick the wrong kind."

"You can't go wrong with morels!" exclaimed Della. She stepped over to an old pine stump, and bending over, picked a small spongy growth, shaped like a tiny pine tree. "They're apt to be any place here, but especially around old logs and stumps or under any type of fruit tree or shrub. Just keep your eyes peeled to the ground."

Even as Della was speaking, Meriel stooped over and picked a couple morels from a knoll. "Like these? Now I see what you mean."

From then on it became a game, seeing who could find the most. Joey was most adept at spotting mushrooms, putting one first in his mother's pail, then one in Meriel's.

Everett, not to be outdone, settled on dropping small pieces of brown bark into his mother's pail and on one occasion, a live toad. By noon Della's pail was full. Then she helped Meriel fill hers.

"Now Della, you'll have to tell me how to fix these for

eating."

"First, wash them in salt water. That way, if there are any ants or other insects inside, they will come out."

"Also any toads!" quipped Meriel.

"Be sure to take them out of the water immediately and dry them. Then cut them in half lengthwise, roll them in flour, and brown in butter in a frying pan."

"Mm-m-m, sounds really yummy!"

"They really are. What's more, they can take the place of meat in a meal and that's a saving."

The two women sat a few moments to rest while the boys played. "You must have many fond memories of growing up in these parts."

"As a girl, yes — but those days seem so far away."

There was a moment of silence, broken by the intermittent warbling of a song sparrow and the distant bleating of sheep.

"I was just seventeen when this dashing fellow, Al Kirt, came along. My folks begged me to wait, but we decided to get married right away." Della hesitated, then went on. "Al left me before Joey was born. My folks were great about taking me in, and they thought the world of Joey. When he was big enough to care for easily, I went to work in town to earn money to support him. My folks thought that was the okay thing to do. Then, all of a sudden, Mom died of a heart attack."

Della stopped abruptly as she choked up.

Meriel placed a hand over hers. "He's a fine boy, Della. You and your family have done a good job raising him."

Back at the house, when the guests had departed, Meriel could sense that Will's morning had been far from enjoyable.

"Might as well move Gibraltar, as budge that stump!" he muttered when questioned.

"If the garden's worked, why don't I go ahead with planting, once we get our seeds, and forget the stump?" suggested Meriel. "It looks like you'll have plenty other work with your animals and field planting."

"We may have to do that," Will allowed. "But whoever heard of a garden with a stump in the middle?"

Since the horses were still hitched, they drove in to Rhodes to pick up the seeds. Every corner of Kettering's store encouraged customers to "think gardening". Large posters showed beaming gardeners holding baskets of succulent lettuce, tomatoes and cucumbers. The aisles were filled with racks of seeds promising sure yields.

While Meriel busied herself selecting packets of vegetable and flower seeds, Will sought out Bill Kettering, the proprietor.

As nonchalantly as possible, he asked, "How do you folks go about getting pine stumps out of a field?"

Kettering grinned slyly. "Having a problem with stumps, eh? You know, a stump is sort of like a snaggy tooth in your mouth. You have to decide the lesser of two evils; whether to put up with the unsightly look of it – or the pain of yanking it out. Now, if you're bound to get it out, Lew Stymick can furnish you with a few sticks of dynamite. He's the stump expert around here."

"Thanks. I'll stop there on my way home."

Lew Stymick sauntered out as the Eschmans turned into his drive. "Can I help you?" he asked, pausing to hitch up his suspenders and spit out a cud of tobacco.

"I was told I could pick up a few sticks of dynamite here, for blasting stumps – " Will stopped short in his speech at the sight of two massive critters yoked together. "Do you use those oxen for plowing?"

"Strictly for pulling stumps," replied the owner.

"Well, these sticks of dynamite should do the trick. Beside, I've got a pretty good team of my own."

"Suit yourself." Stymick disappeared into an old building and emerged a short time later with a gunnysack. "There's your dynamite and a coil of fuse, and here are the dynamite caps." He held out a small paper bag which Will accepted gingerly. After settling for the blasting material, the Eschmans made their way home.

Next morning, Will lost no time getting to the stump. "Be sure and keep Everett inside!" he called as he left the house.

After chopping off the tentacle roots, he placed two sticks of dynamite with caps in a burrow beneath the stump. Using enough fuse for a getaway, he looked around to make sure all was clear.

Then he lit the fuse and retreated toward the house.

The sparks hissed along the fuse to the stump. There was a moment's silence followed by a blast that shook the ground and sent clouds of earth and pine splinters into the air. The horses pranced and whinnied in their makeshift shelter, and a flock of crows mounted to the sky with loud, harsh cawing. When Will walked back to the stump, he found it split in sections. However, most of it was still intact. He hitched the team to a chain girding one section and they started off briskly until the chain tightened with a jolt. Then the horses stopped abruptly.

"It's time they learn not to give up whenever the pulling gets rough!" Will mumbled to himself.

He drew the team back and started over. As they slowed down, he lashed out vigorously with the end of the reins.

"Get up there!" he shouted. "Hi-you, lazy critters! Hi-yuh!"

The team gave a lunge then stopped short in their tracks as the tugs tightened. Nell turned her blind side toward Nick, threw her head over his mane and whinnied.

"What ails you two!" stormed Will as he dropped the reins and strode to the front of the team. Nell was sweating and trembling. Her one good eye stared wildly about.

A sickening wave of guilt swept over Will as he recalled a day on the old home place when he had impetuously spurred his favorite mare, Belle, causing her to stumble and fall on him.

"It's all right, Nell!" he soothed the frustrated horse as he cradled her quivering nose in his arm and patted her sweaty neck. "I guess you two horses weren't meant to be stump pullers. Still I wouldn't trade you for any other team in these north woods."

Entering the house, Will turned to his wife. "Did you say you enjoyed planting around stumps? Well, I guess you're going to get your chance this year. I'll help you measure off the rows, and we'll get at it."

CHAPTER THIRTY

Dawning

𝒯he auction that was to end Guy Sauter's days on the farm was really the turning point of his life. As he watched his live stock and working equipment pass into the hands of others, he became more and more aware that his farm was the last place he wanted to leave.

During the years of farming with his wife and daughter, Della, every fiber of his being was intertwined with his cabin and land. And now, with time on his hands, he became restless to work again and pass his acres and lifestyle along to his grandson, Joey.

But it was the appearance of the Eschmans at the auction that made the real difference. Sauter had taken an immediate liking to Will and the winsome young wife who seemed so genuinely interested in his daughter and grandson. With neighbors like them, life could be full and meaningful again.

Sauter had been offered a good price for his farm because of the stand of pine timber on it. Now, he decided to stay in his own log cabin and reap the benefits of the timber himself. The auction had netted him enough to buy and set up the necessary equipment for a sawmill, and he could use his vacant farm buildings for storing lumber.

Meanwhile, new developments were sweeping the Eschman household. Meriel leaning over her husband's shoulder followed the written lines as he read Annalie's letter aloud.

"Can you believe that?" she exclaimed excitedly, tightening her grip on his neck. "Annalie and Louie are coming here to live next spring. And, oh my goodness! Harold and Reah too! I just can't believe it's true!"

"Hey, woman!" gasped Will. "If you squeeze my neck any tighter, they'll find a 'headless hooligan' roaming these acres when they arrive."

Reading on, he noted the arrival of Annalie's seventh child, a boy named Robby. Meriel sighed in sympathy at the thought of Annalie packing to move with all those youngsters underfoot.

"If only I were close enough to help her. Do you think they will be surprised to find a new little one here when they arrive?" She patted her abdomen which was beginning to show the fullness of new life.

Will's face suddenly became overcast as he read on in the letter. "Dan Meister passed away in his sleep, following a day of work in his field. He was eighty years old."

It seemed to Will only yesterday that Meister had laid an encouraging hand on his shoulder. "Dream big, Will! And don't be afraid to follow your dreams, whatever the cost!"

Meister's shining example was woven into Will's childhood past, along with the precepts of the Mennonite community, his father's guiding hand and his mother's faith. Now, the time had come for him to look to the future and begin building on his own.

Will looked up from the letter in his hand. "You know, Meriel, I've just had an idea. With Sauter starting his sawmill and Fritz working with him, this would be a good time to start building our new house. If we got the framework up this fall, we would have shelter for ourselves and our folks from Iowa would have a place to stay until they got started on their own homes."

Meriel reached over and gave her husband another squeeze. "Oh, Will! Do you really mean that? Pinch me! And tell me I'm not dreaming!"

Meriel found paper and pencils. Soon they were busy sketching and discussing the shape and details of their new home. "I've missed a porch on this place. Let's have a wide, inviting veranda across the front."

As Will spoke, his pencil inscribed an area on one side of his rectangular house. "And with all the cooking we'll be doing, we'll need plenty of cupboard space and lots of windows to make the kitchen light." On his own piece of paper, Everett drew a square topped by a triangle roof with a cat and dog sitting by the door.

Meriel glanced up as she heard the clock strike. "My land! It's twelve o'clock already! I must get some dinner on!"

"I believe we have visitors!" Will exclaimed as a gray horse pulling a dusty buggy turned into the yard. "They probably haven't had dinner. Do we have enough to invite them in?"

"I think so. There's leftover beans and corn bread besides coleslaw and apple cobbler."

"I don't remember seeing them before," Will remarked as he studied the resolute features of the man driving. At his side was a small, pleasant-faced woman holding an infant. There was something more about the outfit that arrested Will's attention.

"Look Meriel. I've never seen anything like that before!" He pointed to the back of the rig.

Suspended from the rear of the buggy between the two back wheels was a crude wooden seat on which sat a freckle-faced girl of eight and a smaller boy in overalls and a torn hat. The two children clung to the back of the buggy as they sat on the suspended seat. Their bare feet dangled a mere six inches above the dusty road.

The driver dismounted from the buggy with quick steps and held out his hand as he approached Will. "I'm Bob Adams, pastor of the Bentley Church, along with two other congregations." He spoke with an infectious smile. "I just couldn't go by without a closer look at your flourishing garden. And, by the way, what is that blazing blue plant or tree in the middle?"

"Oh, you're looking at Meriel's 'heavenly blue' stump."

"Never heard of one before," the preacher answered, puzzled.

"Well, that's my wife's masterpiece. When we couldn't get rid of the stump in the middle of the garden, she simply surrounded it with heavenly blue morning glory seeds, and you see the results — Oh, what's wrong with me? You folks probably haven't had dinner, yet."

The family nodded in agreement.

"Come on in. Nothing fancy to eat today, but you're

welcome to share."

The group followed Will as he led the way to the waiting table. To the Adams family, who barely subsisted on the meager offerings from the circuit parishioners, the meal was a feast.

Following dinner, Adams pushed his chair back from the table. "Brother Will, I've been hearing good things about you and your family. I just had to stop and visit awhile. Are you acquainted with any folks from my church? It's the little white one on the edge of Bentley."

Will confessed that since they lived closer to Rhodes, they naturally gravitated that way when they shopped. And, well, they hadn't taken much time for socializing, except for shopping at Kettering's store.

Adams nodded. "I understand, your being here such a short time. I was about to invite you to come to our church in Bentley. Then it hit me; maybe you were the man for whom I'd been praying to start a church in Rhodes. The need for the Word is great there. Would you be willing to hold church meetings there, if I furnished hymn books, Bibles and Sunday School papers?"

After thinking a moment, Will responded, "I guess that's a pretty good way to thank the Lord for bringing us safely here and getting us started on our place."

"You are a Christian, are you not?"

Will recounted his Mennonite upbringing, his father's uplifted face as he prayed in German at mealtime and his mother's positive faith.

"Aye!" Preacher Adams nodded, "But did you ever meet the Lord in a personal sort of way?"

Will's eyes grew misty, as he glanced across at his wife. "That time came shortly before we were married. I had hit rock bottom after my horse had fallen on me. Meriel prayed me out of the pit of despair and helped me find faith in Jesus."

"That's good!" exclaimed Adams softly.

A little later the Adams family, loaded down with produce from Meriel's garden, made their departure with the young children, Timothy and Abigail, bobbing along at the rear of the buggy like an afterthought.

Will and Meriel had planned to attend Adam's church with the Sauters on the following weekend. However, on Sunday, Everett came out of his room holding his stomach. "Mama, I don't feel too good."

Meriel felt her son's flushed forehead. "Why don't you and Sauters go without Everett and me?"

On hearing that Meriel was not going, Della also decided to stay home, leaving Will and Guy to go alone.

Sitting on the plain polished oak pews, they listened to the earnest preaching of Bob Adams. Glancing over the small congregation, Will found it to be made up chiefly of middle-aged farmers, a few parents with small children and still fewer teenagers. Guy Sauter sat with his eyes glued upon the preacher and a wistful look on his face.

After the service, Rev. Adams led the two men to a small room that served as his study and store room. He had already collected a couple boxes of Bibles, hymn books and papers for use in the Rhodes meetings.

"Just how would you begin this work, if you were me?" asked Will.

Adams thought a moment. "Well, there's Ma Webber in Rhodes. She's tender-hearted. I believe she would be receptive to Sunday services. She's also well-liked and respected by everyone."

"How about the Ketterings in the store at Rhodes?"

"Good idea!" agreed Adams. "You're the right man to approach him. They have a large room over the store, sometimes used as a dance hall. They might let you use it for your Sunday meetings. I'll be praying for you two families in your mission work."

Sauter turned to Will, hesitatingly, as they rode together on the way home. "Did the preacher include me in the church work?"

"He sure did. I'd be pleased to have you for a partner."

"That means I'd have to have some sort of religion to talk about."

"Not religion," answered Will, "but the Lord Jesus Christ as your Savior."

"I haven't the faintest idea how to go about it." Sauter looked up blankly.

"Just admit your past sin and failure, and ask the Lord to take control of your life. Would you like me to pray with you?"

Sauter responded, "Yes."

Will tied the reins loosely about the center upright of the wagon. The team walked on slowly without changing their gait. "Just repeat," encouraged Will, "Lord, Jesus, I know I'm a sinner. Thank you for dying on the cross for me. I need your forgiveness. Come into my life and make me a new person. I will honor and serve you with all my heart. Amen."

"I am a sinner," responded Sauter, "thank you Jesus for dying for me and forgiving me. Show me how and I'll work for you." Sauter looked up with gratitude and a new light in his eyes. The first missionary team, aimed at reaching the Rhodes community, was formed on the front seat of the wagon that Sunday.

CHAPTER THIRTY ONE

Building

In the coming fall, Will and Guy Sauter scooped out the basement for the new Eschman house, just behind the tarpaper one. Cement blocks were hauled from Gladwin and laid in place; then the basement was covered. By mid-September, two huge piles of lumber from the Sauter mill stood in readiness for the building.

Kettering and Stymick joined the crew from Sauter's mill to help raise the rafters. Della had helped Meriel several days ahead baking pies, cakes and bread for the occasion. Ma Webber came out with the men's families to help with the food, and Preacher Adams and family drove out from Bentley to join the neighborly get-together.

The weather cooperated so that a plank table could be set up outside to give the work crew and their families more elbow room while eating the meal at noon.

With dinner over, the men returned to their work, mingling stories and jokes with their hammer strokes....By mid-afternoon, the skeletal frame of the new house gleamed in the autumn sunshine.

When the last rafter was in place, Sauter brought out a guitar and began strumming on it. Immediately the group formed ranks for square dancing. Those not skilled in dancing joined in energetic clapping and stomping in time with the music.

After a time of whirling and promenading to Sauter's chanted directions, the breathless dancers paused to rest.

Will's voice rose above the drone of conversation: "Beginning

211

this Sunday morning, Meriel and I would be glad to have all you folks join us for a get-together at ten o'clock as long as the weather is nice."

"What sort of get-together will it be?" demanded Stymic as he directed a well aimed stream of tobacco juice over the edge of the new flooring.

"Preacher Bob has donated us song books, Bibles and papers," answered Will. "Guy Sauter, here, will be strumming his guitar and leading us in singing. Come just as you are now and see for yourself!" Then raising his voice louder, "Everybody's welcome! Hope to see you all Sunday morning at ten o'clock!"

The week following the houseraising, Will and Meriel left Everett with the Sauters and took the train to Gladwin, where Dr. Glover had his office. A physical check-up assured them that all was fine with Meriel. Dr. Glover felt she should have no problems at delivery time. However, when Will questioned him, he admitted that the distance was too great for him to take care of her unless she stayed in Gladwin when her time was near. "Ma Webber, in Rhodes, is considered a very good mid-wife," the doctor continued. "There's no reason she can't take care of you, providing you feel comfortable with her."

Riding home on the train, Will reached over and took Meriel's hand. "You look worried, honey. Want to talk about it?"

"It's just the thought of having a baby with no doctor around. Am I being childish about it?" Her lip quivered.

"You don't trust Ma Webber?" questioned Will.

"I thought you were the one that didn't care for her," declared Meriel, recalling their argument about leaving Everett with her when they went to do the cleaning.

"I didn't know her too well then," admitted Will. "But we'll handle it whatever way you think best."

"Maybe, when I talk to her, I'll feel better about it all. How about my driving over to see her, tomorrow?"

"Sounds like a fine idea!"

Next day, Will helped Meriel load a basket of cabbage, tomatoes and cucumbers into the wagon. He and Everett waved goodbye as she drove out of the yard. It seemed strange taking off by herself, alone. Since being in Michigan, she was usually surrounded by family and neighbors on all her trips. The time spent driving to town gave her a chance to sort out her thoughts. Mid-wives had been an established part of many cultures since the beginning of time.

"Lord, I can accept that with peace if it's Your will!"

Ma Webber glanced out of the door in surprise when Meriel knocked. Then with a happy cry, she threw her ample arms about her visitor.

"Land sakes, Meriel, it's so good to see you! Come in! Come in!"

"I need some help getting a basket out of the wagon; then I'll stop for awhile, if you don't already have company."

After expressing pleasure with the vegetables, Ma Webber collected herself. "Here, sit down while I fix some coffee for us." She returned in a moment with the coffee and cookies.

"Now, tell me how everything is going out on the farm."

Meriel expressed her appreciation for Ma Webber's help at the dinner for the houseraising, then launched immediately into the trip to Gladwin and the doctor telling them to find a mid-wife. "So I'm asking if you would consider taking care of me." She looked pleadingly at the older woman.

Ma quickly crossed the room and threw her arms about Meriel. "I'd be honored to help out when you need me! I thought when I was at your place, 'That girl is going to need help when her baby comes,' and I was just hoping you would call on me."

Tears of relief brimmed in Meriel's eyes, and a weight fell from her shoulders.

"When will you be needing me?" asked Ma Webber.

"The doctor thinks it will be sometime between Thanksgiving and Christmas."

"You can count on me!" promised the older woman. "Meanwhile, we should get together again to discuss what is needed and what to expect."

Della spent much time at the Eschman home as fall days sped by, and Meriel became heavier and slower. The two women canned bushels of tomatoes that Joey and Everett picked and cut blanched sweet corn from the cob for drying.

Remembering the white marquisette window curtains that Will's mother had given her back in Iowa, Meriel took them from the trunk. Then she and Della hung them over the newly installed window panes in the new house.

"Now, the windows are no longer staring at us!" exclaimed Della as the two women stood back to admire the cozy atmosphere of the room.

Will and Sauter fashioned a number of benches from leftover lumber, then constructed a much higher stand for a pulpit, which they dubbed their "Masterpiece".

They were rewarded for their labors by a good-sized turnout each Sunday for the remainder of the fall. Sauter led the singing with his guitar. Will was impressed with his neighbor's rich baritone voice.

Stymick and his wife came regularly. Meriel provided him with an old glass fruitjar to use as a spittoon, to keep his tobacco juice from staining the new pine floor. The Ketterings brought Ma Webber and the Rose family with their three little ones.

The little ones soon became restless from sitting on benches. So, after the first songs, Meriel and Della took them to the adjoining room. There, Meriel told them Bible stories while they sat on a braided rug in the center of the floor. Robby, Rex and Rachel Rose were soon coaxing their mother to go back to their "Jesus class" with Everett and Joey.

With the coming of November and cold weather, the Sunday services at the Eschmans were terminated. However, Mr. Kettering announced that he would be happy to have the group meet in the hall over his store, come the following spring.

CHAPTER THIRTY-TWO

Enough and To Spare

$\mathcal{D}$ella insisted on preparing Thanksgiving dinner, and for once Meriel did not protest. With delivery time near, her body had become unwieldy so as to make movement difficult. The Sauters had also invited Fritz. He was in a jovial mood, regaling those present with stories of his travels. Pausing between tales, he would suck in leisurely on his pipe as his listeners chuckled.

New curtains with a poppy design, a touch Della had borrowed from the Eschman place, brightened the Sauter cabin, and the crackling flames in the fireplace added to its coziness. Joey kept Everett fascinated with his collection of wood carvings, an art his grandfather had taught him.

At mealtime Guy Sauter bowed his head and prayed, "Thank you, Lord, for all you've done for us, and thank you for these friends. Amen." Conversation became sporadic as the food was passed and guests became engrossed in the roast chicken, dressing, salad and pumpkin pie before them on the table.

Thanksgiving Day had been a day to remember for the simple country folks at Sauter's cabin — the warmth of close friends about the fireplace, the gratitude for daily provisions nourished by the soil, the sun and the rain, and the time to look up and trust their Heavenly Father who had brought them safely through the past.

A few snowflakes were in the air as the Eschmans made their way home in the wagon. With some difficulty, Will helped his cumbersome wife down at their own doorstep. "Remind me to invest in a more genteel mode of travel," he chuckled, once he had lowered her safely to the ground.

"How about fixing a derrick?" she panted, out of breath.

About midnight, Meriel reached over and touched her husband's shoulder. "Will, I think this is it!"

Springing out of bed, Will stepped over to Everett's cot and slipped the boy's coat and cap over his night clothes.

"How would you like to go to Joey's house?" inquired Will, as he added a blanket for extra warmth.

"We just came from there," Everett reminded his father, sleepily.

"Mamma's about to have her baby!"

"I can help her!"

"No, we'll be needing Della and Ma Webber for that. You can stay with Joey and his grandpa for now. That will be a big help."

Will brought Della back to the house, then drove at full speed into Rhodes to pick up Ma Webber. Della had already rekindled the fire in the kitchen range when Will and Ma Webber entered the house. Stepping into the bedroom, Ma patted Meriel's hand, then wiped her forehead and fluffed up the pillow.

"It will be some time, yet," she informed Will, "so you might as well stretch out on the sofa and get some rest."

About 7 o'clock, as early morning light filtered dimly through the window pane, Della stirred up the coals in the range again and prepared coffee, toast and oatmeal for Will before he went out to his chores.

Meanwhile, Meriel's contractions came closer and harder. Her lips were parched and bleeding where she had bitten them to keep from crying out.

Noontime came and passed. Meriel grew weaker, and her gown was wet with perspiration. Ma Webber wiped her brow and motioned Will to the bedside.

"Hold on, honey! You're doing fine! I love you," he whispered, grasping her hand tightly.

Ma Webber spoke encouragement from across the bed. "This is it, Meriel. One more big push!!"

The exhausted woman summoned all her strength for a final

effort. A cry of pain and intense exertion escaped Meriel's lips. Will gathered his wife into his arms and wept with relief as an infant's cry mingled with that of its mother.

"You have a beautiful little girl, Meriel!" Ma exclaimed as she viewed the pink, chubby infant with its fist already in its mouth.

"She's a cute little pumpkin!" Will crooned as he bent over the infant, swathed in a blanket beside its mother.

Outside, the snow had laid a white blanket over the landscape. Inside the tarpaper house was love, warmth and security.

"I insist on staying a couple weeks!" declared Della the following morning as Will prepared to take Ma Webber home and pick up Everett. "I can help with the cooking, cleaning and the baby until Meriel feels stronger."

"What can I say?" answered Will with a grateful shrug and grin.

Beneath Meriel's busy fingers, the pile of family mending soon melted away. In their free time together, Meriel taught her younger friend how to knit. Then, with an array of bright embroidery flosses, she began a wall motto for herself.

Holding the embroidery hoops so as to catch the light from the lamp on the table, Meriel stitched on her flower-bordered handwork.

"Now what are you working on?" asked Will looking up from the book he was reading.

She held up the linen rectangle for him to see. Will could make out the penciled words within the colorful border.

> *"Before me*
> *Even as behind,*
> *God is*
> *And all is well!"*

"H-m-m, that's a neat thought! Where did you find it?"

"In a poem by Whittier, in one of your books. I thought it was precious! Because of what God has done for us in the past, we can trust Him with all our tomorrows. And notice, God is now — just like Jesus said 'I am with you always'!"

Will nodded thoughtfully. "And where are you going to hang it?"

"On our bedroom wall in the new house. That way it will always be a reminder, even when wc wake up in the dark."

Will bent over and kissed her. "I'm always learning something new from the woman I married!"

Della sat unobtrusively across the room from the Eschmans. Her knitting needles clicked rhythmically as the red yarn flowed from them into the woolen wrist of a mitten for Joey. A tear stole down her cheek as the Eschmans continued to talk. "If only Joey's father had been like Mr. Eschman, how different things would have been!"

A few weeks later, the Eschman family again rode the train to Gladwin for a check-up with Dr. Glover. He was enthusiastic over Laurie, the new baby, declaring her to be in perfect health. He asked them to give his regards to Ma Webber. He also checked Everett and pronounced him to be a fine specimen of a boy. Then he prescribed a tonic for Meriel to help build up her system. The return trip to Rhodes was a time of thanksgiving for the Eschman family.

As winter crept across the calendar, Will and Fritz worked at finishing the new house, using a kerosene heater to take off the chill. By the end of January, the walls were plastered and the doors hung.

The last week of February was mellow, a token of gentler seasons ahead. Snow turned to slush and the branches of the willow trees gleamed like gold. Splotches on the hillside turned green, and ragged V's of wild geese etched their way across the sky. There would be more snow and low temperatures later, but nothing could dim the bright promise of spring.

A letter, stating that Harold and Reah, and Louie and Annalie with family would be arriving the first week of April, spurred the Eschmans into a flurry of activity.

The stove and range were moved from the old house to the new, followed by the rest of the furniture.

"Funny how sparse our furniture looks in all this space,"

remarked Meriel when their old household pieces had been placed in the new setting.

Will merely shrugged, "When we have wall-to-wall people here, we'll be glad for the extra space."

Stymick, the stump puller, was engaged to move the old house, once it was vacated. After jacking up all the house corners, he placed log rollers under the building. Then the oxen were hitched to a treadmill turntable that slowly towed the tarpapered house to the desired spot behind the new building.

With the arrival of the Iowa relatives, life at the Eschmans took on the semblance of a perpetual family reunion. Groups of men walked over surrounding fields deciding which were best for planting. Women congregated around washtubs near the back door and hung out endless lines of clothes to dry. Groups of children romped or swung beneath the trees in the yard. Meals consisted of huge kettles of stew, goulash or beans, many loaves of fresh bread and a simple dessert. Meriel refilled the huge bowls with hot food from the range while Annalie and Reah kept them moving at the table.

Seated on wooden benches about the long plank table were Louie and Annalie's brood of seven children ranging from the fifteen-year-old twins to Robby, the toddler. Fritz Zimmerli usually ate with the group, as he was helping Harold and Reah build their house. Everett alternated between running errands and eating with his cousins, and Laurie, in her highchair, banged on her dish with a spoon like a drummer at a circus.

A couple extra bedsteads were borrowed from the Sauters to accommodate the Iowa couples at night. The singles and children spread across the floor on comforters in a glorified camping spree.

The evenings were spent eating popcorn about a lamplit table. While the children played games, the adults caught up on news.

Mary was planning to marry a young minister who had been preaching in the Mennonite community. Sam was teaching at Bromes Dell, and Minnie was "Jill of all trades" around home, looking after Jacob and Anna.

At planting time, Will initiated his brothers-in-law into the fine art of planting crops around stumps, rather than waste time and energy trying to clear the field first. "There'll be time to clear the land later. Besides, you can always get more seeds into a crooked row than a straight one."

Each day Louie and Annalie left their two youngest children at Will's and took off across the adjoining acres with the rest of their family. There they spent long hours making their dilapidated house livable. While Louie and his twin sons carried out the litter and repaired walls and woodwork, Annalie and the rest of the family scrubbed floors, washed windows and put up curtains.

Louie and his wife found their crew of young workers becoming more disgruntled and rebellious as time went by. Finally, one day at lunch, Louie confronted the twins, "What ails you two guys, anyway? It seems you're better at grumbling than anything else!"

Tom mumbled without looking up, "We left a nice home in Iowa for this rat hole. Do you call that progress?"

Louie, already exhausted from work, bristled. His jaw set and eyes glared at his son as he started to rise from his chair.

Sara interrupted, placatingly. "Papa, the thing that's bothering us kids is that all the rest of the relatives have nice new houses and we have to settle for this ramshackle place!"

"Oh, so that's your problem!" interjected Annalie. "Did you notice the tarpaper shanty behind Will's new house?"

The twins nodded glumly. "Yeah, what about it?"

"Well, that's where Uncle Will and Aunt Meriel had been living until three months ago."

The eyes of the children widened in disbelief. "You don't mean they really lived in that shack?"

"That's right! They moved into their new place just before we arrived in Michigan."

Louie's face softened in relief. "If we all pitch in and work together, we'll have a new house too, before you know it!"

True to Louie's prediction, new buildings began to materialize on the Sprenger farm. The first to appear was a spacious barn to shelter their two teams of horses and a growing herd of cattle necessary to support a large family. Louie and his sons were soon recognized as "those Swiss farmers from Iowa".

Dawn and Robby, the Sprenger's two youngest, along with Laurie, made a lively trio during those early settling days. They would spend long periods of time building block towers, then topple them. At other times they would raid the henhouse to get real eggs to put in the mud pies they were making.

Laurie, thriving on the attention from her aunts, uncles, and cousins, grew into an imperious young potentate. She learned that by raising her chubby arms and demanding "Carry me!" she would immediately be given a ride on someone's shoulder. "Carry me!" she called one day as she approached her father.

"How's my little pumpkin today?" quipped Will as he hoisted her to his shoulder.

"I'se Papa's little punkins!" she chanted delightedly, looking down from her high perch. The nickname, Little Punkins, followed Laurie long after she had outgrown her toddler days.

For Laurie and her two cousins, Dawn and Robby, time passed as lightly as the white clouds drifting above the meadow separating their two homes. The children daily crossed the field of clover to play together. During those sun-drenched hours they developed nut-brown bodies and childhood bonds never to be broken.

CHAPTER THIRTY THREE

Revival

*T*hough the Eschman and Sprenger farms bordered each other, the road between was actually a county line dividing Bay and Gladwin counties. The road past Louie and Annalie Sprenger's house led to the village of Bentley, so the children attended Ketchum Hill School in the Bentley area. Through shopping and attending school, the Sprenger family gravitated to the little white church which their schoolmates and farmer acquaintances attended. They soon became an integral part of the congregation, to Pastor Adam's great pleasure.

Harold and Reah accompanied Will and the Sauters to Rhodes and became active in the Sunday services there. The meetings in the hall over Kettering's store began to flourish. The store owner had furnished folding chairs, which were a luxury after the wooden benches used at the Eschmans the fall before. Many of the Rhodes school children found the meetings a new attraction, and they in turn, drew their parents to attend.

Though there was a piano in the hall, Sauter continued to use his guitar as he directed the singing. Harold led the opening, and Will taught the adult Bible class. Harold's wife, Reah, and Della helped Meriel in the children's department which was curtained off at one end of the hall.

Clothilda Grant, who lived across from the school, watched through her house curtains each Sunday as neighbors walked by to the services. However, she herself never "darkened the door" of the meeting place. "Humpf!" she replied when Ma Webber invited

223

her to come. "They say 'Birds of a feather flock together'. Everyone knows Della Sauter is a scarlet woman and since the Eschmans are so thick with her, they can't be very spiritual themselves. I can be a better Christian at home!"

She turned from her visitor abruptly and went flouncing through the house.

With lambing season imminent, Will had cleaned the central drive-through area of the barn and thrown down a large amount of fresh straw from the hayloft. Everett spread the dry, rustling bedding evenly over the ground floor. The late February sunlight, filtering through the open barn door, illumined the rising particles of dust and fine chaff into golden motes, dancing in the air.

Bleating sounds came from the far corner of the area where several ewes, heavy with lamb, were penned by themselves. Other ewes stood outside the door waiting to move in and occupy the dry bedding.

Will paused in his work as two men appeared suddenly in the doorway. The familiar one, Preacher Adams, spoke first.

"Brother Will, this is Alexander Strait, a traveling evangelist, who would like to hold meetings in the area. I told him of your good work in Rhodes, and he felt he could be a real help to your group."

The large burly man with him thrust his hand out suddenly, causing the sheep to scatter away from the door.

"Praise the Lord! I'm sure He has led me to this man!"

Will blinked his eyes, startled at the salutation, but he thought, "I guess the Lord uses all kinds of servants in his work." He acknowledged that the group in Rhodes could use any available help.

"And I'm sure God has led my wife and me to abide under your roof."

"That will be up to my wife," Will answered hesitantly. "Let's go to the house and talk it over with her."

Everett, having finished scattering the straw, put up his fork and followed the men from the barn.

"This is my son, Everett," stated Will, placing his hand on the boy's shoulder.

"Hallelujah!" exclaimed Strait. "Did you know that children are a heritage of the Lord?"

"Yes, God has blessed us with two fine children," Will answered.

Meriel agreed to keep the Straits during the meetings.

"Amen! Blessed art thou of the Lord!" exclaimed the evangelist.

Will braced himself, wondering how many more of Strait's biblical responses he could take before something within him snapped.

On Sunday evening, the gas lights were lit in Kettering's upper hall. The seats began filling up, half an hour early. Since several inches of snow had fallen, Louie and Annalie hitched their team to a sleigh and picked up the Sauters, the Eschmans, and the Brownings for the service. Clean straw, comforters, and heated soapstones provided warmth for the riders, as the horses trotted with sleigh bells jangling.

The room was warm and crowded with an underlying scent of stale alcohol. Several men had been tippling to bolster their determination to come. Sauter had been informed before the meeting that he and his guitar would not be needed, for the evangelist's wife, Enid, would be playing the piano.

Following the singing, Evangelist Strait began his sermon. "The Lord has sent me to this place of darkness, and I have found it filled with diamonds. Yes sir! That's what you all are — diamonds in the rough. Hallelujah! I am here to polish you for the Lord."

Will discovered that once Alexander Strait was inside their home, most of his bombastic manner disappeared, and his energy was spent keeping his wife appeased. It was the wife, Enid, that nettled Will.

Enid found the new Eschman home much too drafty for her comfort. Meriel rounded up extra bedding so she could sleep warmly. In the morning when seven o'clock breakfast was served, Strait explained Enid's absence by saying her delicate health required extra hours of rest.

Meriel rid the table of dishes, washed them and waited. At 9:30, when Enid appeared in hair curlers and a pink, flowered housecoat, Meriel prepared a new breakfast of eggs, toast and oatmeal. Enid then stated that her doctor had insisted on her having fresh fruit each morning, preferably oranges or bananas.

Meriel relayed the need to Will. Before he could explode, she laid a finger on his lips. "Honey, this will all be over in a few days!"

Ketterings had no fresh fruit of any kind on hand. Will finally settled for a can of pineapple which he brought home for Mrs. Strait.

The lambs began to arrive during the day, keeping Will busy and Everett delighted. When Everett came to the house to report on the last lamb, Meriel bundled up Laurie to have a look at them. She also invited Enid Strait to go with them to the barn.

"Mercy, no!" she exclaimed. "A trip to the barn would put me in bed with an attack of asthma."

Monday evening when Louie and Annalie came by in the sleigh, the Sauters were missing. Enid reluctantly got into the sleigh. She was used to riding in a carriage, though she did admit later that the sleigh was warmer than a carriage in winter.

The attendance was low at the meeting that night, and the offering small. When the ushers brought back the plates for Strait's blessing, he looked hard at them and then prayed aloud, "Lord, I hear you telling me that some folks out there forgot to put their money in the offering, so we're passing the offering plates again."

Stymick turned around to see who was sitting behind him and if he could leave without being noticed. He finally slouched down to be as inconspicuous as possible. The majority of the congregation sat staring ahead as the collection plate passed them the second time.

The ushers circulated through the congregation once again with the plates and brought them back with the same amount in them.

Following the meeting, Will excused himself as soon as they reached home. Changing into old clothes, he went to the barn to be with his ewes in their lamb delivery. Next morning, he returned to the house weary, chilled and stiff.

Enid Strait, in hair curlers and flowered house coat was eating her breakfast of poached egg, toast and canned pineapple.

She turned as Will entered the kitchen.

"I was just telling your wife about my vision last night. The Lord called me to go to Africa!" She paused for effect. " – Just as plain as I'm telling you, He said, 'Go! And I will give you the gift of tongues, so that all who hear you will turn to Me'."

Will fixed his eyes on her and answered cooly, "Mrs. Strait, I believe when you go to Africa, you will have to do like my friends who are on the mission field. Take time to learn their language and culture before they will understand what you say to them."

Enid rose from the table and gathered her housecoat about her. "Well! That is the first time an infidel has called me a liar or disputed what the Lord said to me!" So saying, she flounced to the bedroom where she remained most of the day with her husband.

Will's eyes blazed. He opened his mouth to speak when he noticed Meriel watching him. She shook her head and placed her finger on her lips. Will turned and strode out of the kitchen, slamming the door behind him.

Mealtimes were strained and quiet. Laurie glanced from one to another perplexed. Everett kept his eyes lowered to his plate. Only Meriel spoke, urging ham, scalloped potatoes and custard pie upon the silent group.

Will did not attend the services that evening and was in the barn with his sheep when they returned home later that night.

When he entered the kitchen next morning, Enid Strait, red-eyed and thin-lipped, was in her usual place, eating breakfast. Stepping to the range, Will placed on the oven door a small bundle, wrapped in an old blanket.

Mrs. Strait ate on, pretending not to notice until the bundle gave a lurch and one spindly, wooly leg emerged.

She jumped from her chair with a start. "What's that?" she shrieked.

Meriel explained calmly, "That's a new-born lamb that was separated from its mother and got chilled last night."

Disgust and revulsion spread over Enid's face. "This is the first time in my life I've had to share quarters with – with – barn critters!"

Will spoke up, "Our Lord Jesus didn't complain about

sharing a stable with such critters when He came to earth."
Wailing loudly, Enid called for her husband to take her away from such an awful place. Alexander appeared, grim-faced, and stated tersely that it was time for them to leave.
Will had already hitched up the team. When they reached Rhodes, Strait asked to be let out at Kettering's store.
Clothilda Grant was inside shopping. She listened to Enid Strait's wild story. "You poor abused, godly people!" she commiserated. "You're welcome to stay at my house."
That night, the hall over Kettering's store was packed full as Alexander Strait preached his final message. Fritz Zimmerli related it later to Will and Meriel, who had remained at home.
Quoting Alexander Strait: "Satan and his hosts have worked against these meetings from the very beginning. He has thwarted my words and slandered my wife. He has contaminated our services with drunkards, adulteresses and liars. He has used all sorts of excuses to disrupt our meetings, and to some, he has even sent lambs to keep them away. I hereby dust off my clothes and feet from this evil place forever."

CHAPTER THIRTY FOUR

Huckleberrying

"*I* can't really explain it," Meriel confessed when Will voiced concern over her recent low spirits. "I just feel like the Straits have left some evil cloud hanging over our home and community."

"Don't let them bother you," Will soothed as he stroked her shoulder. "The way they growled, like ungrateful dogs, after all you did to keep them comfortable and well-fed, they should be on their knees asking forgiveness!" Will stopped abruptly as he felt his anger rising even though "Strait's revival" had occurred five months before.

Strait's meetings had left repercussions throughout the congregation at Rhodes. The Sauters no longer attended since Clothilda Grant had taken over his song leadership. Even more devastating were her snide remarks about Della's questionable past.

Will now seldom attended the services, stating that his absence was preferable to going with animosity seething in his heart. Meriel's brother, Harold, now taught the Bible lesson in his slow, patient way that seemed to shed criticism like a loose garment. Meriel, with a heavy heart, would get the children ready each Sunday and ride to the meetings with Harold and Reah, all the while longing for the time her husband would again take his place of leadership in the group.

The early February and March lambs had thrived in spite of Strait's curse upon them. Most of the ewes had delivered twins and some even triplets. Gentle spring rains had produced lush pasture

229

for them, and with extra feedings of grain, they were finished off in time to bring top price on the spring and early summer market. Will was elated with the income from the lambs. Not only was he able to pay off the indebtedness on his house and barn but to lay some aside for future needs.

Louie and Annalie had built their house and barn during the summer. With the combined building activities of the three related families, their corner of the county had blossomed into a prosperous looking community.

"Ever been huckleberrying?" asked Sauter as he pitched a forkful of second-cutting hay up on the wagon to Will.

"Can't say that I have. What's special about it?"

"You owe it to yourself to get out in the huckleberry marsh for at least one day of the year not only for relaxation but for a supply of good eating through the winter. Huckleberries taste great any way you fix'em, whether raw, in cobblers or canned."

"Sounds like a good excuse for a family get-together," Will observed later to Meriel, hoping a break in their work might lift her spirits.

"How about a picnic this Friday?" Meriel answered. "We could invite the Sprengers and the Brownings and, of course, the Sauters."

After a summer of hard work, all the family members were enthusiastic about taking a holiday. Friday forenoon, three wagons formed a mini-caravan in Eschman's driveway.

"We men-folk might as well ride together," Will motioned to the others as he swung up on the seat beside Sauter. Harold and Louie joined them on the improvised board seat behind, glad for the chance to discuss farming alone.

The women-folk followed in the second wagon with Della driving and Robby, Dawn and Laurie protesting that they had to ride with old folks instead of the big kids.

The "big kids" brought up the rear with the twins driving the Sprenger team. Louie looked back to where his five offspring, plus Everett and Joey, were bouncing around in the wagon. "Hey, you kids," he reminded the effervescent bunch, "better settle down a bit, before someone falls under a wheel and gets hurt!"

The caravan moved out with Sauter leading the way. His gray team stepped eagerly along over Big Molasses Creek and up the sandy road to the marshlands. Leaving the road, Sauter followed a faint wagon trail that meandered around knolls and through bogs. He finally stopped beneath a clump of jack pines. The other wagons joined him. Amid mild confusion, folks dismounted, children scattered and women began unpacking food for the picnic. By the time the men had unhitched and fed the horses, the women had spread dishes of fried chicken, beans, coleslaw and chocolate cake upon the cloth-covered ground.

With the picnic over, pails and kettles for picking berries were distributed to all down to tin cups for the youngsters. Sauter gave final directions.

"Everyone take an extra drink of water out of the cream can because the rest of it goes to the horses. And you kids, keep in sight of another person. With a few turns or tumbles in these marshlands, every tree and hummock looks alike, and it's easy to get lost."

The pickers were soon raking handfuls of the luscious blue berries into their pails and the pails when filled, were, in turn, emptied into larger containers on the wagons. Even the cream cans were partially filled with berries as the weary group made their way home.

The men returned to the fields next day, leaving the women and children with the tedious job of sorting and canning the berries. For Annalie it was a cinch with three pairs of children's hands for cleaning berries and thirteen year old Sara as efficient as a grownup at supervising children and canning fruit.

Meriel thought of Reah facing the canning chore alone and sent Everett up to the hilltop house to invite her to join them. In a surprisingly short time, Harold delivered Reah, berries, pans and fruit jars at Meriel's doorstep. Reah's red-rimmed eyes gave mute evidence that she had been crying.

Meriel quickly organized pans and chairs about the kitchen table. "Shall we just wash and can all our berries together? Then we can divide the jars when we are finished." Reah nodded in agreement.

After skimming the floating leaves and imperfect berries from the top of the water, the rest was pleasant pastime as they scooped handfuls of blue berries shining like Aladdin's jewels.

"I've been thinking of you," Meriel remarked as she let a handful of berries slide into the partially filled kettle on the table before Reah. "How are things going up on your hill?"

Without warning, Reah burst into tears. "I'm sorry! I didn't mean to cry while I was here, but I've been so lonely and homesick for Iowa I could just die!"

Meriel's eyes grew misty and concerned. "Hasn't Harold been good – or kind to you?"

"You know Harold. He couldn't be anything but kind. He's slow and easy going. Doesn't say much, but he's sweet! It's when he's out working in the field; I get so lonesome I could talk to the nails in the woodwork. And when I look out, there's nothing but pine stumps!"

Meriel's arms were about her sister-in-law. "I'm sorry, Reah! I've been so occupied with my own home and children, I should have thought about you being alone on the hill. We can plan on doing more things together this coming winter, maybe even do some quilting."

While the berries simmered in kettles on the stove and were ladled into jars, Reah and Meriel reminisced about family and friends back in the golden state of Iowa.

CHAPTER THIRTY FIVE

As Sparks Fly Upward

With the corn crop harvested and out of the way, Will enlisted Lew Stymick to rid his field of stumps. Stymick arrived early in the morning with his oxen, Bif and Boz. The critters stepped along briskly for their size, their heads nodding in unison beneath the yoke. Louie and Harold had come to gain pointers for when they were ready to clear their acres of stumps.

Taking off the heavy yoke, Stymick laid it in the wagon, then tied the two animals so they could eat hay until needed.

The men gathered around a huge stump in the field and watched closely while Stymick, enjoying his role as showman, bored holes beneath the stump and set his dynamite charges. He next attached the caps and fuses. After studying the setup a couple minutes, he spit out a wad of tobacco and lit the end of the fuse. The men hastily retreated to a safe distance. Stymick followed them at a leisurely pace.

The stump erupted like a volcano, shaking the ground and darkening the sky with soil and pine fragments. The horses near the barn galloped around the lot. Chickens flapped their wings and scurried off cackling. The oxen raised their white faces and gazed stolidly ahead.

When the debris settled and the air cleared, Stymick yoked the ox team to a split section of the stump. "Gitchee- yup!" he yelped at them. The massive beasts moved calmly away from the stump. When the tugs tightened, the oxen merely stretched their hind legs and leaned forward, as if preparing to lie down. With the combined force of two tons of bovine weight and muscle, the long pine roots gave way, and with a mighty crunch, left their empty sockets in the earth's jaw.

Stymick repeated the blasting and stump-pulling throughout the day. By evening, what had formerly been a Michigan field bristling with stumps now resembled a battlefield with craters and ragged pieces of pine roots scattered over the area.

Clearing the field was another occasion for a neighborly get-together and cooperation. While the young folks gathered the small pieces of pine for kindling and "quick cooking wood" with teams and wagons, the men criss-crossed the field with their teams and tow chains corralling the blasted stump roots into a mountainous heap in the middle of the field. The men left their job of jockeying stump roots only long enough to snatch a bite of the outdoor dinner the women had prepared for them; the stump-pile had to be finished soon to leave time for burning the same day.

"Be sure you stick around for the bonfire," Will reminded the group as they were finishing the potato salad, boiled ham and pie.

"Aren't you going to wait until dark to light it?" asked Everett in a disappointed voice.

"There'll be plenty of flames and sparks left after dark!" Will replied. "When that pile takes off with a roar, we want to see everything around, just to make sure nothing else is ignited by flying sparks." Will placed some kerosene-soaked pieces of splintered pine under the edges of the pile and lit them. Small flames licked up through the roots. Soon a powerful updraft of flame and smoke shot skyward through the middle of the pile like a mighty smelting furnace. The surrounding group of people, with one accord and red faces, melted back from the intense heat.

The blazing intensity of the stump fire subsided as evening approached, and as dusk deepened, the family members were irresistibly drawn back to the crackling flames. They sat in awed silence about the stump pile and watched as the flames danced upward. At times the showers of sparks seemed to be reaching for the stars above in the velvety dome of the heavens. An occasional streak of light would brighten the upper horizon; the group would hold their breath, wondering if it were a meteorite about to visit earth or an exuberant firebrand trying to find a more celestial orbit.

As the bonfire flickered lower, the children turned to more active pastimes – chasing each other in tag games around the circle of light. Will called in a word of caution, "Watch out you don't run too close to the fire or push anyone toward it!"

Sauter struck a few chords on his guitar and the grownups joined him singing "Swanee River" and "Beautiful Dreamer". As a voice rose from the circle singing "Rock of Ages", the melodies changed to the old hymn. Sauter quickly adapted his strumming to accompany them.

A smoldering root broke and fell into the ashes, sending upward a shower of sparks. Sauter stopped strumming for the moment. "Somewhere, I heard that 'Man is born to trouble as the sparks fly upward'."

"That's true!" stated Annalie. "It's from the Book of Job. Papa also quoted where, 'The same God calls all the stars by name and heals the broken of heart'."

They were interrupted by the older boys asking if they could sleep out by the bonfire. Will and Louie not only consented, but agreed it might be a good precaution to have a few pails of water on hand to keep the fire from spreading in case the wind shifted during the night.

Will was in high spirits as he and Meriel walked down the lane toward the pasture on Saturday. The hillside before them spread like a tapestry of gold, scarlet and burgundy, flocked with ewes bearing next spring's lambs. On the right lay the cleared cornfield, now rid of stumps, and as neat an acreage as any in the state of Iowa. On the left, a bright yellow field of navy beans waited to be harvested.

He squeezed Meriel's hand. "Did you ever see a more beautiful layout? Things have fallen into place this year like a magnificent jigsaw puzzle. This coming week, we'll harvest the beans. They should bring us enough to pay off all remaining debts. Then we can relax this winter for a change."

Meriel wanted to remind Will of the desperate need for his leadership in the Rhodes Sunday services but held her peace. It would keep for a later date. There were times a man needed to bask in the light of his dreams and accomplishments without being doused with a bucketful of cold reality and obligation.

She snuggled close to him as they followed the path homeward. "Don't you wish we could hold on to this autumn day forever?"

CHAPTER THIRTY SIX

Grim Harvest

*W*ill was in the beanfield early on the following Monday, determined to finish the harvesting before the weather broke up. The horses stepped along briskly as the bean puller plowed through the golden field, leaving neat rows of uprooted beans in its wake.

"One more day," he thought as he fell asleep that night, "and the last crop of the year will be ready for market."

Toward morning Will woke to a dripping sound. As he became fully aroused, he made his way to the window and peered through the darkness at a heavy downpour of rain.

"Oh no!" he groaned with a sense of betrayal. "Why God, couldn't it have held off one more day?"

At breakfast time, he sat glumly as Meriel placed oatmeal and toast before him on the table. "Do you want to ask the blessing?" he asked Meriel, as the children joined them at the table.

Meriel glanced about the table at her troubled husband and sleepy-eyed offspring. "Our Father," she began "Thank you for your care during the night and for this another day. Lord, you know how to cope with this harvesting problem ahead of us; Will needs your guidance. Watch over and protect each one in our family. In Jesus name. Amen." Then she added silently, "And give us peace in our hearts, especially Will!"

"I'll take the children to school today," he stated after breakfast.

"Should they go in all this rain?" questioned Meriel.

"The rain will probably be over soon," he answered,

wishfully. "Find that old oilcloth to put over our heads and shoulders," he called as he left the house.

Meriel quickly packed a couple sandwiches, cookies and apples in two lunch pails while Everett found the yellow oilcloth. A few minutes later, Will stopped at the door with the team and spring wagon. The children mounted the seat on either side of their father, and the three rode off looking like a shiny mushroom beneath their oilcloth covering as the horses splashed down the muddy road.

The rain, driven by a strong west wind, pelted against the window as Meriel cleared away the morning dishes and straightened the house. When Will had not returned by noon, she fixed herself a cup of strong tea to drink with a sandwich. She put on Will's extra chore jacket, a red scarf on her head, and bracing herself against the gale, made her way to the barn. There was a mingled mooing of the cows as she opened the door to their warm, steamy quarters.

After throwing a little fresh hay in their mangers, she went on to the chicken house carrying a bucket of cracked corn with her. Again she was greeted with sounds of gratitude. The hens clucked and scratched as she scattered their grain on the straw-covered floor. The rooster tossed his head and crowed lustily as she gathered eggs to take to the house.

"All right, Caesar," she addressed the cock. "So you have everything under control — just like a man!"

The rain had let up somewhat, but the wind had turned much colder. She was glad it was at her back as she dodged mud puddles on the way to the house.

Once more in the comfortable house, she replenished the wood in the range and cut up vegetables to cook with a soup bone for supper. The gloomy, wet day had deepened into twilight when Will returned with the children after school.

"I'm sorry I couldn't let you know what I was doing," he apologized.

"Of course you couldn't, without a phone," agreed Meriel. "A telephone is one Iowa convenience we could use!"

"I met Stymick in Kettering's store this morning, and he gave me the lowdown on how to deal with harvesting beans in wet weather. In fact, he said I could cut the poplar saplings from his land to hold up the beans for drying. That's what I was doing today until school was dismissed." He waved his hand toward the wagon outside, rounded up with long poplar stakes.

At the sight of the enormous task Will had accomplished in spite of pouring rain, Meriel's resentment over his brusque morning behavior melted into admiration and concern.

"I can't believe you cut all that in the rain today! Now, you'd better get out of those soaked clothes before you catch pneumonia."

"Just as soon as I tend to the animals for the night."

Meriel reheated the kettle of vegetable soup while Will finished choring. With the meal over, the family relaxed around the kitchen table as the copper teakettle simmered on the range. Laurie built spelling words from alphabet blocks; Everett sketched castles and knights from his history book while Will browsed through a collection of orations dating back to Forum meetings at Bromes Dell School. Meriel hummed to herself as she stitched on quilt blocks. The peace she had prayed for earlier in the day had indeed settled on the Eschman family.

By morning, the heavy rain of the previous day had given way to intermittent drizzle. "Mind staying home from school today, Everett?" asked his father. "I really need you to help in the field."

"Naw, I think I can stand it!" Everett answered with a grin.

As soon as Will left the house, Meriel bundled Laurie and had Everett take her to Harold and Reah's house. "Just tell them I'll be busy and would appreciate them keeping her for the day."

A short time later, Meriel appeared in the sodden bean field where Will and Everett, in mud-covered boots, were driving stake holes and setting the poplar saplings along the bean rows.

"What in thunderation are you doing out here?" demanded Will regarding his wife, outfitted in his chore jacket, overalls and a red scarf as she plodded through the mud in oversized galoshes.

"Sh-h-h-h," she silenced him as she lifted a manure fork in one hand. "Now, tell me how you want this done."

"Just stack the beans around the sapling until it looks like a tower." Taking her fork, he stacked the bean plants into the semblance of a pillar around the support. "And be careful it doesn't turn into a leaning tower of Pisa!" He pushed the column with the fork into a more upright position. "By the way, what did you do with Laurie?"

"Oh, she's fine, keeping Reah company," came the masculine voice of Harold, who had just joined the group. "I thought maybe you could use a little more help."

"Thanks!" Will grinned in appreciation, "I'm not turning anyone away."

The group worked doggedly down the long, muddy rows, lifting forkfuls of soggy beans and stacking them around the poplar stakes. As the afternoon wore on, the drizzle finally disappeared, and the sun peeked sheepishly through the slate-colored clouds. Gloves and boots became stiffer, and fingers and toes numbed as the temperature dropped.

By evening, the beanfield bristled with hundreds of bushy columns rustling in the frigid air.

While the group shed their stiff, muddy clothes for dry ones, Meriel sliced potatoes, onions and ham into a chowder seasoned with pepper, butter and a little milk.

Everett walked home with Harold after supper and soon returned with Laurie. When the children entered the kitchen, Will was mixing hot toddies from honey, hot water and whiskey, kept on hand for medicinal purposes. "Mm-m-m-m-, that smells good!" commented Laurie sniffing at the aromatic brew. "I'll take some, too!"

"It's just for folks coming down with a cold."

Laurie immediately began a hard, barking cough. Will shut his eyes and twisted his mouth into a wry expression after a sip from his steaming cup.

"Oh, you folks!" Laurie exclaimed in a disgusted tone of voice. "I can tell you're all just wearing your make-believe sick faces."

Whether it was the potency of the brew or strong constitutions, all seemed to escape any bad effects from the day in the field — that is, except for Meriel, who woke up next morning, weak and achy.

"It's probably just a touch of the grippe," she commented. Her head swam as she held onto the edge of the range and tried to get breakfast.

"Woman, you belong back in bed!" With that, Will slipped an arm under her shoulder for support as he walked her to the bedroom.

"We can rustle some food for ourselves; might even bring you a bite if you mind and stay down!"

Meriel slept through the day and the following night. Next morning she awoke somewhat refreshed.

"Feel my gown," she said as she pulled the soggy garment from her shoulders. "It's as wet as if it had been through the wash."

"With all those impurities sweated out of your system, you should soon be on the mend," Will sighed with relief as he found a fresh gown and warm kimono for Meriel, then helped her to a chair by the heating stove.

The pink flush on her face and the locket about her neck accented the blue kimono and added a fragile beauty to her features.

Tilting his head, Will began to sing in an exaggerated tenor,

"Beautiful Dreamer, waken to me
Starlight and dewdrop are waiting for thee."

Meriel grinned at him, "Thank you, I think — " A spasm of coughing interrupted further speech.

"This must be the second phase of the grippe," she wheezed when she could finally regain her breath.

Will helped her back into bed. There was a gentle knock at the door and Della stuck her head in.

"Paw said you weren't feeling too good, so I came over to help a spell. Just go ahead and sleep; I'll visit before I leave."

When Meriel roused from her sleep, Della was picking up clothes scattered about the house.

"How can we ever repay you for all your kindness?"

Della shrugged, "Just trying to even the score a bit for all you've done for us. I'll take these clothes home to wash. You don't need any more moisture in the house until you're over your cold."

Annalie kept Laurie much of the time insisting that she was good company for her two, Dawn and Robbie. Reah came almost daily with her quilt blocks and visited as the two stitched away. Meriel would soon grow drowsy and nod off to sleep. "Sorry!" she apologized. "I make dull company."

"That's all right!" put in Reah. "Don't try to talk and get to coughing. I can talk enough for both of us."

With Christmas near, Meriel concentrated on making gifts for the family. She cut out a rabbit from white outing flannel to give Laurie and stitched together two Dresden plate quilt blocks to make pillows for the women. Gifts for men folk were harder to come by. She finally settled on monogramming initials on the sweaters Will had bought for Everett and himself. Reah took over the stuffing of the rabbit and the pillows since the fine cotton fibers brought on coughing spasms.

Will spoke up as Meriel sank into a chair, exhausted from a hard fit of coughing. "It's high time we get you to the doctor."

"We might as well wait until after Christmas," she gasped. "He'll probably just order more cough medicine."

"Only if you promise to start eating more, so the wind won't blow you away!" insisted Will as he wrapped the loose folds of her house coat about her frail body.

"How about starting with an eggnog right now?" put in Reah. She broke an egg into a bowl and beat it until frothy, then added milk, sugar, and a few drops of vanilla. Within minutes she had poured the tasty beverage into a glass for Meriel.

"That does taste pretty good!" agreed Meriel as she sipped half the contents of the glass.

CHAPTER THIRTY SEVEN

Christmas Interlude

Christmas morning dawned with the peace of Bethlehem permeating the Eschman home. After breakfast, the family gathered around the small pine tree decked with strings of cranberries and popcorn. Will opened the Bible to Luke's account of the first Christmas, and in a voice choked with emotion, read how the Son of God left his royal realms above to enter this weary, sin-cursed world through the birth canal of a lowly Jewish girl in a crude Judean stable.

In her favorite rocker, Meriel smiled upon the small circle of loved ones about her. Everett proudly distributed his gifts; a wooden doll carriage with spool wheels for Laurie, a tie-rack trimmed with pine cones for his father, and a cat-shaped matchbox holder for his mother to hang over the kitchen range. Strips of sandpaper covered its back with the words, "Scratch my back!" underneath.

Laurie squealed with delight over the white bunny, complete with pink ears and shoe button eyes and promptly put it in her doll buggy. Will and Everett admired their specially monogrammed sweaters.

After presenting each of the children with a new book, Will handed Meriel a small box. "I hope you don't mind. I couldn't resist getting this."

Meriel stared in amazement as she opened the box. "Why Will, it's almost identical to the locket I'm wearing — flower and all!"

"I know!" he admitted sheepishly. "I couldn't resist buying it when I saw it since you've almost worn the design off your old locket by wearing it to work in the kitchen and fields. You needed a new, shiny one for dress up occasions."

Opening the new locket, she read the exact words penned in the time-worn one about her neck. "To Meriel — I love you forever, Will."

"Bless you, honey!" Further words failed her as she threw her arms about his neck.

The Eschman's, along with Harold and Reah and Fritz Zimmerli, were invited to Louie and Annalie's for Christmas dinner. It was a time of lively celebration. Stories and laughter rang about the food-laden table. After the children had left the table to play with their Christmas toys, the adults lingered to visit over coffee and dessert.

Sensing the weariness of his wife, Will glanced at his watch and announced that they should be heading for home. With hearty thanks and good wishes for the holidays, the Eschmans departed, leaving behind a group of anxious relatives.

As the Eschman rig pulled out of the yard, Sara voiced the concern of all present. "I just can't stand seeing Aunt Meriel wasting away like that! Don't they realize how sick she is?"

"Yes, they realize," Annalie responded sadly, "only too well."

Early next morning, Will was wakened by the creaking of the bed as Meriel, raised on one elbow, shook in the throes of coughing. Her gown was again wet with perspiration.

"Can I help you?" he asked, bouncing out of bed.

She gasped, trying to catch her breath.

Making his way to her side of the bed, he noticed that the phlegm she raised was flecked with bright red spots. A cold shudder shook his frame. This was what he had been fearing in a blind sort of way.

He stepped into Everett's room and roused his son. Then he sent him with a message for Harold to ride into town and try to reach Dr. Glover, in Gladwin, by phone. If he was in his office,

Meriel and he would take the train that very day for an office call.

While waiting for a response, Will built the fires in the range and heating stove and began fixing oatmeal for breakfast. Reah returned with Everett and finished getting breakfast. By the time the meal was over, Harold was back, stating the doctor would see them if they could make the train trip to Gladwin.

While Reah helped Meriel dress for the trip, Will glanced at Laurie and Everett who were standing by, watching in bewilderment. "Why don't you two spend the day at Annalie's? And Reah, how can I thank you?"

The trip to town seemed like a bad dream as Will supported Meriel on the seat beside Harold with an extra blanket to keep her warm.

Kettering greeted the couple warmly as they waited in his combination store, post office and depot for the train to arrive.

"By the way, Will, you have a letter here from the grain elevator. Must be about your bean crop."

"Thank you, sir!" Will replied, as he put the letter in his pocket without opening it. He presumed Kettering already knew the size of his bean check, as on earlier occasions he had watched the storekeeper hold business letters up to a bright light to read the contents. The last thing Will wanted to discuss on this day was his bean harvest.

He assisted his wife to the train as it slowed to a grinding halt, and the two made their way to one of the red plush seats. The train had covered several miles of its trip toward Gladwin before Will pulled the envelope with the enclosed check from his pocket. After studying its contents for a moment, he shook his head in mingled amazement and irony, then handed the letter to Meriel. "Would you believe it? Those beans brought top price on the market!" There was no joy in his short laugh.

Dr. Glover glanced soberly at Meriel as he recorded ninety-five pounds in his clinical data. "And what is your normal weight?"

"One hundred twenty-five pounds, up to a few months ago."

"You also seem to be running a low grade fever." With stethoscope in hand, the doctor scanned each minute area of her chest, front and back, then retraced his movements while Will watched with mounting apprehension. "And when did the coughing begin?" he continued.

"A couple months ago."

Laying the stethoscope aside, the doctor rubbed his moustache and cupped his chin in one hand as he studied his notations.

"I'm afraid I have bad news for you. Your wife has all the symptoms of tuberculosis."

Will recoiled as a man just sentenced for manslaughter.

"If only I had sent her back to the house, instead of allowing her to help in the rain-soaked beanfield last fall!"

The doctor laid a reassuring hand on Will's shoulder. "Don't be hard on yourself! T.B. germs, or bacilli, have a way of lying dormant in the human body, sometimes for years. If one condition doesn't trigger them off, another will.

"Our concern from here is how to treat it. Unfortunately, not too much progress has been made, so far. Some say complete bed-rest in a sanatorium. I believe the patients do better with their own folks, providing they have complete rest. Our Michigan weather is notably bad for T.B. sufferers. I recommend a drier climate."

"Would Iowa weather be better?"

"Well, at least it's better than Michigan. Before prescribing any treatment, I'd like you folks to see Dr. Seeley, a T.B specialist in Bay City this coming week. I'll take a sputum specimen today, for tests. I can also set up an appointment with Dr. Seeley."

He picked up the phone and arranged their appointment in Bay City.

The following Wednesday was circled on the January sheet of a brand new year. Will and Meriel waited and wondered what the trip would bring forth, what Dr. Seeley would be like, and what verdict he would give.

Dr. Seeley was a stocky built man with a bald head receding back from a round, pink face. He moved his stethoscope with short, deft strokes over Meriel's chest and back, then glanced at the records and sputum tests he had received from Dr. Glover by mail.

"Did Dr. Glover make any other recommendations?"

"Besides sending us to you, he suggested that my wife return to Iowa where her mother could take care of her."

"Sounds like a good idea to me."

"Is that all you have to offer?" Will's eyes grew flinty with impatience at the idea of a wasted trip to his office. Before he could say more, Meriel exploded into a spasm of coughing.

Dr. Seeley regarded her with deepened concern as she finally stopped, exhausted and beaded with perspiration.

"I'll give you some cough syrup to help suppress that cough and a tonic for your appetite. Understand, this is not a cure for T.B., but it should help relieve some of the symptoms. And you would do well to make arrangements for your mother to care for you as soon as possible."

As they left the doctor's office, Will extended his elbow for Meriel to hold. "Mrs. Eschman, we haven't had a night out together since our honeymoon. We're long overdue for a time of relaxation. So, let me escort you to the Wenonah Hotel for the evening until our train leaves for Rhodes in the morning."

"But Will, that would cost − ."

Will silenced her with a raised hand. "Speak nothing of expenses! Remember our bean check."

He led her to the curb where a taxi was parked and asked the cab driver to take them to the Wenonah Hotel. Trying not to appear as novices on their first automobile ride, they leaned back in the seat as the taxi began moving. They were amazed at the comfort and warmth of the vehicle, the smoothness with which the rubber tires rolled over the pavement, and the short time needed to reach their destination.

As dusk was deepening on the outside, a warm glow welcomed them into the coffee shop on the first floor of the hotel. When they entered the dining room with its snow-white table cloths, red napkins and gleaming silverware, they were tempted by aromas of spices, baked goods and cooking meats from the kitchen. As the waitress filled their coffee cups and took their orders, even Meriel found her appetite stimulated for the roast beef dinner that followed.

Leaving word with the desk clerk to be wakened early in the

morning, Will and Meriel took the elevator to the second floor and found their room, another study in luxurious living. Crystal lights glowed on the dressing table and deep-piled carpeting cushioned their footsteps. The double bed, soft and inviting, was topped with a white, embossed candlewick bedspread with a pastel eiderdown comforter nestled at the foot.

As they sat on the edge of the bed together, Will gathered his wife into his arms. "Meriel, oh Meriel!" he whispered brokenly, as he recalled the doctor's appointment that had brought them there.

Drawing back enough to study his troubled face, Meriel lightly traced his eyebrows with one forefinger, letting it slide down the bridge of his nose and around his lips. Then reaching over, she planted a kiss on his neck.

"Remember, honey, God is in control! And He cares for us. Nothing can happen to us that is out of His will."

They sank into the enveloping softness of the bed and pulled up the down comforter — "light as a dream".

The future might be threatening and unknown.

This night belonged to them, alone.

CHAPTER THIRTY EIGHT

Mending Fences

Fritz strode into his sister's kitchen, brandishing the newspaper he had picked up in Bay City the day before. The May 7, 1915, headlines screamed:

LUSITANIA SUNK OFF COAST OF SOUTHERN IRELAND
Loss 1198 - Americans 128
War Clouds Loom Over Entire World

Fritz's face was red with determination. "I tell you, that spells war for our country, too. And when war does come, I'm enlisting to help teach Kaiser Wilhelm a lesson!"

The long, bony fingers of war were reaching out over the world, eventually also to grasp the United States in its bloody grip. But a more threatening battle and testing field loomed; not on a geographic map, but in the terrain of Will's heart.

Following the consultation with Dr. Glover, Will had written Meriel's mother. She had agreed to come to Michigan in May and take Meriel and Laurie back to Iowa with her. Everett would stay with his father.

Reah and Annalie helped Meriel rearrange cupboards for easy access when Will and Everett prepared meals alone. They packed extra clothing from the closets into boxes, leaving only what Will and Everett would be needing. They also took tucks in all of Meriel's clothes, so they would fit more becomingly.

Grandma Browning's arrival was like balm on sunburnt skin. If she felt any shock over Meriel's frail appearance, she concealed it. After gathering her grandchildren into her arms, she reached into her satchel and pulled out a toy telephone for Laurie. It was glass, filled with candy pellets. Thrusting her hand into the bag again, she came up with a pen and pencil set for Everett.

Luella Browning's stay of a week in Michigan was filled with visiting friends and family. Her small being quivered with enthusiasm over the new buildings and neat community. "This is more than I ever expected to see!" she confided to her son, Harold. "My, my! To see you all in new houses! You folks must be making out real good!"

Harold responded modestly, "We owe most of it to Will and Meriel. They took us all in so we could start building right away. Also the Sauters and Fritz helped a lot."

To Annalie, she spoke more soberly. "See to it, won't you, that Will and Everett get along okay? Men folks are never too handy about the house."

Annalie responded with a hearty hug as she promised she would.

The time of departure for Luella and her charges arrived too soon. Will had borrowed Louie's carriage to make the trip to town more comfortable for Meriel and her mother.

"We might have a carriage of our own on your next visit here," Will addressed his mother-in-law.

"Who knows? We might even have an automobile of our own!" put in Everett, hoping to sound really impressive.

Spring had never been more breathtakingly beautiful, and yet heartbreaking, than on that May day Will drove his family to the train depot. Wild cherry trees danced on every hillside, and their lacy, white boughs shimmered in the sunlight. Robins and swallows darted back and forth, intent on building their nests, and red-winged blackbirds whistled from the cattail swamps.

Will had hoped for a moment of privacy for their final goodbye at the station. Instead, a large crowd of well-wishers had gathered at Kettering's store.

Several of the women gave Meriel embroidered handkerchiefs, and others, small bottles of perfume, a necklace and a brooch, all bought at Kettering's store. When Meriel had a problem holding on to all her remembrances, Kettering stepped forward with a handsomely woven totebag. "Take this with my compliments. It will hold your other goodies."

Lew Stymick, misty-eyed, stepped forward from a group of men and shyly handed a medium-sized bottle to Meriel. "This has helped my woman get over all her chest colds." He swiped his sleeve across his mouth and rubbed his chest with his hand. "Just rub it on like this."

"Oh no!" came a hoarse whisper from the background. "Not Stymick's skunk oil again!"

"Thank you, Mr. Stymick," Meriel smiled as she slipped the bottle into her totebag with the other tokens of remembrance. "That is very kind of you."

As a whistle announced the approaching train, Ma Webber stepped up and hugged Meriel. "We'll all be waiting here when you get back!"

The train ground to a halt. Will followed with the suitcases as Luella and the conductor helped Meriel and Laurie up the train steps. After arranging the luggage on the rack, Will shook hands with his mother-in-law. "Thanks for everything!" He planted a kiss on his daughter's upturned face. "Bye little Punkins!" He then held Meriel a long moment. "I love you!" he breathed brokenly. He released her only as the train gave a lurch. The train had begun moving toward Bay City as he hopped off.

Everett looked up into his father's face as the team jogged homeward, "Papa, how long will Mamma be gone?"

"I don't know, Son — I don't know!" Will clasped his hand over Everett's shoulder. "I'm glad I have a reliable son like you. We men are going to have to pull together."

And pull together they did, with Everett preparing simple meals and doing dishes while his father chored and supervised the field work. Through planting time and hay season, Everett was his father's right hand helper.

Reah washed Will and Everett's clothes with her laundry and kept them supplied with fresh-baked bread. Everett attended Sunday services in Rhodes regularly with his uncle and aunt.

Annalie frequently invited Will and Everett over for meals, and the lonely pair never refused. There was always the comfortable feeling of belonging in the large Sprenger family. With plenty of food on the table for nine hearty appetites, two plates, more or less, never posed a problem for Annalie. Her heart overflowed with love; ministering to the hungry and hurting came naturally for her.

The highlight of each week for Will was a letter from Meriel, always assuring them that she was feeling better that day. There was news of visits from John and Miriam. Minnie had brought Will's parents to see her. Oh yes, Minnie was now keeping steady company with Tom Burrows's son, Sam.

"How about that!" chuckled Will to himself and Everett. "Sounds like wedding bells will be ringing for my little sister, after all!"

Back to Meriel's letter: "Laurie will be entering school in Pulaski, this fall. Everett, I'm glad for the good reports of how you're helping Papa. I love you both, so much! Love, until we're together again."

"Do you think Mamma and Laurie will be home for Christmas?" asked Everett, looking hopefully into his father's face.

"One thing for sure," promised Will. "We'll all be together for the holidays, either here or in Pulaski."

August proved unbearably hot. The old-timers referred to the weather as "Dog Days". The letters from Meriel were farther apart. Will could understand that. Such weather would discourage anyone from writing. Everett returned to school in September; Will spent the warm fall days cutting corn. He missed Everett working at his side.

As October's weather turned cooler, Sauter helped Will harvest his crop of potatoes. As he straightened his back at the end of the row, Sauter stopped to talk. "Hear about the stray dogs getting into Stymick's flock the other night?"

"That reminds me," Will answered. "Guess it's time for me to be checking the fence of my sheep pasture soon."

Stopping at the mailbox, Will was pleased to find a letter. However, the pleasure was overshadowed by premonition as he noticed unfamiliar handwriting on the envelope. It was from

Meriel's sister, Eadie, in Sioux City, Iowa. Between her last two visits to Pulaski, she had noticed decided deterioration in Meriel's condition. "It would be well if you came before too long. Best regards, Eadie."

"Oh, dear God," groaned Will inwardly. "Why my Meriel?"

He made plans with Harold to look after his livestock while he and Everett were away. Then, remembering Sauter's warning about stray dogs, he decided to mend the sheep pasture fence the next day.

Rev. Adams left his horse in the barnyard and walked down the lane to where Will was working. When Will raised his eyes from stapling the fence, he found himself looking directly into the pastor's face. The face was thinner and more deeply lined than he had remembered it before. A wave of guilt swept over Will as he recalled giving up church attendance after the Strait meetings.

"All right, Preacher, let me have it and get it over with!" Will challenged his visitor.

Deep sadness filled the minister's face as he spoke. "Only the other day did I learn of Meriel's illness. I've just stopped to tell you how sorry I am. Is there anything I can do to help?"

"Nope! Not that I know of." Will looked at Adams with pain-filled eyes. "Her letters always sounded so cheerful. I thought she was getting better. Then last week her sister wrote that she had been steadily failing." Will stopped speaking and looked away.

"I've never known a kinder, more Christlike woman than your wife," Adams spoke comfortingly. "That sounds like Meriel, not to complain."

Will continued to pound staples into the post, not trusting himself to look up as tears welled near the surface.

"Ever have a wolf get into your flock?" Adams asked abruptly, changing the subject.

"Nope! Stray dogs have been molesting Stymick's flock. I aim to keep them away from mine!" He emphasized the point with a hard hammer stroke.

"I would classify Alexander Strait as a wolf." Adams continued the analogy. "A wolf in sheep's clothing. I'm sorry I didn't recognize it before I introduced him to you. You had to find out the hard way; the majority of the Rhodes group are grateful to you."

"Barring Clothilda Grant, of course," chuckled Will.

"I guess we need a few pickled saints like Clothilda here on earth so we'll enjoy heaven more, later on," observed Adams dryly. "Just as a wolf leaves some wounded and torn sheep behind, so has Strait."

"Meaning?" Will was beginning to see the Strait episode in a new light.

Rev. Adams continued, "I believe you're a mature enough Christian to rise above Strait's attack and grow stronger through it. Now take Sauter, for instance, who's new in the Lord; to him it was a major catastrophe. He feels, if that's the way Christianity operates, he wants no more of it. If I were to urge him to return to Sunday services, he would consider me part of the religious system, pressuring him."

"So you're asking me to — ?"

"You've done a fine job encouraging him. He trusts you!"

Will considered the matter a few moments before answering. "Since you put it that way, I'll talk it over with Sauter, next time I see him."

The minister grasped Will's hand in both of his and exclaimed, "God bless you, Brother!"

Will watched his pastor walk back to the buggy and drive off. The granite wall of bitterness in his heart had disintegrated. With tears flowing down his face he prayed, "Lord show me what to do and I'll do it."

CHAPTER THIRTY NINE

The Valley

*W*ithin a few days Will and Everett were on the train retracing the route to Iowa. Will gazed out of the coach window on late-harvested shocks in hazy cornfields. He responded briefly to Everett's remarks about the passing scenery. His mind was miles ahead, wondering what to expect at the journey's end.

At Pulaski the two left the depot, and with their grips in hand, walked the short distance to the Browning home. The sky was hazy, and early November sunshine filtered down through the few yellow leaves left on the gaunt tree branches. A light breeze was laden with scents from the coal-burning train and wisps of leaf smoke that curled up from bonfires.

Will knocked at the open door of the Browning bungalow. "Anybody home?" he called out in tones used in his courting days. Luella came bustling to the door, wiping her hands on her apron. Laurie followed close behind her.

"My land! Are you ever a good sight for the eyes!" After an appreciative hug, Luella led the way to the bedroom where Meriel lay propped up by several pillows. Her dark eyes brightened and a broad smile spread over the thin features of her face. "Will! Oh Will!"

She reached out her slender hand toward Will. Sitting on the bed beside Meriel, he gathered her frail body into his arms. "Darling!" he whispered, burying his face in her dark hair.

Laurie crept shyly from the side of the bed and edged her way into the fringe of their embrace. Noticing Everett in the background, Meriel motioned for him to join them. "Your father wrote what a wonderful helper you've been!" Everett approached hesitantly. "Mamma!" The word formed brokenly on his lips as he took her hand in his.

"She hasn't been out of the house for days," remonstrated Luella next day, when Will broached the subject of taking Meriel for a buggy ride, "but we can ask Doc Shelton when he calls in the morning."

On the following day, Will noted that the doctor walked at a slower gait and that his shoulders were more stooped than when he had delivered Everett at Golden Acres. However, he was still faithfully making the rounds to the third and fourth generation of his patients. He checked Meriel with a stethoscope, closing his eyes beneath shaggy gray eyebrows as he listened.

Will's question about the buggy ride did not surprise him.

"I see no harm in Meriel riding a short time, if she feels like it. You should lift her in and out of the buggy and use plenty of pillows to prevent jarring her bones. You can find a comfortable buggy at the livery stable."

Remembering how they had enjoyed the smooth taxi ride in Bay City, Will almost hired someone to drive them in a car, then decided against it. Their time together was too precious to be shared with a third party.

The day was warm and balmy for November. With one arm about Meriel, cushioned in pillows beside him, Will allowed the horse to pick its own gait over the familiar Iowa roads. They stopped at Golden Acres farm where they had begun their married life and where their son, Everett, was born.

Looking back, those days seemed like another era to them. The sun shining through the hickory and cottonwood trees cast a glow of peace and tranquility over the landscape.

"Are you sorry we didn't stay here?" Before the words were out, Will felt he had spoken unwisely. If they had remained at Golden Acres, Meriel still might have had her health.

She squeezed his hand, "What, and miss out on the arbutus, the mushrooms, the huckleberries and the sheep on the hillside?"

"And pine stumps in the garden," quipped Will.

"Yes," agreed Meriel. "Pine stumps and all the beautiful people who lived among the stumps!" She looked up into his face. "I hope you know by now that wherever you are is home to me, even among the pine stumps."

"I love you so much!" Will enveloped her, pillows and all, into his arms.

With the coming of cold November rains, Meriel was confined to bed. The congestion in her chest tightened and the coughing spasms occurred more frequently. Following one such spell, she motioned to Everett who was watching through the bedroom door. He approached slowly, and she embraced him gently. "You've grown into such a fine, dependable boy."

"Uh huh!" he responded self-consciously.

"Later on, Papa is going to need all the help he can get! Laurie is still too young to realize what needs to be done about the house. Suppose you could look after them for me?"

"Uh huh, Mamma!" were the only words he could manage, as his throat tightened and his eyes brimmed with tears.

Thanksgiving was a day of muted family togetherness. Eadie and her husband were home for the holiday. Minnie brought Will's parents, Jacob and Anna, for a short time. However no attempt was made to visit, as even breathing was labored for Meriel.

Will sat holding his wife's hand as she lay propped up on pillows. The rose-adorned locket accented her blue housecoat. A slight smile played over her lips. "You know, I was just thinking of that first birthday card you sent me before we were married."

Will squeezed her hand. "You'll never know how much pride I had to swallow before I sent it. That was a wise move we made setting our wedding date on November 25, your birthday." He rose to his feet. "There, I almost forgot again." He left the room and returned in a moment with a ribbon-tied box which he handed to Meriel. "Happy Birthday from all of us!"

"It's lovely!" she murmured as Luella joined them and lifted the white knitted shrug from the box. The others in the house gathered at the door and sang "Happy Birthday" while Luella draped the shrug over Meriel's shoulder.

Suddenly Meriel was seized with another coughing spasm and

the raising of crimson phlegm. Dr. Shelton was called. He arrived as she sank, exhausted, into a deep coma.

By midnight, the warm, valiant spirit had left Meriel's frail body. The date was Thanksgiving, November 25, 1915.

As one in a dream, Will, accompanied by John and Minnie, made the necessary funeral arrangements. Anna and Luella chose Meriel's burgundy wedding dress and the rose locket for her final viewing.

Lew Browning looked down upon the peaceful features of his daughter in the casket. "My little girl!" he whispered brokenly, then turned away, his weathered face contorted with grief.

The little white church in Pulaski was packed for the funeral. Both town and country folks gathered with mingled love and sympathy to support Will and his family in their time of bereavement. Pastor Mueller from the Mennonite Church shared the service with the young Methodist minister.

Will sat dry-eyed, looking straight ahead as Pastor Mueller lauded Meriel's many virtues and pictured her in the presence of her Savior. His heart was constricted, as with an iron band. If only he could take a deep breath. But a deep breath would have burst his heart, iron band and all.

Laurie and Everett sat on either side of their father, their bodies pressed tightly to his, as if drawing strength from the close physical contact.

The graveside committal followed at the village cemetery, with the sound of dark, damp clods of prairie soil falling upon the casket in the ground. Then the family slowly made their way homeward beneath a shrouded, November sky.

Josef Schillig edged up to Pastor Mueller as he was leaving the cemetery. "Did you notice?" his thin voice rasped. "Willard Eschman never shed a tear at his wife's funeral."

The usually mild pastor eyed his parishioner sternly. "There are some depths of sorrow too deep to be washed away with tears. Only a kind heavenly Father and time can assuage such pain."

Pastor Mueller turned abruptly from Schillig with a shrug of impatience, "But you wouldn't understand that. Never measure a man's grief by his tears!"

CHAPTER FORTY

Lonesome Road

"*Y*ou can't spend Christmas alone!" persisted Meriel's mother when Will spoke of leaving for Michigan soon after the funeral. "Think of the children, if not yourself!" At Luella's insistence, Will agreed to wait until after New Year's before returning to Michigan.

A short time later, Eadie sought Will out alone in the family gathering. A single strand of matched pearls relieved the severity of the black satin dress she had worn to the funeral.

"Forgive me if this is the wrong time to bring up the subject." Eadie laid a soft arresting hand on Will's arm. Will glanced from the daintily manicured fingernails on his coat sleeve into the face of his attractive auburn-haired sister-in-law, and the memory of Meriel's hands, encased in heavy men's gloves as she pitched bean plants in a mud-sodden field, flashed across his mind.

Eadie resumed speaking, "I realize this must seem abrupt, but I had to talk to you about Laurie before we leave for home in the morning. Richard's farm supply business in Sioux City has done exceedingly well so that we are comfortably situated. However, we have never been able to have children of our own, and that has caused an emptiness in our lives."

Eadie's lips trembled as she paused. "If you could see your way clear to let us raise Laurie, we could do so much for her in providing a home, clothes and schooling, besides meeting our own needs."

Will's first impulse was to say "No!" How could he part with this child who reminded him so much of her mother with the dark brown hair and eyes, the tiny nose that crinkled when she questioned something that was said, and the way she snuggled her head on his shoulder when she was distressed.

However, his better judgment reminded him that this was probably the answer to his prayer on how to properly care for Laurie in the days ahead. Knowing Eadie, he could visualize his daughter in the bright, frilly dresses his sister-in-law would choose for her. Yes, every little girl needed a woman's touch while growing up.

His answer to Eadie came slowly. "It's a hard decision you've asked me to make on the spur of the moment. However, I'm grateful to you. If Laurie is willing, I'd be obliged to you for keeping her – at least, until we see what the future holds for Everett and me."

"Thank you, Will!" Eadie threw her arms impulsively about his neck. "You'll never regret it!"

As Will moved from one family household to another around Pulaski, he became aware that time had taken its toll in his boyhood community as well as in Michigan.

His mother, who had always been so swift at supplying every need of the family, now moved cautiously to avoid tripping and falling.

"Let me run up to the attic and get those comforters for you!" offered Will when Anna spoke of needing more bedding on the downstairs beds.

"Nonsense! I'm used to going up and down these steps every day. I'll be back in a minute!" She was already pulling herself up the steps by gripping tightly to the handrails on the wall.

Anna reappeared some time later with a doll in her arms and a sheepish grin on her face. "You know, I forgot what I went up after, but I did find this doll of Minnie's. It's for you, Laurie. Every little girl should have a doll of her own."

"Oh, thank you, Grandma!" beamed Laurie as she held the doll tightly and ran her hand over its shiny porcelain head.

Will slipped up the stairs and soon returned with an armful of comforters. "This should keep everyone warm for the night."

"Ach! I don't know why I should be so forgetful these days!"

sighed Anna.

Will gave his mother a quick hug. "Think nothing of it, Mamma. I hope I can do so well at your age."

"Such a good boy!" She patted her son's back gently. The soft pats carried Will back to childhood days when his mother's touch could wipe away any childish hurt. If only they could soothe his raw, torn heart now!

Life had revolved full cycle to the place where family roles were now reversed. His father's voice of authority had given way to a nod of acquiescence as he blinked his misty, blue eyes in agreement.

Will studied his family through the painful barbed wire of his "No Man's Land" of mixed emotions. He was deeply aware of the debt of gratitude he owed them all. They had lavished love and gifts upon Laurie and Everett during the holiday season and had included him in all the family activities.

And yet, there were days he could scarcely restrain himself from running down the railroad tracks toward Michigan where he could begin weaving the frayed threads of his life back together again.

At last the day of departure Will so longed for had arrived. A skiff of fresh snow covered the Iowa landscape as the family rigs gathered at the Browning house on January 2. Will and Everett were ready to return home to Michigan, although it wouldn't feel like home with Meriel's grave in a cemetery north of Pulaski. However, the time had come to look ahead and move on. The family had gathered at Grandpa and Grandma Browning's to see Will and Everett off.

Aunt Eadie slipped an arm around Laurie and gently drew the child toward herself. "You know, I've always wanted a little girl just like you."

Laurie drank in the fragrance surrounding her aunt and snuggled up closer. "M-m-m-m, you smell nice!" she confided with childish candor, crinkling her nose.

"I have it all planned," Eadie continued. "A room of your own with pretty dresses and dolls. Wouldn't you like that?"

"Uh-huh, it sounds pretty," responded Laurie, looking up

into her aunt's face.

"Then, you'd like to go home with me?"

Laurie shrugged her shoulders. "It sounds nice," she responded again – but without enthusiasm.

Eadie sought within herself to find the right words to win this child of Meriel's, not only for the child's sake, but as a way of compensating for some of the misunderstandings between Meriel and herself in the past. This would be one way of making amends.

Brother John laid a hand on Will's shoulder. "I don't want to rush you, but it's getting near train time."

Will and Everett gathered their luggage in preparation for leaving. Then putting his grip down, Will stepped over to his daughter and knelt down to her level.

"Well, Little Punkins, I guess this is 'goodbye'! How about a hug before I leave?"

Laurie looked deeply into her father's eyes, then threw her arms tightly about his neck in a vise-like grip. "I want to go home with you, Papa!"

There was silence in the room at the sudden reversal of plans.

Aunt Celinda was the first to break it as she sputtered in the background, "Believe me, no seven-year-old child of mine would tell me what she was going to do with her future life. How does she know what's best for her?"

A glimmer of hope flickered in Will's eyes as he turned to Meriel's sister. He spoke apologetically, "I'm sorry, Eadie. I hope you can understand and forgive this abrupt change in our plans. If Laurie wants to go home with us, we'll be needing her suitcase."

Eadie nodded her head as she pressed her lips tightly together. A tear seeped from between her closed eyelids and slid slowly down her cheek.

CHAPTER FORTY ONE

Homeward Bound

$\mathscr{A}$s the train pulled away from the weathered Pulaski Depot, Everett and Laurie pressed their faces against the coach window for a last glimpse at the group of relatives who were waving a tearful goodbye. Will joined the children, waving mechanically, but his mind was racing miles ahead of the train. "Home!" he repeated fervently to himself. "Going home at last!" He appreciated the concern of his Iowa friends and family for the welfare of the children and himself over the past weeks, but the time had come for decisive action.

Within a couple hours, Will and the children had reached Burlington and boarded the Chicago-bound train. Very slowly, as if in trepidation, the locomotive eased itself onto the bridge spanning the Mississippi River. Its wheels glided smoothly over the rails high above the ice-sheathed waters below. Once on solid ground beyond the bridge, it accelerated in loud puffs as the engineer opened the throttle and was soon thundering across the frozen plains of Illinois.

It was time to relax for the long hours of travel ahead. Laurie, still clutching the doll from her grandmother, fell asleep with her head on her father's lap. Will folded the child's plaid coat for a cushion. As he placed it under her head, she stirred slightly and sighed in her sleep.

In the opposite seat, Everett pored over a book he had received from his Uncle Sam. He turned the pages rapidly as he followed the story of his hero, William Tell.

Resting his head against the red plush seat, Will watched the snow-flecked farms reel past the coach window and recalled the scene, ten years earlier, when with his wife, Meriel, and two year old son, he had traveled the same route.

Beneath the quickening touch of spring, the fertile Illinois acres had then been dotted with green corn sprouts, and blooming lilacs spilled from every farmyard. The hearts of the young Eschman couple had likewise bubbled over with high hopes as they journeyed to their new home in northern Michigan.

Vignettes of those early days flashed before Will's inner eye: the first glimpse of their Michigan farm, a stump-studded acreage with a tarpapered shanty. He chuckled now as he remembered tearing off the side of a loose window frame to help Meriel measure the length of curtains needed for the house. Other events burst forth in kaleidoscopic array: the birth of their daughter Laurie; the thrill of moving into their new house; the arrival Annalie's family from Iowa along with Harold and his wife, and...

A sudden lurch of the train jarred Will into the present reality. Meriel, his faithful wife and companion, the mother of his children and keeper of his house was gone! No longer could he expect to see her smiling at the door as he came in from the field, nor feel the soft caress of her hand on his face as she reached up to kiss his cheek. No longer would he hold her warm body close in the night. She was gone!

He placed a hand over his tightly closed eyes as a dry sob escaped his lips. A shudder shook his frame, and a tear slid down his cheek.

Everett glanced up quickly from the book in his hand, and Laurie raised her head in shocked surprise. "What's the matter, Papa?" they asked in unison. "Are you all right?"

Will pulled a handkerchief from his pocket. He wiped his eyes and blew his nose hard, then straightened his shoulders. "Yes, I'm all right, now!" he answered, forcing a weak smile. "With two fine children like you, we're going to make out just fine!"

The conductor, walking down the aisle, announced that within a few minutes they would be at the Chicago station. Will welcomed a time of activity. He and the children followed the flow of passengers streaming into the waiting room of the Union Station.

Leaving Laurie and Everett to watch the luggage, Will stepped immediately to one of the ticket windows. A slightly balding attendant there leafed through Will's tickets. "They're all in order!" he stated with a smile and a nod. "You have a couple hours to wait before your train leaves for Michigan."

Thanking the man, Will returned to the children. "You've done a good job guarding the luggage! Now how about you two taking a breather and looking around a bit before train time?"

"You mean go walking by ourselves?" Laurie asked, as she crinkled her nose incredulously.

"Just keep close together and don't talk to strangers! Be back in half an hour," Will added. Reaching into his pocket, he pulled out his gold engraved watch and handed it to Everett. "This should help you gauge your time!" As an afterthought, Will pressed a dollar bill into each child's hand. "Just in case you find something you like in the souvenir shop!"

"Gee, thanks, Papa!" Everett stretched to his five foot stature as he left and Laurie, with a broad smile, clutched tightly to her brother's coat sleeve.

Will watched the pair as they made their way past the lunch room, then disappeared into the souvenir shop. A couple moments later, two policemen with nightsticks at their side walked briskly in the same direction. Uneasiness clouded Will's mind. "Should he have turned his children loose in the crowded depot of a great city like Chicago?" Reason told him that he could depend upon Everett. Besides, the children had been sitting still since early morning. They needed some exercise.

Meanwhile, Everett and Laurie gaped in amazement at the resplendent array of treasures in the gift shop. Gold chains shimmered on a black velvet background. Nestled in clusters about them were pendants, earrings and bracelets, glittering with sets of rubies and diamonds, pearls, sapphires and emeralds — all securely locked in a glass showcase.

The nearby shelves were filled with curios from the orient: fans, incense burners, temple bells and miniature elephants. A small ivory pagoda caught Everett's eye. "May I see that little temple?" he asked, pointing to the intricately carved artifact.

The matronly clerk took the small curio from the shelf and held it close for Everett's inspection. "How much is it?" he asked as he lightly touched its lustrous surface.

The woman adjusted the spectacles on her nose, turned over the price tag and read slowly, "Two hundred and fifty dollars." She added, "It's genuine ivory, imported from China."

"Oh my!" The shocked boy drew his hand back quickly. His face turned red with embarrassment. Then he reached into his pocket and slowly pulled out the bill his father had given him. "Do you have anything here for a dollar?" he asked earnestly.

The clerk looked down fondly at the two children before her, recalling from the dim past two such young ones of her own. With an understanding smile, she answered as if it were the most commonly asked question of the day. "Oh yes! Right over there!" she pointed. "On that counter by the window you'll find many articles for a dollar or less."

"Thank you!" Everett answered solemnly. Then pulling his father's engraved watch from his pocket, he exclaimed to his sister, "We'll have to hurry if we get back when Papa said!"
The clerk watched misty-eyed as the two children hurried away to the toy and notion counter.

As the clerk had said, there was a nice collection of puzzles, books and dolls, many of them under a dollar. Everett chose a jigsaw puzzle of the United States for ninety-eight cents. Laurie's eye was taken with a doll's comb and mirror set, only seventy-nine cents. Putting their change together, they had enough for a couple boxes of Crackerjacks.

Will breathed a sigh of relief as the children bounded back to him.

"And to think!" Laurie chattered excitedly as they displayed the treasures to their father. "We even had three cents left over!"

Once aboard the Michigan-bound train, the family group slept until they were roused by the conductor's call of "Jackson". The aroma of strong, hot coffee greeted them as they entered the depot out of the pelting snow and ice. Will mechanically stepped to the lunch counter and ordered doughnuts for the three of them. The children ate theirs with milk while Will sipped his hot coffee.

Turning to Everett, Will asked, "Do you remember eating doughnuts here before?"

"Why yes! The waitress put some kind of box on the stool to make it high enough so I could reach the counter!"

"Where was I when all this was happening?" demanded Laurie, miffed that she had been left out of the family discussion.

"Well Punkins!" teased Will as he mischievously pulled one of her braids, "You hadn't been thought of yet!"

A dull red sun peeked over the horizon of Saginaw Bay as the train carrying Will and his children left Bay City on the final leg of their journey home. Cy Matthews, the aging conductor on the Gladwin line, stared in surprise as he paused to punch Will's ticket.

"Will Eschman! What a pleasant surprise, meeting you and your children here! And how is your lovely wife doing these days?"

Will choked as he attempted to answer. "Hadn't you heard? Meriel passed away in Iowa on Thanksgiving Day." His voice sank to a bare whisper.

Matthew's jaw dropped in shock. "No! You don't say!"

Will nodded dumbly, blinking hard to keep back the tears.

The conductor shook his gray head sadly, "I'm sorry!" Then laying a hand on Will's shoulder, he continued, "If there's anything I can do to help, let me know."

"Thank you!" Will grasped his hand gratefully.

In a short time the scrub pine and cottonwood thickets were broken by a clearing that surrounded the town of Rhodes. Ma Webber's two-story square rooming house loomed on the left, and on the right, stood Kettering's General Store with a couple horse-drawn sleighs in front. The team at the nearest sleigh stretched their necks and whinnied, with vapor rising from their frosty nostrils, as Will and the children approached.

Just then a familiar figure emerged from the store.

"Louie!" exclaimed Will as he greeted the man with a red

muffler wound about his upturned coat collar. His brother-in-law grinned broadly. "It's sure good to see you folks again!" Reaching out, he shook Will's hand vigorously. "Do you need anything at the store before we leave town?"

"Nope!" responded Will. "The sooner we get home, the better!"

CHAPTER FORTY TWO

Journey's End

$\mathcal{S}$o eager was Will to reach home that he felt his brother-in-law was dallying too long before leaving Rhodes.

Louie carefully tucked Will's two children under the blanket in the straw-lined sleigh bed with heated soapstones to keep their feet warm. He placed the Eschman luggage in the four corners of the sleigh to hold down the blanket. He then handed an extra blanket to Will.

"What's that for?" asked Will with impatience tingeing his voice.

"To put around your shoulders," Louie stated simply. "After spending hours in a heated train coach, you're going to find the ride home a mite chilly."

Louie finally turned the team homeward, and the horses started off at a brisk pace with sleigh bells jingling. Will had to admit that the blanket felt good, as the icy north wind stung his face and penetrated his clothing.

Will found his excitement rising as the horses trotted closer to his farm. When his neat A-frame house appeared with a thin column of smoke rising from the chimney like incense toward heaven, his heart pounded with anticipation.

"Whoa!" he called suddenly as Louie's team passed by his driveway. "Did you forget that I live here?"

"We're going to my place first!" answered Louie. "Harold and Reah are already there, and Annalie has dinner waiting for us. That way, we can catch up on the news while we're eating." Louie continued talking fast as he noticed disappointment cloud Will's face.

"The women folks have straightened up your place and stocked your cupboards, so you'll have plenty to eat for a few days. And with a fire going, it should be cozy when you turn in tonight."

Annalie paused from her cooking as Will and his children entered the kitchen. After wiping her hands on her apron, she greeted them with outstretched arms. "Welcome back! It's so good to see you again!" Her round face beamed as she hugged each one tightly, Will first, then Everett and Laurie. Harold and Reah joined in the greeting; then the group seated themselves about the long table. As bowls of food were passed around the table, conversation arose above the light clatter of silverware.

Will shared the latest news of the family in Iowa, even to the details of Meriel's funeral. In the retelling of his wife's last days, the numbness in his heart began to ease a little.

With the Sprenger children in school, Laurie and Everett sat silently, waiting for the meal to be finished. Aunt Reah looked down at the subdued child beside her. "It's sort of lonely without Dawn and Robbie to play with, isn't it?" Laurie looked up at her aunt and nodded in agreement. The vivacious woman gave her a quick hug and smiled. "If I have a little girl, I hope she's just like you!"

Laurie puzzled over her aunt's comment. "Did she mean she was planning to have a baby girl, or did she mean she wanted me to be her girl?" Laurie decided it would be fun to go up the hill to Aunt Reah's often. She could play with the dog, Old Shep, and pretend she was Aunt Reah's girl while she was there.

Shortly after the meal at Annalie's, Harold and Reah left for home, stopping at Will's place on the way. Harold unlocked the door leading into the warm, cozy kitchen, then handed the key to Will.

"I think you'll find everything pretty much much as you left it," he said. "Your stock is in my barn. I could watch them better there while you were away. We can bring them over tomorrow. Let us know if we can help you!" Harold turned and was gone, leaving Will and the children alone.

Will's first reaction was one of release and satisfaction. It felt good to be back in his own home where he belonged and was in control. He began a tour of the house with the children following close behind, like puppies. Thanks to the thoughtfulness of Reah and Annalie, everything was spotless and in place. The copper teakettle was still warm on the range. Will replenished the fire in the kitchen stove, using some of the kindling from the well-filled woodbox.

The barrel-shaped cookiejar on the cupboard ledge had been filled. "M-m-m!" exclaimed Laurie, taking a bite from a round, sugar-coated tidbit. "This is Aunt Annalie's special kind!" Will and Everett followed suit, each taking a couple cookies from the jar.

When the snack was over, the group resumed their tour of the house. Their footsteps echoed through the master bedroom with its brass bed covered with a candlewick spread made by Meriel. In the next room, a red, white and blue quilt added a patriotic touch to Everett's bed, and still farther down the hallway, a small dressing table with a pink ruffled skirt matched the ruffled flounce on Laurie's cot.

On all sides were reminders of the devoted mother, who with insight and patient stitches had fashioned a home in the wilderness. The family's conversation became hushed, as if listening for her gentle voice to answer.

With the coming of night, Everett lit the lamp and set it on the dining room table. Long, grotesque shadows stretched across the opposite wall as the occupants moved about.

"Well, children!" spoke Will. "This has been a long day! What do you say we turn in for the night?"

Laurie disappeared for a moment, then returned dragging a blanket after her. Climbing onto her father's lap, she looked up, pleadingly, into his face. "Papa, sing me to sleep!"

"What shall I sing?"

"I Wandered, Today."

He gathered the bedding about the child and carried her across the room. Settling into the rocker, he began to sing:

"I wandered today to the hill, Maggie,
To watch the scene below;
The creek, and the creaking old mill, Maggie,
As we used to do long ago!
The green grove is gone from the hill, Maggie,
Where once the wild daisies sprung.
The creaking old mill is still, Maggie,
Since you and I were young!"

The rhythmic creaks of the rocker kept time with the lyrics of the old ballad. When Laurie's relaxed body and even breathing told Will the child was asleep, he carried her down the hall to her small bed. She immediately stiffened as he placed her on the cot, and her arms reached for his neck.

"Don't leave me alone tonight, Papa!" she pleaded.

"Well, all right, Punkins!" he conceded. "But just for tonight."

Gathering the blanket about Laurie, Will carried her down the hallway to his room, then slid her under the covers on one side of his bed. By the time he had tucked the comforter snugly over her shoulder, she was sleeping soundly again.

Will blew out the lamp and climbed wearily into bed. Not only had it been a long day, he had advanced from a disheartening, yet predictable past into an awesome unknown future. How would he ever cope with his children's needs: their meals, clothing and schooling?

Suddenly, he realized his son was standing in the shadows at his bedside.

"Papa, are you awake?"

"Yes, son!"

"It's so dark and cold in my room!"

Will threw back the covers of his bed. "Come on, son. You can climb in with me."

Quickly the lad slid in between the covers and promptly fell asleep.

Rest did not come so easily to Will. His thoughts tumbled like a muddy, tumultuous stream as he wrestled with his aching loss. "Oh God!" he groaned inwardly, as he stared up through the darkness. "Are You there? It's so dark and cold down here! Please give me some assurance of Your presence..or of Meriel's."

As he listened, the stillness of the night was broken only by the even breathing of the children beside him in bed.

He shut his eyes and breathed deeply, trying to rekindle some ember from the past. He recalled Meriel slipping her hand into his — on their wedding day and on many occasions later. Half singing and half speaking beneath her breath, she'd repeat the simple, unfailing truth: "He leads His dear children along!"

The rest of the words eluded Will except for the last two lines of the chorus they had sung in church:

> "Some through deep sorrows; But God gives the song,
> In the night seasons, and all the day long!"

The Lord, indeed, had led them to this promised land — their Canaan. Through the years, Will and Meriel had worked valiantly to reclaim it from the wilderness. Cleared of stumps and all indebtedness, their farm was now as permanent as the land itself..or was it?

Time was marching on with new demands. In a few months, Everett would be finished at the one-roomed school in Rhodes. Will had vowed that his children would go through high school. (Young minds were too precious to waste!) The nearest high school was in Gladwin, twenty miles away. If Everett were to attend there, Will and seven-year-old Laurie would be left alone to run the farm.

The chilling thought arose that he might be forced to leave the farm to keep his family together. "Never!" he exclaimed so emphatically that his children stirred in the bed beside him.

There had to be another way! He could lease or rent his acres for a few years until he was able to return. The land would still be his. He tossed as he wrestled with options, to go or stay on the farm.

Gradually, a thought took form in his mind: the words Meriel had taken from a poem by Whittier and embroidered into a wall motto. Even now, it was hanging in the darkened room above the bed where he was lying.

"Before me
Even as behind,
GOD IS
And all is well!"

Wearily, he relinquished his load of worries. "Lord, if You are as trustworthy as Meriel always claimed You were, I'm turning my future and my children over to You. I'm just too tired to go on by myself!"

So saying, he drifted off to sleep. **Tomorrow is another day and, Lord willing, it will be brighter!**